I0652510

The World
in 2000 Years

also translated and introduced by Brian Stableford:
Anonymous: Sâr Dubnotal vs. Jack the Ripper; *Anthologies*: News from the Moon; The Germans on Venus; The Supreme Progress; The World Above the World; *Henri Allorge*: The Great Cataclysm; *Cyprien Bérard*: The Vampire Lord Ruthwen; *Richard Bessière*: The Gardens of the Apocalypse; *Albert Bleunard*: Ever Smaller; *Félix Bodin*: The Novel of the Future; *Alphonse Brown*: City of Glass; *André Caroff*: The Terror of Madame Atomos; *Félicien Champsaur*: The Human Arrow; *Charles Derennes*: The People of the Pole; *Renée Dunan*: Baal; *Henri Duvernois*: The Man Who Found Himself; *Achille Eyraud*: Voyage to Venus; *Henri Falk*: The Age of Lead; *Paul Féval*: Anne of the Isles; The Black Coats ('Salem Street; The Invisible Weapon; The Parisian Jungle; The Companions of the Treasure; Heart of Steel; The Cadet Gang; The Sword-Swallower); John Devil; Knightshade; Revenants; Vampire City; The Vampire Countess; The Wandering Jew's Daughter; *Paul Féval, fils*: Felifax, the Tiger-Man; *Octave Joncquel & Théo Varlet*: The Martian Epic; *Jean de La Hire*: The Nyctalope vs. Lucifer; The Nyctalope on Mars; Enter the Nyctalope; *Lamothe-Langon*: The Virgin Vampire; *Gabriel de Lautrec*: The Vengeance of the Oval Portrait; *Georges Le Faure & Henri de Graffigny*: The Extraordinary Adventures of a Russian Scientist Across the Solar System (2 vols.); *Gustave Le Rouge*: The Vampires of Mars; *Jules Lermina*: Panic in Paris; Mysteryville; The Secret of Zippelius; *José Moselli*: Illa's End; *Marie Nizet*: Captain Vampire; *Henri de Parville*: An Inhabitant of the Planet Mars; *Gaston de Pawlowski*: Journey to the Land of the 4th Dimension; *Georges Pellerin*: The World in 2000 Years; *P.-A. Ponson du Terrail*: The Vampire and the Devil's Son; *Maurice Renard*: The Blue Peril; Doctor Lerne; The Doctored Man; A Man Among the Microbes; The Master of Light; *Jean Richepin*: The Wing; *Albert Robida*: The Clock of the Centuries; The Adventures of Saturnin Farandoul; Chalet in the Sky; *J.-H. Rosny Aîné*: The Givreuse Enigma; The Mysterious Force; The Navigators of Space; Vamireh; The World of the Variants; The Young Vampire; *Marcel Rouff*: Journey to the Inverted World; *Han Ryner*: The Superhumans; *Jacques Spitz:* The Eye of Purgatory; *Kurt Steiner*: Ortog; *C.-F. Tiphaigne de la Roche*: Amilec; *Théo Varlet*: The Xenobiotic Invasion; *Paul Vibert*: The Mysterious Fluid; *Villiers de l'Isle-Adam*: The Scaffold; The Vampire Soul; *Philippe Ward & S. Miller*: The Song of Montségur.

The World
in 2000 Years

by
Georges Pellerin

translated, annotated and introduced by
Brian Stableford

A Black Coat Press Book

English adaptation and introduction Copyright © 2011 by Brian Stableford.

Cover illustration Copyright © 2011 by Jean-Pierre Normand.

Visit our website at www.blackcoatpress.com

ISBN 978-1-61227-058-6 First Printing. December 2011. Published by Black Coat Press, an imprint of Hollywood Comics.com, LLC, P.O. Box 17270, Encino, CA 91416.
All rights reserved. Except for review purposes, no part of this book may be reproduced or transmitted in any form or by any means, electronic or mechanical, including photocopying, recording, or by any information storage and retrieval system, without permission in writing from the publisher. The stories and characters depicted in this novel are entirely fictional.
Printed in the United States of America.

Introduction

Le Monde dans deux mille ans, which bears the signature Georges Pellerin, here translated as *The World in 2000 Years*, was originally published in Paris by E. Dentu in 1878. It attracted little attention in its own day, although it was cited as an example in an essay on futuristic speculation by Charles Richet, *Dans cent ans* [In a Hundred Years] (1892) and that citation—noted by Pierre Versins in his *Encyclopédie de l'utopie et de la science-fiction* (1972)—has been copied by other historians of speculative fiction without any further detail being added. It is also mentioned briefly in P.-M. Brin's *Histoire de la philosophie contemporaine* [History of Contemporary Philosophy] (1886), where the author is discussed as a "Fourierist," although the text only adopts one specific idea from the voluminous Utopian writings of Charles Fourier (1772-1837) and is at odds to some extent with Fourier's fundamental political philosophy.

The novel is open to the criticism of being a futurological tract lightly disguised with the aid of a tokenistic fictional frame, but the frame does add an extra dimension to the work that distinguishes it from other works in the same subgenre—whose august prototype is Louis-Sébastien Mercier's *L'an deux mille quatre cent quarante* (1771; tr. as *Memoirs of the Year 2500*). Although all such works make explicit comparisons between the present day in which the author is working and the imaginary future he is constructing, *Le Monde dans deux mille ans* places a heavy emphasis on the "double vision" of its mesmerized protagonist, and the fictional frame allows the comparisons to be further developed in dialogue and interrogation. That facet of the work is one of the features recommending it for reading now, when it has—arguably, at least—become a more interesting text than it was at the time of its writing, by virtue of the inevitable tripling of that vision. Whereas readers in 1878 could only make a simple comparison between their own world and the world of 3878 murkily glimpsed by the savant Monsieur Landet, contemporary readers can make a third comparison with the world of 2011, which adds an additional perspective of considerable significance to anyone interested in the science on which the story is based.

The last qualification is perhaps an important one. Although *Le Monde dans deux mille ans* is a work of "science fiction" in the purest sense, the science in which its speculations are firmly and cleverly based is economics, which is very rarely used as a basis for fiction published under that label, partly because its reputation as "the dismal science" is not entirely unjustified, at least in terms of its potential as a source of action, adventure and melodrama. Even some modern readers interested in economics might consider that the science has made so much progress since 1878 that one would require an esoteric interest in the archeology of ideas to find much fascination in it. There is, however, one significant argument that can be deployed in answer to that view.

Because the natural sciences are purely descriptive, they contain no ready-made basis for futuristic speculation, except insofar as physical and chemical theory open up scope for imaginable new technologies. Although our understanding of biological evolution has made vast strides over the past two centuries, the relevant analysis provides no basis for anticipating the future course of that evolution, and all speculative fiction of that sort is, in essence, pure fantasy. Economics, however, is not merely a descriptive science but a prescriptive one, not in the sense that it provides vulgar prophesies, but in the sense that it attempts to map out strategies of individual and political action by means of which certain particular goals might be efficiently attained. It is a deeply frustrating science because, as we know from the bitter experience of hundreds of years of economic history, such plans, no matter how well-laid they are, usually go awry, sometimes because the actions in question have unintended consequences that were simply not anticipated, but mostly because individual economic interests are routinely—perhaps inevitably—in conflict, and whatever plans are made, individually or socially, one can be certain that active attempts will be made to exploit, pervert and subvert them. As its analyses become more sophisticated, economic theory gives further scope to such perversion and subversion, thus continually undermining itself.

The economic theory on which *Le Monde dans deux mille ans* is based is not the economic theory nowadays taught in universities; there is a sense in which it is definitely obsolete. It is, however, not obvious that it is merely incorrect, because its obsolescence lies not so much in terms of its notion of cause and effect as its specification of fundamental objectives. Economics as currently taught and practiced is basically the science of making a profit; it takes it for granted that the ultimate objective of any economic enterprise, individual or collective, is not only to make money, but to make as much money as possible, and its advisory strategies are geared to that objective. In the future described in *Le Monde dans deux mille ans*, by contrast, the primary objective of economic policy is the prevention of the accumulation of money in the hands of relatively few individuals or institutions. While making money remains an objective, it is subsidiary to the determination to steer it in the "right" direction—which is to say, to redistribute it in such a way as give every member of society the opportunity to earn a living free of hardship and strife.

The question of which of these two applications of economic theory is "right" is a political one, although it is worth noting that the author of *Le Monde dans deux mille ans* does not think that it is a matter of mere opinion, or even a matter of pure self-interest, because he believes that human beings have a literally God-given mission to fulfill, which takes precedence over any private judgment of purpose. The chief interest of the text, however, does not lie in that political choice, but in its analysis of how, once the choice has been made, the goal might be effectively pursued and achieved. Unlike many Utopian writers, the author of *Le Monde dans deux mille ans* is not primarily concerned with designing an "ideal society"—a notion that he considers to be essentially relative—and is certainly not foolish enough to believe that, if ever such a plan were agreed, such a society could simply be legislated into existence at a stroke. His concern is not so much with the goal as the possible route, the mapping out of a process of politically-guided social evolution that might at least get us out of the mess we are currently in (whether "currently" means 1878 or 2011) and move us in a direction that is, at least arguably, that of improvement.

Although he does concede the inevitability of future Revolutions and one exceedingly bloody World War, the author of *Le Monde dans deux mille ans* sees Revolutions as rapid discharges of accumulated social tensions and wars as disasters worsening over time by virtue of technological sophistication; he would prefer to see a pattern of change in which gradual evolution eventually takes the place of periodic revolution, thus minimizing the price to be paid for social change in bloodshed. He believes that sage economic policy might and must do that, even if it will inevitably take time. He does not imagine that it will be easy, nor that the process is likely to be uninterrupted, but he does believe that, by proceeding one step at a time, the eventual sum of those steps can, will and must be "forwards." Unlike most Utopians, he is prepared to go into detail about the steps themselves as well as the philosophy behind them. Like most intellectuals of his day and nation, he subscribes to the philosophy of progress, but not in any simple linear fashion, and certainly not without a deep sense of anxiety—an anxiety that impregnates his text and helps to modernize its flavor.

The reader does not have to agree with the specific notion of improvement fundamental to *Le Monde dans deux mille ans* to find some interest in the reminder that the "technology" of economics—whether on an individual level or that of political planning—can and inevitably will be applied in different ways, according to the objective in view. Perhaps there is nothing specific to be learned from the text about possible solutions the world's current financial crisis, in spite of the fact that some passages will seem strikingly modern to readers used to hearing exactly the same complaints, and the novel's discussion of the politics of public debt in relation to the imagined financial crisis of 1959 certainly has some echoes of current debates; even if the relevance is slight, however, it is nevertheless interesting to see the financial crises and challenges of the fictitious world analyzed and tackled, if only to gain a better appreciation of the fact that the issues involved are far from new and by no means narrow. It is interesting, too, to see such issues placed in a much broader historical context—which, within the text, extends into the distant past as well as the not-so-distant future. (The figure of two thousand years is, of course, entirely arbitrary; there are inevitably some aspects, unpredictable in 1878, in which the world of 2011 has already seen far greater changes than the world of 3878 glimpsed in the story, although there are other aspects in which it has not changed at all.)

For these reasons, this translation of *Le Monde dans deux mille ans*, although devoid of action, melodrama and even of satire, is by no means lacking in interest to contemporary readers. Although it is basically a fictionalized tract, the fictionalization process adds a valuable extra dimension to it. The use of hypnotic "animal magnetism" as a technology of time travel is a mere literary device, but it is not used entirely casually, and the author takes care firmly to distance his notion of the potential range of soul-travel from the notion, broached by Louis-Sébastien Mercier in "Nouvelles de la Lune" (1788)[1] and popularized by Camille Flammarion, that disembodied souls would be capable of interplanetary travel. Although his central focus is on economic policy, the author is sufficiently conscientious to pay attention to the wider corollaries of his narrative device, going so far as to include an account of the inevitable end of the world within a general cosmological frame.

---

[1] Translated as "News from the Moon" in the eponymous collection, Black Coat Press, ISBN 978-1-932983-89-0.

The text also presents, if only indirectly, a puzzle regarding its authorship. Ordinarily, it is possible in introducing a book to say something about its author, but in this particular instance that is awkwardly difficult.

A search through the references preserved in Google Books readily reveals three Georges Pellerins who were active at the time the book was published. It is highly unlikely, however, that the book was written by Georges Pellerin (1851-1935) the margarine manufacturer of Malaunay, and just as unlikely that it was written by the Georges Pellerin (1856-1918) who worked in and eventually took over the last active *imagerie* in Épinal. In addition to their alien professional affiliations, both those individuals were surely too young to have written a book in the 1870s that gives every evidence of being the work of a mature individual. The third Georges Pellerin manifest in that record, a lawyer who represented both the *Societé des auteurs dramatiques* and the *Societé des gens de lettres*, in association with one Gustave Roger, seems at first glance to be a likelier candidate, but the timespan of his mentions imply that he too was probably too young in the 1870s to be the author of a book like *Le Monde dans deux mille ans*. Furthermore, one of the most conspicuous absences from the text, in spite of the inclusion of almost every other field of human thought and endeavor, is any mention of contemporary literature; that appears to be a subject of utter and total uninterest to the author of the text.

That uninterest is also odd when one considers that the signature "Georges Pellerin" can be found on two other near-contemporary volumes of fiction: *Le Roman d'un blasé* [The Romance of an Unfeeling Man] (1879) and *Le Comtesse rouge* [The Red Countess] (1883), the latter of which was issued by the same publisher as *Le*

Monde dans deux mille ans. Neither of those texts is available on *gallica*, but reviews of both of them can be found there in a periodical called *Le Livre*. The reviews—both scornfully dismissive—do not go into great detail about the contents of the books, but what they do say implies that the works in question are so very different in kind and attitude from *Le Monde dans deux mille ans* as to make it hard to believe that they are the work of the same author. *Le Roman d'un blasé* is the story of a bored socialite who adopts a daughter with a view to making her his mistress, but ends up marrying her instead—not at all the kind of book of which the author of *Le Monde dans deux mille ans* could be expected to approve. *Le Comtesse rouge* actually contains two stories, and bears two authors' names, the other being Charles DesLys, a fairly well-known writer best known as a dramatist; the review does not speculate as to whether each story might be by a different author rather than either or both being collaborative, or which author might be responsible for which story if they are not collaborations, but is content to write both off as crude exercises in stereotyped popular fiction.

The Georges Pellerin credited on *Le Roman d'un blasé* and *Le Comtesse rouge* might well have been the Georges Pellerin who represented the principal Parisian literary societies in rights disputes; that author obviously knew Charles DesLys and must also have been a friend of the well-known journalist and popular historian Eugène d'Auriac, who contributed an introduction to *Le Roman d'un blasé*. Whether those two Georges Pellerins are the same person or not, however, it does not make it any likelier that they or he wrote *Le Monde dans deux mille ans*, which seems to be very obviously the work of an academic economist, probably a specialist in political economy. Perhaps the choice of "Georges Pellerin" as a by-line on *Le Monde dans deux mille ans* was merely a coincidence, or perhaps the lawyer and/or novelist actually lent his name to someone who wanted to take extra precautions to hide his identity, but the internal evidence of the text certainly suggests that it is unlikely to have been written by any of the Georges Pellerins who were otherwise manifest at the time.

If so, who did write it? In all probability, we will never know—but there is one tiny anomaly in the text that might be construed as a clue. The novel's protagonist is fond of quoting from sources other than contemporary literature, his favorites being Virgil, Blaise Pascal and Aesop, and the author is conscientious in including references for almost all the quotations (although the three from the Bible are all puzzlingly incorrect). There is, however one exception: a quotation from Gustave Dupuynode's *Études d'économie politique sur la proprieté territoriale* [Studies in Political Economy in relation to Property in Land] (1843). Dupuynode's surname is mentioned *en passant*, but there is no footnote giving a specific reference to the book. Gustave Dupuynode was born in 1817, and would therefore have been much the same age as Monsieur Landet, the protagonist of the story, in 1874—which is the date when the story is notionally set and when the author presumably began to write it. Dupuynode did not die until 1898, and was therefore easily capable of writing a book in the mid-1870s, at which time he probably retired from teaching, and he was an academic economist specializing in political economy. Insofar as can be judged by the references of which snippet views are offered in Google Books, his ideas were fully in agreement with those expressed in *Le Monde dans deux mille ans*.

All of that might be pure coincidence. Then again, it might not. Gustave Dupuynode is, at least, a likelier author for *Le Monde dans deux mille ans* than any of the four (or possibly only three) Georges Pellerins cited above.

This translation was made from the version of the Dentu text reproduced electronically on the Bibliothèque Nationale's *gallica* website. The only difficulty it posed was in relation to the specialist terminology of economic science, which varies markedly between French and English (in that parallel terms cannot be translated as they would be if they were common nouns) as well as over time. I have tried to clarify the meanings in such a way as to make them comprehensible to modern English-language readers without distorting their idiosyncrasy excessively.

Brian Stableford

Chapter One
ANIMAL ELECTRICITY

On Monday, February 12, 1874, the Marquise de Roche-Houdion was receiving visitors at her town house in the Faubourg Saint-Honoré. A long file of carriages was stationed by the sidewalks from the Place Beauveau to the doors of the house, level with the Rue de Berri. A flood of guests turned up on the steps of the perron as the minutes went by. In the vestibule, two gilt-edged Swiss Guards presented their halberds to the newcomers.

The Marquise, like all superior women who have doubled the cape of 50, fatigued by the frivolous pleasures of social life, had opened her salon to illustrious figures in politics and literature. When a woman can no longer reign by charm, she reigns by intelligence.

Did she want to resuscitate the shade of Madame Récamier[2] and like her, guide ministerial movements from the depths of her drawing room? That was an indiscretion that the Marquise did not disdain to repeat. People even went so far as too affirm that it was in her house that the fall of the last minister had been decided. Extreme in everything—in love, it was said, as in distractions—after having been crazy about dancing, she could no longer tolerate it on the part of others. The wor-

---

[2] Following her return from exile imposed by Napoléon, Madame Récamier (1777-1849), a close friend of Madame de Staël and Chateaubriand, hosted a salon at the Abbaye-aux-Bois in the Rue de Sèvres, where the cream of Restoration society met.

thy Marquise was a trifle egotistical. In her salon, people talked.

It was the rendezvous of famous people. Her guests called her house the Hôtel de Rambouillet,[3] and by a flattering comparison, nicknamed her the Duchesse de Montausier. It was there that the orators of the future were formed. It was there that the destiny of young authors was in play, and it was necessary that they had proved themselves there before any claim to ability could be admitted.

The sentences of that court could not be appealed; its infallibility was based on two formidable powers: money and wit. It was, moreover, very difficult to obtain entry into that choice milieu, where the gravest social questions were debated in the guise of jovial conversation. An invitation to the Marquise's Mondays drew one into the High Life, like a ticket to a première at the Théâtre Français. The postulants were many and the elect few.

Whether by virtue of her name, her affections or her opinions, the Marquise was a Legitimist, but not one of those retrograde Legitimists who shine in the Chambre

---

[3] The Hôtel de Rambouillet was constructed in the Rue Saint-Thomas-du-Louvre to a design provided by the Marquise de Rambouillet (1588-1665). The salon the Marquise maintained there, whose regulars included Madame de Sévigné, Malherbe, Corneille, La Rochefoucauld, La Fontaine, Scarron and Bossuet, had a considerable influence on the development of 17th century literature. Its star was the Marquise's daughter, "the adorable Julie," who consented to become the Duchesse de Montausier after 14 years of competitive courtship. It was Julie who inspired Molière to write his biting satire about the salon, *Les Précieuses ridicules* [Ridiculously Precious Women] (1659), although not everyone found her ridiculous.

and the Senat by their untimeliness; she was a liberal Legitimist. Understanding and admiring the work of Progress, she knew enough to make the Republic the concession of its interests, but she only admitted the progress sanctioned by divine right in the person of its representative. A sublime Utopia, combining two principles, each of which is the opposite of the other! Extreme, always extreme, the worthy Marquise! In a word, she dreamed of the monarchy restored by Louis XVIII and overturned by the intolerance of Charles X—and, bizarrely, she applauded 1848 because 1848 was the punishment of 1830. She had not forgiven the Orléans monarchy its original task.

In her salon, the Marquise is enthroned in the midst of an animated circle of men and women of all ages, all ranks and all positions. She is 60 years old, although her tall and proud figure, which she hides beneath a dress in the Watteau style, makes her seem younger, and her hair, as white as snow, lifted to the top of her head and falling back in long ringlets on either side of her face, makes her seem older. She has what is required, however, to balance the contrary opinions exactly: a fine and imposing face, slightly wrinkled, a Bourbon nose with a slightly arched profile and blue-gray eyes that the habit of observation has endowed with a penetrating gaze.

Around the vast winged chair in which she is pontificating an entire petty court in grouped, of which she is the pivot; there are old aristocrats in ruffed coats powdered with Spanish tobacco; old women who, like her, regret the good old times; young ones who are waiting for some piquant tale of a gallant adventure of the Restoration; and, finally, men of various ages flattering her, some by virtue of confidence in her long experience, others by ambition, knowing that her influence is all-powerful with some minister or other. There are also some in that number, people of intelligence, who find a certain charm in listening to the words falling briefly and abruptly from the Marquise's lips. What pleases them most about her is that the tone in which she retraces her memories is redolent with conviction—a rare thing today.

In November 1873, the petty court of the Hôtel de la Roche-Houdion had obtained the government's consent to make an approach to the Comte de Chambord.[4] His return being already certain, the senior functionaries of the future sovereign were designated in advance, and the Marquise was congratulating herself on the triumph of her dearest hopes when the question of the flag suddenly put an end to communication between Versailles and Frohsdorf. The Comte de Chambord refused to substitute the flag of the usurper for that of his family, and for that consideration alone, paltry in appearance but decisive in reality, preferred to retain a voluntary exile.

That news fell upon the Hôtel de la Roche-Houdion like a thunderbolt. All hope was henceforth lost. However, little by little, confidence returned as events trans-

---

[4] The Comte de Chambord was the grandson of Charles X, who should have succeeded that monarch in 1830 after his father and elder brother stepped aside, but the Duc d'Orléans, whose job it was to proclaim him king Henri V, failed to do so and was given the crown himself, hence giving rise to the "legitimist" opposition. After the fall of the Second Empire, the Legitimistists and the Orléanists settled their differences, the latter consenting to the childless Comte de Chambord taking the throne, on the understanding that their own heir, the Comte de Paris, would succeed him, but the deal fell apart, allegedly—as the present text states—because the Comte de Chambord refused accept the tricolor as the flag of France.

pired and a new conspiracy was organized by a small committee in the Marquise's house, whose friends, with one exception, had adopted liberal ideas.

That opposition came from none other than Monsieur Landet, a senator, member of the Institut—the Académie des sciences morales et politiques—Officier de la Légion d'honneur, etc. A Federal Republican, he extolled the system of the United States and rejected with all the force of a tight dialectic the incessant attacks that the Marquise and her aides-de-camp launched at him. Why was Monsieur Landet, in spite of the stripe of his Republicanism, one of the Marquise's Monday regulars? That was a mystery that we shall not even attempt to plumb. At any rate, a conversation without debate becomes monotonous; Monsieur Landet revived it with his savant controversy, and perhaps he had only been admitted to add a grain of salt to the charm of the meetings. Still, he was the wolf in that sheepfold, in which he had become the most exquisite guest.

A large head, framed by long, graying hair, with small green eyes as piercing as a drill, fleshy lips, strongly-chiseled features, the whole set on a thin body wrapped up in a black frock-coat buttoned up to the neck, only allowing the passage of the narrow border of a white cravat—that was the man, physically: one of those individuals withered by study to whom one almost does not dare to attribute a sex. Beneath that frail envelope, however, the multiple intelligence of a fine and satirical mind was hidden, with an astonishing profundity of insight. In the matter of opinions he never gave his own, for fear of having to retract it one day. If I said, just now, that he was a Federal Republican, it was because the elegance he deployed in all circumstances in bringing out the advantages of the government of the

United States gave grounds for believing that he had a marked preference for that system.

He was one of those people who only make pronouncements with careful reservations and who finds the means to be something under every regime. He was a charming conversationalist, a distinguished economist, a witty and erudite writer and a refined man of the world.

From time to time, the Marquise looked at the clock, giving signs of impatience. She had announced a surprise.

The conversation was animated; people were talking about the politics of the day, current plays and new novels.

Monsieur Landet, closely surrounded, was playing with his listeners like a cat with a mouse. He was talking a great deal but saying nothing. It would have taken a fine mind to divine his secret thoughts.

Suddenly, over the general brouhaha, a domestic announced "Monsieur Hobson."

As that name passed through the drawing-rooms, all eyes were turned to a man of about 40, tall and slim and as flexible as a reed. A thick forest of black curly hair darkened his head. Profoundly ensconced beneath his eyebrows, coal-black eyes as shiny as carbuncles, with a gaze of unsustainable fixity, illuminated his face. All of the extraordinary person's life seemed to reside there.

A murmur of astonishment greeted his entrance. Who had not heard talk of the celebrated American magnetizer and spiritualist, Hobson? This, then, was the surprise that the Marquise had planned for her guests!

With the perfect ease of a man accustomed to being examined from head to toe, Hobson went straight to the Marquise.

"You have done me the honor of sending me an invitation, Madame," he said, bowing deeply. "Here I am."

"I was almost despairing of your response, my dear Monsieur Hobson," the Marquise replied, indicating a chair beside her.

"I beg you to excuse me, Madame, if I am slightly late; I was retained this evening by a spirit."

"By a spirit!"

The word ran through the assembly as if borne by an electric wire.

"By a spirit, Madame, yes—does that astonish you? It is by the intermediary of spirits that I am in daily communication with the other world."

"With the other world! I confess that that surpasses the limits of my convictions."

"I'm not talking about other planets; I mean the world of the dead. Spirits, detached from their bodies after death, wander in the sphere of terrestrial attraction, waiting to be given, by virtue of a new incarnation, a new enterprise in life, in a new body, appropriate to the demands of the epoch into which they will be reborn on Earth."

"You seriously believe in metempsychosis, then?"

"Certainly, Madame. It is the basis of creation."

"And from our world, you claim to be in correspondence with the dead?"

"Yes, Madame. Death is merely the transition from this life to another. The body finishes therewith, but the soul that has been that body's spark during the trajectory of human existence, deprived of its carnal bonds, is purified in the atmosphere until the Supreme Being judges it appropriate to continue the proof of existences in a society relative to its improvement. During that intervening period, it is not completely isolated from beings who have been dear to it, or who are linked to it by blood, and the magnetic attachments that still chain it to the Earth permit it to remain in permanent communication with them."

"So you see magnetism everywhere, then?"

"Everywhere, as you say. Magnetism is the invisible agent that attracts and repels, which engenders sympathy and antipathy, the ultimate motive of all sentiments."

"I'll wager that you find it in love?" a joker put in.

"More than anywhere else," Hobson replied. "Is not love, insofar as it is a sentiment, the most sudden, the most poignant and the most irresistible of all those that take possession of the soul; like any passion of the senses, is it not an unconscious attraction, to which we all submit, the great and the pretty alike, save for certain strong minds who make a game of defying nature, or when another passion—ambition, for example—absorbs it completely? 'Love comes without one thinking about it; the mind goes to it of its own accord; nature wishes it, and issues the command.'[5]

"The Creator has formed, with a material and perishable substance, two essentially contrary beings, with the goal of bringing them together for generation, but he has animated both of them with the same immortal fire: the soul. The soul is a parcel of his divinity; it is the hyphen facilitating the joining together of a man and a woman.

"Why unite two different beings and make reproduction a linking of two components? Because in nature, everything follows an invariable law; in the same way

---

[5] The author adds a footnote crediting this quotation to Blaise Pascal's *Discours sur les Passions de l'amour* (1652-53).

that, in physics, a negative pole attracts a positive pole, in love, the woman attracts the man, and reciprocally.

"How can that immutable attraction of the man toward the woman and the woman toward the man be explained, if not by a sort of magnetic current, which we may call animal electricity? We all possess within us a certain dose of fluid emanated from the ethereal, invisible, impalpable substance that forms the soul. We transmit that fluid by the pressure of the hand, by the contact of the body, and above all by the force of the gaze, which is its most subtle and active agent. Hence the influence of a superior will upon an inferior one, a necessary consequence of love. It is in the order of things that one dominates the other, for, when that magnetic superiority no longer makes itself felt, love is gradually annihilated, to make weary for a sentiment of another kind: amity, which is the lot of old age. This transmission of fluids operates its cohesion by means of hooked atoms, according to the system of Descartes.

"Love does not always encounter reciprocity. It is often the case that only one of the two is subject to the fluidic influence, and that the other does not feel the effects of the magnetic transmission. That is because animal electricity, more developed in one than the other, is unable find a sufficient force of cohesion in the subject that it dominates because another current is drawing it in another direction—for in nature, all is proportionate, and a man and a woman are only truly united by love when the transmission operates on both parts with equal spontaneity, without the effort of thought. Unshared love is thus not true love; it wearies, softens and fails of its own accord.

"It is wrong to give the name of love to the violent sentiment that is born in the imagination and is merely the fruit of a temporary impression; that ought to be given the name of passion, for love and passion are totally different.

"Love derives from the soul; it is the impression produced on our soul by another soul. Passion derives from the senses; it is the impression produced on our senses by the attraction of a momentary charm. How little beauty counts for in true love! It is a more or less graceful frame, which strikes the eyes, but contributes nothing to the natural impulse that constitutes love. These two quite distinct sentiments should not, therefore, be confused, and the accessory should not be mistaken for the fundamental. Passion only lasts as long as caprice; love is eternal. One obeys the soul, the other the body."

"But then," the Marquise objected, "if this exchange of transmission is absolutely necessary to produce love, instinctively, without the effort of thought, many people risk not encountering their counterpart."

"That is because people cannot wait," Hobson continued. "If a man is wise enough to leave himself to his natural impressions, he will encounter the counterpart that is destined for him—but if he tries too hard to find it, in the course of that pursuit of the ideal, he excites his imagination, wearies his heart, falsifies his judgment and ends up realizing that the further he goes, the more he deceives himself. It is thus that one sees the dangerous game played by those who record in their journals as many love affairs are there are months in the year.

"To return to the role of magnetism in human organization, however, the man or woman who knows the influence of the will does not make use of it too often for a momentary caprice.

"Certain women, generally nervous by nature, emit such a quantity of fluid and enjoy such a subtlety of gaze that they inundate and transpierce the men who approach them with it, and inculcate an invincible passion in them, purely by virtue of that magnetic pressure. The existence of the sirens of antiquity, so long debated, becomes easy to understand. Their enchantments were merely the abuse of a fluidic force with which they enveloped the travelers attracted by the charm of their voices. But that sudden passion is extinguished as soon as the dazzled man is no longer in the power of the woman he thinks he loves, because the current to which he has fallen victim has not found a corresponding current in his soul—or, rather, because the currents that are exchanged emanate from a material substance."

"You're making love into a sort of fatal combination to which we are condemned by invariable laws," said an old dowager, shocked by the magnetizer's argument. She was English by birth.

"Yes, Madame; love is the principle of generation. We are all subject to it. It is, therefore, logical that the atoms of souls are interlinked according to the law of sympathy, or repel one another, following the contrary law."

"So, to you, everything in this world is magnetism," said a writer, who was following Hobson's reasoning attentively.

"Everything," the latter replied, "in material beings as in simple substances. Water advances and recoils under the influence of lunar rays; that is flux and reflux. A stone, detached from the summit of a mountain and rolling down its side, obeys the force that tends to draw it toward the center of the Earth. A tourist who climbs a steep slope is seized by vertigo at the sight of the gaping precipice at his feet, an irresistible impulse pulling him into the depths of the gulf; it is the magnetic force that is attracting him, like the stone to the center of the Earth. The meeting of two currents in the atmosphere produces a detonation: a lightning-bolt; again, it is the magnetic fluid, which here takes the name of electricity."

"All that is purely and simply physics," Monsieur Landet interjected in his turn. "The magnetic effects of which you speak are those which experience demonstrates to us—but I don't believe that the soul is subject to the same principle. A body, of whatever sort, by virtue of the material elements that comprise it, gives off a sort of atmosphere endowed with magnetic properties, exercising on another body the influence of a superior or inferior force. That is what causes the terrestrial nucleus, swollen by the molecules aggregated around it, to attract as if to a common center, by virtue of the Earth's rotation, the bodies that are within its radius of attraction. But that such a power, emanating from a simple substance, obtains identical effects on a substance of the same sort I cannot conceive. Common sense refuses to admit the attractive and repulsive force of something impalpable and invisible. To obtain a physical force requires a body constituted of material molecules."

"You're speaking as a philosopher, Monsieur," Hobson retorted. "Personally, I'm speaking as a practitioner convinced by long experience. Philosophy is all very well, but it is sometimes found wanting. When you have heard me out, and especially when you have seen me at work, perhaps you will consent to alloy magnetism with psychology—I might even say with metaphysics."

"With metaphysics! That's deifying matter."

"Would you care to do me the honor of witnessing an experiment? Better than that—would you care to be the subject of one?"

"Do you intend to put me to sleep?"

"Why not?"

"Oh! I'll wager that you'll never manage it."

"Who knows?"

"You're serious, then?"

"Very serious. You've proposed a wager—I accept it. What is the stake?"

"Well! You're American to the tips of your fingernails. It will be, if you wish, a lunch at the Café Anglais."

"Agreed."

"When is the séance?"

"Today."

"Today? Where?"

"Here."

"In this drawing-room? You don't mean it."

"The wager was made in public; it's necessary that the experiment likewise be in public."

"So be it!"

A frisson ran through the drawing-rooms, and the guests, enticed by that strange wager, flowed into the principal room. Conversations stopped, gazes fixing upon the magnetizer and the savant.

"Install yourself comfortably in this armchair, as if you were about to undertake a long railway journey," said Hobson. "The rest is up to me."

Monsieur Landet sank into a vast wing-backed chair and waited.

Hobson retreated to the far side of the room and, after a few minutes of meditation, to isolate his thoughts, he folded his arms across his chest and raised his eyes, which he darted at the savant with a grim fixity.

He was no longer the same man. His long, thin body was animated by a superhuman force. His nerves, taut with the effort of his will, curled his bony fingers. His body was agitated by a febrile tremor. The muscles of his face contracted, his shining eyes projecting an unsustainable glare, like that of an electric fire. They had phosphorescent gleams, and caused all gazes within the range of their radiation to be lowered. They plunged upon Monsieur Landet and pinned him to his armchair.

Everyone was breathless with impatience and astonishment.

The patient's head slumped on to the back of the armchair, his eyelids lowering. He was asleep.

Hobson approached the sleeping savant, passed his hands over his face several times from bottom to top, in order to dispel the superabundance of fluid; then he sat down facing him and took his hand.

"What question do you desire to ask, Madame?" he said to the Marquise.

"Ask him what the world will be like in 2000 years."

"You're overreaching the limits of human faculties, Madame," observed a bishop *in partibus*[6]—the Marquise's confessor—respectfully. "The future belongs only to God."

"What does it matter, Monsignor? You'll give me absolution for it tomorrow morning."

The worthy prelate raised his eyes to the heavens and uttered a profound sigh.

"It will be tiring, Madame," the magnetizer replied.

---

[6] i.e., a bishop without a see, holding the title in name only.

"Will our dear friend be in any danger?"

"He might be, if he were in any other hands but mine. The further the somnambulistic subject is transported from his own sphere—the further he penetrates into the future—the greater is his fatigue. His mind labors, seeks, travels. He appropriates all that he sees; science no longer has any secrets for him; it requires all the energy of the magnetism, and all his attention in following it, if no accident is to occur. If an extraneous thought were to disturb me during the experiment, the subject, abandoned to himself, incapable of sustaining himself by his own strength and deprived on the fluid that I am directing at him constantly, would exhaust himself in such a distant double vision. Reassure yourself, though, Madame; I'm sure of myself. There will be no danger."

"Nevertheless, Monsieur, if we were risking the precious life of Monsieur Landet to satisfy a frivolous curiosity..."

"Have no fear on that subject, Madame, I repeat."

"Go on, then."

Hobson beckoned a servant, and sent him to fetch two individuals who were waiting in the antechamber.

"Who are these gentlemen?" asked the Marquise.

"These gentlemen are stenographers, who accompany me everywhere."

"Stenographers? Why?"

"To write down the curious relation that you are about to hear. Monsieur Landet, in his capacity as a statesman, will reveal to us things that it would be regrettable to abandon to forgetfulness. It is for his sake, much more than mine, that I am taking this precaution."

The stenographers sat down at a small table in front of the clock, pencils in hand, ready to take turns in playing their role.

The séance, introduced in the guise of an eccentric wager, took on a more serious character.

"Are you asleep?" Hobson asked the savant.

The latter shook his head painfully, and passed his hand over his forehead. "Yes," he replied.

"Are you lucid?"

"Yes."

"Would you like me to clear your mind before commencing?"

"Yes. My head is heavy; my ideas are colliding confusedly in my brain."

With one hand, Hobson made a few long downward passes over the savant's body. "Is that better?"

"I'm fine now. What do you want of me?"

"Will you abandon yourself completely to my will?"

"I'm abandoning myself."

"Why are you speaking so softly?" the Marquise interjected. "Just now, you claimed that it was necessary for him to the under the empire of your will."

"I need to store as much influence as possible within him, and gradually lead him to submit to it. That superiority, overwhelming him to begin with, would gradually weaken him in his research." Addressing himself to the savant, Hobson continued: "So, a distant voyage through the centuries doesn't frighten you?"

"Not at all. You know how interested I am in progress. Moreover, the story that these gentlemen will write"—he indicated the stenographers, immobile at their post—"will enlighten my studies."

"And serve your ambition my dear Monsieur Landet," said the Marquise. "Admit it."

"Who does not have his small seed of ambition?" the savant replied. "Ambition is the noblest human passion. It elevates one, aggrandizes one, and forces one to develop one's intelligence. Then again, cannot ambition be applied in the interests of humankind?"

"Very well," said the magnetizer, in the midst of a solemn silence. "Isolate yourself from our present world, follow my thought, and transport yourself through 2000 years."

The savant appeared to sink into a profound meditation. His lips moved, as if to count the centuries; his hands stirred, as if to palpate the space. Then his head, wearied by that frightful journey, slumped on to the back of the armchair.

Hobson, attentive to the slightest movement, never took his eyes off him; his thoughts became confused with the other's; he became incarnate in his subject's person. From time to time he revived the other with his fluid, by passing his hands lightly from the head to the extremities. The savant was reanimated then. His lips moved and his hands stirred again; he continued the journey he had begun.

"Are you there?" Hobson said, finally.

"Not yet; I've only covered 1500 years."

This time, Hobson placed one hand on his forehead, the other on his breast, and blew lightly on to his temples. The savant recovered a new vigor.

"Are you there?" Hobson asked, again.

"I'm there."

"Can you see the world clearly, as it will be in that epoch?"

"I see it—but let's take things in order."

31

"Always logical," the Marquise remarked, smiling.

"Where would you prefer to begin?" the magnetizer asked. "With politics, finance, industry, commerce or metaphysics?"

"With the family, which is the principle of society."

"Write, gentlemen," said Hobson, turning to the stenographers, "and don't miss a single word."

Chapter Two
THE FAMILY

Marriage and Natural Law

"The primary cause of the anarchy that divides society," the savant began, "is the dismemberment of the family. Before societies were constituted as States, the family was the nucleus around which the generations were successively grouped. Composed of members issuing from the same origin, the same ancestor, having the same worship and the same tomb, the family was a sacred line, which it was sacrilege to break.

"Human ambition had not yet invented politics. Every family governed itself according to its own laws, and recognized no other authority than that of its own patriarch. The insolence of strangers did not cause offense within its customs. Religion was its base, and that religion, which belonged to it alone, informed it with the sentiment of fraternity in regard to others and respect in regard to its chief, the depository of all political, moral and religious power.

"After his death, that family chief became a protective divinity whom posterior generations invoked, with the certainty that he would assist them in their joys as in their difficulties. Superstition in wellbeing is a barrier to the baser human instincts, which are better governed by prejudice than by force. Humans recoil before the dread of the unknown.

"Soon, isolated and independent families felt the need to come together; they were organized into groups, then into tribes, and finally into nations, while conserving their primitive subdivisions. It was then that, envy taking old of everyone, the religious sentiment that united people weakened over time, and the strongest imposed themselves on the weak. That discord, bursting forth in the bosom of the family, engendered war. War set the weak conclusively beneath the yoke of the strong, and the fragmented family established the State. That was the product of patriarchal life.

"As the centuries went by, the bonds of association broke and egoism proclaimed individual liberty.

"So long as the family was assembled in a cluster, it lived peacefully and happily; it was strong in its unity, because it enclosed within itself all the necessary elements of life. From the day when each member was freed from its laws, society, broken at its base, followed the current of the passions.

"Previously-unknown needs made themselves felt; wealth, held in common until then, was divided and became the source of constant jealousy. Power was the prey of the most audacious,

"Man was created with one objective: relative perfection. Without that objective, there is no reason for being, and the Creator's work is regulated with too much intelligence for futility within nature to be conceivable. Futility, the fruit of human idleness, is the stigma of his imperfection. It is in progress that we lend ourselves gradually to the objective of human life. A long time will pass before we are permitted to attain it. Human beings can only be purified in the course of a succession of centuries. They are obviously born better than they are today, but, yielding to the penchants of their free will, often enjoying impunity in this world, they have been emboldened in evil and have deviated from the

34

simple and straight path that their conscience, the reflection of a Supreme Being, has clearly traced for them. Life has therefore become an ordeal for them.

"There will, however, come an epoch of reaction, in which the comparison of good and evil, the series of deceptions through which they will have passed, will return them fatally to their primitive state—with the difference, however, that what existed in them to begin with in the form of instinct will be the result of the maturity of their immortal souls. They will reenter eternity happily, as they emerged from it, as perfect as they were meant to be. The future will therefore reconstitute the family.

"For the same reason that humans have declared themselves strangers to one another, the bitterness of their egoism will reunite them again. That is the work of progress."

"What about Creation?" the Marquise interjected.

"Let us take things in order," the savant went on, pitilessly. "Everything in its turn. When I get to metaphysics, I shall talk to you about Creation, within the limit of my conceptions."

This was no longer Monsieur Landet, the diplomat of ambiguities, the political equilibrist, whom one wit had nicknamed "the comfortable sofa-bed of politics," the man of the world amiable to the point of insipidity. Transfigured, the savant had become curt and incisive.

"Don't be astonished at the change that has taken place in Monsieur Landet's manner," the magnetizer observed. "A man in the power of magnetism loses the urbanity acquired by education; he abruptly sets aside everything that deflects him from his enterprise. It's better to avoid questions; they will confuse his ideas and injure the lucidity of his double vision."

"I can see the world in 2000 years," Monsieur Landet continued. "The age of iron and the age of silver have passed; the age of gold is on the way back. Humans, instructed by the experience of the centuries that have gone by, have discarded their envelope of egoism. They have come together again; the general interest has succeeded individual interest; the family circle has tightened again. That immense progress has brought back mutual confidence.

"No more suspicion, no more ulterior motives, no more fraud; everyone, sensing himself to be honest, assesses others according to his own aspirations. It is rare for any dispute to recall the judges to their post and reawaken laws from their torpor. Justice has shut down and, fortunately for humanity, judges do not work by reason of their appointment.

"How little resemblance modern Paris bears to the Paris I have before my eyes! Everywhere, activity, work, joy. No more hazardous speculations; utility, always utility. If fortunes have not been leveled out, however, it is because the problem of compensation is insoluble down here; necessity itself is not felt in equal proportion by all human beings. Envy, that needle envenoming passions, has, if not deserted at least considerably neglected the human mind. The finger is pointed at rebels against progressive perfection; they are counted.

"I shall only occupy myself with intelligent Paris, with moral Paris. What good would it do to describe the marvels I am contemplating? You can divine them as well as I can. What is the point of telling you that the streets are lit by electricity, that machines are also powered by electricity, by the force of the wind or the heat of the sun; that balloons have replaced omnibuses, that locomobile carriages have succeeded vehicles drawn by horses, and that submarine vessels are plowing the depths of the seas while hulled vessels are plowing their surface?

"There are as many improvements as modern industry allows us to suppose, and about which I shall tell you when the time comes. Walls are still walls. There is, therefore, no interest in pausing over details that add nothing for the intellect or the heart. Besides, in matters of comfort, is not the present century the last word? As for nature, it only transforms its bark into another bark of the same sort.

"I'm passing through a crowd of busy people going to their occupations or chatting about matters of general interest, trying to improve themselves by communicating the various particularities of their intelligence. I'm going into a building, which seems to me the most appropriate one to bring out the advantages of this peaceful and laborious life.

"The family is gathered around the hearth. It's evening. The children are playing games in a corner, which are already awakening in their souls the idea of work in an agreeable form. The parents and grandparents are conversing about current events, but they hardly mention politics. It's a gentle, easy discussion, devoid of acidity. Why should they be dogged in defending their opinions when no partisan hatred divides them? For a long time now, individual ambition has been considered a crime, and people govern themselves by themselves, employing people of their choice for that purpose. A nation without rules eats itself away; leaders are still necessary, in accordance with the fable of 'The Limbs and the Stomach,'[7] but the leaders are not exempt from the

---

[7] The fable in question is attributed to Aesop.

permanent control of those who have appointed them to protect their interests."

At this point, Monsieur Landet began to smile.

"They are talking about our epoch," he continued, "and are not sparing us. They consider us to be barbarians, effeminates and bandits. To judge by what I hear, tradition has exaggerated historical truth somewhat. Has it not been the same in all times? The future, grafted on to the past, judges according to its constitution.

"It's strange: the word 'money,' which, in our day, is the motive of all intelligence, the practical emblem of power, has not been pronounced. People make it in order to live, and to help others in need, not to become rich. The only luxury that they permit themselves is necessity in a larger measure. Whence comes this indifference to superfluity? From its abuse. It's very true that extremes connect. Humans having reached the ultimate degree of their moral degradation, have turned back on themselves; they reflected on the result of their easy pleasures, and, disgusted, risked a different path. The happiness that they had pursued for so long, which followed them like their shadow, has appeared to them in all its simplicity. They found close at hand what they had sought far and wide. Luxury and debauchery have been a school for them, whose severe instruction they have appreciated. In a word, they have learned to be content with the bounty of nature, the source of true felicity in this world."

"Then you see humankind perfected?" said the Marquise

"Perfected is not the word," the savant replied. "Perfection only belongs to the Creator, the principle of all things. Created beings cannot elevate themselves to the level of their maker. The imperfect cannot conceive the perfect, Saint Anselm says,[8] because the perfect implies the idea of infinity, and infinity surpasses the bounds of human intelligence, which only has an intuition of it by virtue of the divine imprint engraved in the soul. The human beings I am describing for you have not yet reached their highest level of relative perfection. They are approaching that goal, but many centuries will elapse before the Supreme Being deems their mission accomplished."

"And how long still separates them from that end?" the Marquise put in.

"There are things that ought not to be investigated, Madame," the savant replied, severely. "If I wished to fathom the secrets of destiny, I could not do it. I can only reason from hypotheses. Besides, we'll talk about it when the time comes. Have the patience to wait, Madame—that's all I ask of you."

For the second time, the Marquise pinched her lips.

"I warned you, Madame," Hobson objected. "In the best interests of this communication, it's preferable to let the somnambulistic subject follow his own train of thought."

"A young man is coming into the family living-room," Monsieur Landet continued. "It's the daughter's fiancé. He's been waiting for two years. Don't be astonished by that delay. The prudent custom of betrothal, lost by us, has resumed its ancient right. Today, it's not hearts that are allied, but matching fortunes. Marriages are concluded in haste, for fear that some unforeseen

---

[8] In the *Proslogium* (1077-78), which sets out the most comprehensive version of the ontological argument for the existence of God.

incident might occur to break the ongoing negotiations. Everyone fears the devaluation of his merchandise.

"It's not the same here; marriages of convenience have fallen into disuse; the happiness obtained from the intimate union of souls is considered more noble than the aggregation of fortunes—but before fusing two individuals in a common existence, they wish to be sure that their natures are compatible, and their souls suitable for combination.

"What is more painful in a household, after all, than two characters in incessant conflict? Youth passes over this discord when the attraction of material pleasure furnishes a sufficient compensation, but on the day when age paralyzes those relations, nothing remains in confrontation but the antipathy of two opposed characters—an antipathy increased by daily contact—and when a shared caprice no longer balances out the dissonance of souls, hatred quickly succeeds antipathy.

"That is why our descendants have returned to the ancient custom of engagement. They only give their children after having studied a suitor profoundly. That study, in order to be scrupulous, requires at least two years. A man who is strong enough to conceal his weaknesses for six months cannot hide the chinks in his armor for two years. These engagements are, therefore, the public consecration of a pledge given on both sides.

"However, as the objective of life is only accomplished by the union of two souls, the serious question of physical aptitude is not neglected. Sparta, whose far-sighted laws we hold up to ridicule, owed its strength to them for as long as its vigor lasted. It ordered that only those individuals recognized as being appropriate to fulfill the duties of marriage be coupled. Our descendants, searching ancient constitutions and collecting what was best from them, have exhumed that forgotten law. It is thus that future centuries will finish off the work of past centuries.

"Humans, as created beings, must employ the sources of life that they bear within them for the reproduction of their species. To dissipate such a precious deposit in futile pleasures is an act of the utmost ingratitude to toward the Creator, whose confidence it betrays. It is a sort of misappropriation, prejudicial to humanity. The people of early times, according to the calculations of science, were more solidly built and much taller than those of the present day, but the social gangrene of debauchery, corruption, abuse, exhausting the generative principle, have diminished humankind over time; the further we go, the more diminished we are.

"What has enabled the English aristocracy to remain so beautiful and so vigorous is that it has been able to reserve itself for marriage, and has only married within itself. The French aristocracy, by contrast, so strong and powerful in the Middle Ages, has debased itself and bastardized itself by misalliances, and even more so by the scandalous excesses of the reigns of François I, Henri II, Louis XIV and Louis XV, to such a point that the people, ashamed of bowing down before such despicable masters, have shaken off the yoke and proclaimed their independence.

"We are going through an awkward period at present. Society, badly shaken in 1789, has not yet broken with tradition; it is not sufficiently solidly constituted to enjoy its conquest. Accustomed to submit to those whom, in good faith, people believe to be above them, society allows its sage resolutions to be blocked by ancient errors. On the day when it has cast down the ambitious men who undermine it, its work will bear fruit.

"As I said before, there is nothing in creation that resembles a beginning so much as an end. If human morality were to regain its point of departure, human physique would also recover its primitive vigor. Excess has debased it; sobriety will re-elevate it, and generations to come will benefit progressively from the convalescence of their forebears.

"The people of the milieu in which I find myself have already profited from that amelioration. Hideous maladies do not carry them off before old age; they are almost all born healthy and well-built; they die of old age. Disease is the result of human depravity. Medicine has therefore become a sinecure. The lifespan has been extended, the death that youth is spare only strikes before its time by accident. The mean lifespan is fixed at 80 years; people often surpass 100.

"That is not to say that there are no exceptions. The wounds of vice, although much reduced, are not entirely scarred over. Nature itself, unequal in its distributions, does not accord all its privileges to everyone. It disgraces hunchbacks physically but compensates for its negligence by giving them a strong dose of intelligence, and *vice versa*. Then again, the Creator has conserved rights over humans that He has not revealed to us. The retarded minds and abortive beings that I distinguish in this regenerated world do not exist without a reason. Their contrast stimulates other people; their moral inferiority is proof that their time of expiation is less advanced and that they will pass through many more incarnations before their sins are completely effaced.

"In contrast to our era, the majority holds sway. In anticipation of exceptions society has elaborated laws full of wisdom, and, among others, stipulates an examining committee formed of members of two families, with matching numbers of men and women, assisted by a government inspector. This committee is responsible for establishing, in view of marriage, the physical aptitudes of the future spouses. No more secret affections, consequences of irregular conduct, which are only revealed when the most important of life's actions has been accomplished! The young man and the young woman are subjected by the competent commission to a minute inspection, and when they are declared fit for the duties of marriage, the engagement begins.

"In marrying their children, the parents are working to ensure the work of generation. Any other consideration would seem monstrous to them. No importance is attached to love if it is devoid of utility, even less to fortune; everyone's work is sufficient for them; they only make use of that of others, without preference, in order to assist one another to live; there is no unemployment. Protective law appoints suppliers for everyone, organized by a supervising council. It thus regulates the provenance of resources and makes the accumulation of disproportionate fortunes impossible.

"The aspirant spouse who is deemed inappropriate for marriage by the examining committee is condemned to celibacy. He is permitted, however, by way of compensation, to espouse a woman afflicted by the same ostracism, on condition that they adopt a young orphan. Both devoid of utility, they are, at least, good for bring up poor individuals deprived of their parents and educating them in the duties of life.

"A man, once married, is the master of his household; he has the upper hand in all things, but he has enough common sense to leave domestic sovereignty to his wife and to content himself with the role of provider for the family. Nearly 4500 years before the epoch of which I speak, a man of superior merit—Xenophon, a disciple of Socrates—drew up an admirable plan for household life in his treatise on *Economics*. And, surprisingly for that time, if one considers that the ancients placed their wives at the rank of servants or household utensils, the husband he places center stage elevates his own to his own level. He treats her as an equal and informs her of the first principles of order, the bases of domestic economy:

"'Nothing, my wife—the most beautiful in the world—is more useful than order. A choir is a union of individuals; were each one to sing the part that pleased him, what a disagreeable confusion there would be for the audience! But when all are carrying out the prescribed measures and singing in harmony, what charm there is for the ears and eyes alike!

"'It is the same with an army; if all its components behave independently—donkeys, hoplites, light troops, baggage-carts, cavalry, chariots—everything will be in disorder; hence, universal confusion and all service become impossible, with dishonor assured and victory certain for the enemy. In any maneuver carried out, everything gets mixed up; runners are impeded by marchers, those in ranks by runners, horsemen by chariot, chariots by mules, hoplites by baggage-carts. How can a battle be fought in the midst of such chaos? Those who are constrained to flee the enemy that is coming at them inevitably collide with armed me in their flight.

"'By contrast, what is more beautiful than a well-organized army? What enemy will not tremble, on seeing hoplites, cavaliers, peltasts, archers and pikemen all distributed in distinct bodies following their officers? I believe that I form an accurate idea of the confusion when I imagine a laborer heaping barley, cheese and legumes together in the same store-room, and then being obliged, if he wants pastry, bread or a plate of vegetables, to make a triage in order to find what he needs

"'Spare yourself such confusion, my wife; will you please administer our house in such a way that, if I ask for something, you can to find what is necessary, and offer it to me easily? Let us try to put everything in a suitable place. That triage once made, my wife, regard yourself as the preserver of the law in our household. Like the commandant of a garrison inspecting his troops, or the Athenian Council its horses and cavaliers, proceed, when you deem it necessary, to inspect our furniture, to see whether the items are sound. A queen in your house, use all your power to honor and praise whosoever merits it, to reprimand and chastise those who provoke your severity.'[9]

"To describe the duties of the wife in the household, I do not believe I can do better than borrow that sublime passage from Xenophon. He was the first to make woman the companion of man, at a time when she was merely a machine indispensable to reproduction. That profound thinker was certainly ahead of his time. Who knows whether the Supreme Being might send beings superior to their contemporaries among us in order to activate, thanks to their genius, the march of Progress?

"Our descendants, such as I see them at this moment, have put Xenophon's doctrine into practice. They have organized the household according to his instructions. They have raised women to the same level as men

---

[9] The author adds a footnote here crediting this quotation to chapters VIII and IX of Xenophon's *Economics*.

without, as today, placing them on a pedestal, without making them conventional divinities that we intoxicate with our banalities and homages. Is it not depreciating them to adore them in a servile manner? Is it not to offend their dignity to affect to live at their feet? It is not to make them feel their weakness cruelly to accept voluntary servitude under their yoke?

"Whereas the ancients made them domestic objects and the moderns make them an item of luxury, our descendants will make women companions. The prejudice that excludes them from the thinking mass is in contradiction with the sentiment of respect that everyone experiences for his mother. Nature is the only voice to which humans should listen.

"Women do not possess, however, an intelligence equal to that of men; theirs is more refined, more active and more impressionable, but also lighter, more variable and more superficial; it lacks depth. That of men, in conformity with their physical constitution, which destines them for hard work, is profound, reflective and stubborn—so it is true that there is a direct relationship between the physical and the mental. To women, the cares of the household, which only require mechanical attention; to men, the burden of public affairs, which demanded multiple combinations and logical reasoning. If the Supreme Being has made one sex strong and the other weak, it is because, in His infinite wisdom, he wanted to indicate the absolute superiority of men over women. Two forces endowed with equal power would be exposed to daily collisions.

"To conclude from this that instinct replaces the soul in women would be to add a paradoxical deduction. Two beings created to live together, to perpetuate one upon the other the admirable work of creation, necessarily entails their having the same elements. The dissimilarity only exists in their sex. Their souls conceive the same thoughts, are subject to the same passions, recognize the same Creator; if it were otherwise, they would not be able to join together in the unity of marriage, with a view to forming a complete whole.

"Differently dosed, according to their roles in this world, but regulated by the supreme, infinite, universal soul from which it is derived, their souls are formed of the same simple substance, unique and indivisible.

"Two beings, thus fortified by laborious life, having taken the trouble to study one another reciprocally, cannot fail to be suited to one another. They have employed the phase of their engagement to weigh their qualities and their flaws, and it is only after mature reflection that they have legalized their choice before humans, the Supreme Being sufficing to sanction their choice by means of conscience, that sensitive entity he had placed in every heart as the delegate of his authority, as an intermediary for communication with his creature. With accord assured there is no longer any fear that either of the two spouses will break their oath; their happiness is in the hearth. The adultery foreseen by the Code only presents itself in a proportion of three per cent; the cause then lies is the weakness of a momentary lapse or the premeditated agreement of two perverse natures.

"The law, however, competent as it is in general affairs, in internal and external politics, commercial, industrial and financial questions, does not extend its jurisdiction to the family. It is up to the family to repair what has been done; it alone is responsible, it alone being experienced in such matters. It has seen the spouses develop in its bosom; it had sound knowledge of their characters; it is able to judge them. The law limits itself to ratifying its decision. The guilty party is thus bought before the tribunal from which nothing is hidden.

"There, a great difficulty presents itself: the children. Separation grants them to the more worthy, divorce causes them to enter into a strange family; it is not, therefore, a practical solution. Absolute divorce, in the society that I am describing, is only admitted in cases where the marriage is sterile, and even then, before pronouncing it as a last resort, the family waits until the woman's condition has passed beyond the possibility of an initial pregnancy.

"If there are children, the law, not attributing to both spouses the fault of one alone, authorizes the plaintiff to remarry. If it is the mother who is at fault, she remains in the home of her remarried spouse, the mother of his children, but having lost her conjugal rights. It is the same for the father; justice has no preference. If the guilty party removes himself or herself from the difficulty, he or she is excluded from the social circle and sent to populate a distant colony; there are no more children, the individual being a pariah."

"But that situation," the Marquise put in," acceptable for a man, is not so for a woman."

"Either is free," Monsieur Landet replied, "to choose between the alternative judgments—to live independently within another's household, under the protection of the law, contenting herself with the link that still binds one to one's family: the children; or, if pride refuses that foreign hospitality, that one renounces one's children and accepts exile. It is up to the individual. Better to deprive children of a parent than conserve a bad one. The law has no leverage on the heart."

"And what if a woman, once remarried, weakens in her turn?" riposted the Marquise.

"There would no longer be any reason for the conclusion," the savant went on. "The woman would then, as of right, revert to her first husband, by the very fact of her fault."

"And what if there are children of the second marriage?"

"The mother does not leave her children. She remains, once the divorce is pronounced, in the home of her second husband, with the first, with the entitlement of a mother, just as he is installed there with the entitlement of a father."

"But a family might gather parasites indefinitely, by virtue of repeated adulteries by its members!"

"In our society, perhaps, but not in that one. You're forgetting, Madame, that the laws are one in effect because they are the consequences of a society better than ours. Laws are corollaries of the epochs that they regulate. This legislation, Utopian today, is the work of 20 centuries of progress. It astonishes you as much as ours would astonish the feudal lords of the Middle Ages if they returned to the world as they had quit it."

"I understand perfectly that our laws would be monstrous in the society that you are describing," the Marquise replied. "According to your theory, laws conform to the tastes, tendencies and needs of the epoch, following humans through the different periods of their incarnations, adapting to their transformations—but in any society, there inevitably exist material difficulties raised by exceptions, difficulties that the law needs to anticipate in its broadest extension. In cases of adultery, you say, a guilty woman, having lost her conjugal rights, remains in the home of a stranger, the father of her children. If the other, remarried spouse similarly fails in his duties, the two guilty parties return to one another; I admit that too. But what becomes of children born of the adultery?"

"I was getting to that when you interrupted me," the savant replied, dryly. "It would certainly not be just for poor little children, innocent of their parents' sin, to be condemned to suffer its effects, without support, sustenance or family. The law, benevolent but reluctant to mingle legitimate children with bastards, tales them into its care in special houses, and assigns them to the households of those refused by examining committees, who adopt them. They only know the mother and father that adoption gives them; too young to regret their natural parents, they learn to love those that the law attributes to them. Gratitude substitutes in their hearts for the voice of blood. Take note of the wisdom of this measure, which sets aside the bad example of their birth.

"Natural children are a more frequent exception. Two young people love one another, their souls are sympathetic, they do not have the patience to wait for the expiration of the engagement—or perhaps, not being affianced, they succumb to the violence of their sentiments. A child is born of that clandestine union. Should that be made a crime? No. Does human consent have the power to condemn the impulse of nature? No. Human consent is necessary to establish a fixed regulation on the disorder of passions, but there is no sin so long as the heart commits no perjury.

"They are both free, those young people; no oaths impose other duties upon them; the responsibility for their being led astray is incumbent on them alone. Let them repair their weakness in consecrating their premature action by marriage! If one of the two refuses, the law then exerts its rights; it demands. The deflowered woman cannot be the only author of her sin; the Creator, believe me, will not damn them for that. After all, they have not deceived anyone. Free, they have followed the impulsion of a mutual sympathy, having no other judge than their conscience, no other sanction than their word. Society is therefore incompetent to reproach their lack of strength. They have not done any wrong. It is prejudice that imprints the forehead of the fallen young woman with shame. If we did not have our petty weaknesses, we would be as perfect as the Creator, and that is inadmissible.

"Everything depends on circumstances. If the two young people succumb without having an intention to marry, or if a lover abuses his mistress with false promises, the law is inflexible in that regard. In the former case, it proceeds with a marriage or sends the lovers to the colonies, as they choose; in the second, it researches the paternity. And, indeed, why should the law allow the responsibility for a child to remain entirely with the woman, a weak and passive individual? Why, on the one hand, make her a victim, and on the other, favor the egoism of a debauchee by according him impunity? The fault is his as well as hers, and his more than hers, since he was the one who provoked and accomplished the bad deed. Whence comes the noxious breath of debauchery that infects our present society with gangrene? From the fact that the law, being too partial, does not research paternity. If men had the fear of being burdened with a child, they would reflect, and the evil, cauterized at its root, would gradually diminish.

"A man notices a woman; she pleases him; he seduces her, leads her astray, ruins her and enjoys her until the day when he runs the risk of being compromised—and when a child is born o their relations, when the woman is most in need of his support, he abandons her

51

and disappears in a cowardly fashion. Sometimes, he even has the audacity to shelter behind the letter of the law and reply to objections made to him that his position, his future would be injured if he recognized the child. Who can prove, in the final analysis, that the child is really his? With the reputation and future of the young woman he is unconcerned. What does that matter to him? Should he suffer for it? It isn't worth the trouble, for a caprice, of hindering his career.

"Thus there is an unfortunate young woman, ruined forever. She has no other resource but to accept the equivocal role of mistress. Always under the threat of the unforeseen, her mind works and become embittered; she suffers from the illicit situation that proscribes her from her family, attempts to free herself, and is further ruined.

"If her lover abandons her on the fatal day, so much the worse. She has no other prospect than poverty—and yet she is a mother; a new sentiment has taken possession of her; she loves her child. It is necessary to nurse that little creature, to live for the child if not for herself. First she despairs; then resigns herself and works. She can scarcely earn enough to meet her most essential expenses. That lasts until privation has sapped her energy. Then discouragement takes hold of her; she glimpses a easier way of making a living. She is young and pretty; she sells herself.

"In selling herself, however, her modesty revolts at the idea of setting herself to rights with the moral police. To submit to a weekly inspection, to be mingled with the rejects of society, rolling in the mud, to be classified, with her order number! Never! She still conserves an appearance of dignity. She despises herself, but does not want her shame to be inscribed in the register at the prefecture. The police, however, on the lookout, catch her *in flagrante delicto* in vagabondage, take her to the Station, and after a few days spent in that horrible place, set her free, on the promise that there will be no backsliding.

"She continues her infamous trade and, caught again, is taken back to the Station and from there to Saint-Lazare. Henceforth, she is public property; she is no longer a woman but a number. The few generous sentiments battling in her favor desert her heart as soon as she has crossed the threshold of that filthy redoubt. She gradually adopts the kind of life of the women with whom she finds herself in daily contact, acquires their habits, their language, their cynicism. She emerges from there transformed. What does the world's esteem matter? One can live without that. She receives a police license and exercises her trade under the tolerant aegis of the law, which assigns her a perimeter to exploit, outside of which Saint-Lazare will punish any act of insubordination.

"That life becomes her element. She rivals her peers in scandal, speculates on men, whom she hates in memory of her first lover, and only adores one God: money. Her child is a hindrance and is handed over to a nurse, then to an obliging boarding-school, and finally, when old age opens the prospect of poverty again, if the child is a girl, she recruits her to her infamous trade; if he is a boy, she teaches him to profit from an even more infamous trade: trafficking in women.

"That creature, more to be mourned than blamed, would have been a good mother without the deadly counsel of despair. What is the first cause of her debasement? The man, who sows victims on his route, protected by the text of the law.

"Registered prostitution and licensed brothels are the remedies that modern civilization has brought to bear on the invasion of debauchery. Instead of restraining it, they propagate it.

"Our descendants have cut off the evil at its root. Placing all the responsibility upon the man, they have thus stifled the seed of prostitution at its inception.

"To anticipate the imperious needs of nature they have instituted marriage at an appropriate age: men at 25 at the latest, women at 22, the age of legal majority in either case being fixed at 21. A man who exceeds that limit loses his civil rights; he no longer is an integral part of society. A woman is afflicted in what she holds most dear: her dignity. She is placed under police surveillance for fear that her desires, suddenly sharpening, might cause her to disturb the security of families.

"The paternal consent that is, in our day, a hindrance to the union of two young people, often without sufficient motive, is submissive to the decision of the family council. In case of refusal, the young people may appeal to civil justice, which arbitrates the conflict as a last resort. At 21, they are free to go their own way, without respectful notice; there are precautions in that instance reserved to the law, but to which such a well-organized society does not dream of having recourse. Is not the spirit of the law to cater for the worst possibilities?

"Every family has its internal government in miniature, under the arbitrage of the government, which only gets involved in its affairs at the final extremity, like the Supreme Court.

"In the beginning, as I have said, before empires, before cities, before curia, before tribes, there as the family. The family, in multiplying, formed curia, cities, empires. Society began with the family; it with the family that it will end."

At this point, Hobson made a sign to indicate that the savant had done enough. As if to put him to sleep, he gathered all his energy and made several passes in an inverse direction over his eyes. Then, to disengage him, he blew lightly on his forehead and finally, by means of sweeping passes from the head to the extremities, all along the arms and the legs, he expelled the fluid to the earth.

The Marquise's guests, stirred by the fantastic séance, watched without saying a word. The smiles had left the lips of the most incredulous. The Marquise herself had the serious and reflective expression of a woman who has just attended a religious ceremony.

Monsieur Landet uttered a profound sigh, like a man relieved of a heavy burden. He rubbed his eyes, opened one and then the other, and looked around him in bewilderment.

"Where am I?" he murmured.

"We can see that you've come back from far away, dear friend," said the Marquise, recovering her liveliness. "You're in the home of your old adversary."

"It's astonishing," said thee savant, who was beginning to collect himself. "I don't know what I'm experiencing, but it seems to me that I'm emerging from a dream. I'm exhausted."

"And you have, indeed, been dreaming," Hobson replied.

"Bah! I was dreaming, that's true—I don't, however, remember..."

"Stenography has remembered for you," said Hobson, handing him the work of the stenographers.

"Here—read it yourself. That language isn't algebra to you, and even if it were, you'd understand it."

"What!" the savant exclaimed "I said all this? But that's amazing! I'm no longer dreaming! You can assure me that I'm no longer dreaming?"

"No, you're wide awake."

"There's an entire theory here, an entire world! Utopia now, verity later. Oh, my dear magnetizer, you'll render me immortal."

"You already are," said the Marquise.

"Oh, what is academic immortality in comparison with that which awaits me!"

"And your wager?" said Hobson.

"What wager?"

"You don't remember that you doubted magnetism two hours ago?"

"Why, that's true!" exclaimed the savant. "But this time, my dear sorcerer, I shan't leave you again until we have given birth to the dream of the future."

"The lunch, then..."

"Is settled—more than ever." Monsieur Landet held out his hand, adding: "Above all, don't forget the stenographers."

Chapter Three
METAPHYSICS

The next day, Monsieur Landet and Mr. Hobson, flanked by the two stenographers, did battle with an excellent lunch in a private room at the Café Anglais. The numerous uncorked bottles and the debris scattered on the plates testified to the gastronomic capabilities of the two gentlemen.

They were taking coffee, and inhaling the perfume of authentic Havana cigars in the manner of connoisseurs.

"Do you know, my dear sorcerer," said Monsieur Landet, whose small eyes were beginning to blink, "that one could get a great deal out of magnetism, in politics?"

"Assuredly," Hobson replied. "I'm not far from believing that several of our statesmen make covert use of it in diplomacy."

"For myself, I confess that I'm your fervent disciple and that if ever a ministerial conspiracy assigns me to foreign affairs, I shall not take any initiative without having abandoned myself, on the sacred tripod, to the inspirational breath of your magnetic pressure. I shall be my own Pythoness and you will be my Apollo. Is that now how one can explain the oracles of the Pythoness at Delphi and the Sibyl at Cumaea—oracles whose realization were a marvel of antiquity?

"Those priestesses must have been nervous, impressionable women prepared early in life for the role destined for them, submitted to the fluidic influence of some skilled high priest who—like you, my dear Monsieur

Hobson—fulfilled the office of the divinity with respect to them. The vapors escaping from the gulf over which the tripod was laced, the convulsive tremors that agitated the somnambulist priestess, were an ingenious complement to the great scene of inspiration, imagined with the objective of making an impact on the ignorant mass and revealing the presence of the divinity by means of physical effects in harmony with the superstitious ideas of the epoch. And those hallucinations often spoke the truth; at least, history reports that." The savant had become pensive. He added: "Who knows whether, by publishing this perception of the world in 2000 years, we might accelerate the match of progress?"

"Don't believe it. It's an anticipatory study that will interest intellectual society, but which the ordinary public will regard as a utopia and perhaps condemn it without having taken cognizance of it, on the strength of rumor. What is written in the book of destiny is not effaced by human desires. If the term of 2000 years is fixed for the degree of perfection that you have glimpsed in the somnambulistic state, the world will take 20 centuries to effect its transformation."

"Yes, we're not sufficiently mature, more's the pity!" said Monsieur Landet, with a half-smile. "And yet, between ourselves, I like it better that this transformation will only take place when I'm gone—my little operations on the Bourse would suffer thereby."

The fumes of the wine must have gone to Monsieur Landet's head for him to be so frank.

"Oh, you're very much of your century," Hobson replied.

"Eh? I'm not so discontented with what my century provides."

"Because your century doesn't treat you so badly, it seems to me. You're a senator, a member of the Institut, rich and decorated. What more could you want?"

"I should like, while alive, to reform society, without that posing any threat to my interests."

"Have a little patience. In a few centuries, you'll return to Earth as an actor of the theory that you have prophesied."

"Oh, but then," Monsieur Landet replied, with the mischievousness of a sophist, "I'll be reborn with the sentiments of my new epoch, and, improved by successive incarnations, I shall have no regrets."

"I'm vanquished by my own weapons," said the magnetizer, bowing.

"Do you sincerely believe that we are subject to different incarnations after death?" the savant went on.

"Didn't you just say that to me that yourself?"

"I said it to you for the sake of the argument, to vanquish you with your own weapons, as you just put it. That's a child's game. Socrates invented it 500 years before Christ."

"But haven't you denied the existence of Christ in a pamphlet entitled *Errors of tradition*?"

"Once, when I had nothing better to say."

"Then you make your opinions a question of dialectic?"

"I might believe in it one day."

"When?"

"On my death-bed" the savant sighed, speaking half-seriously and half in jest. "If Christ existed after all, it would be prudent to have my passport validated for the other world."

The good lunch, copiously washed down, had definitely betrayed the secrets of Monsieur Landet's philosophy. Never had he shown himself so communicative. "But we're forgetting the principal motive for our rendezvous, my dear master," he went on. "*Time is money*, the English say, and they're right; they think like practical men. For us, time is glory; I'm not young enough to put it off until tomorrow."

"As you wish," Hobson replied. "Install yourself in that armchair as you did yesterday, and now you have faith, go to sleep without resistance."

"It seems to me that yesterday, as well as today, you found me as docile as a lamb."

"Mental resistance, I meant."

"Does that impede the action of the fluid?"

"The energy I deploy in overcoming that resistance tires us both. That prolongs the passage, already difficult, from the waking to the somnambulistic state; it weighs upon the brain before it has begun to work."

"Let's go! I abandon my free will to you—but don't abuse the deposit."

"My power doesn't extend that far," said the magnetizer, gathering all the force of his will. "Now, not another word."

The savant let his head fall back on to the back of the armchair. In less than a minute, he was asleep.

Hobson took his hand and began the customary interrogation, making a sign to the stenographers to take up their post.

"Are you asleep?"

"Yes, I'm asleep. I feel quite well; I'd like to remain in this state permanently."

"You mustn't. Shake off that torpor; it will numb you."

"What's the point? I prefer to savior this delightful repose in peace."

"What about the world in 2000 years?"

Monsieur Landet started in his armchair. "That's true!" he exclaimed. "Science! Science before everything!"

As on the previous day, Hobson waited for the savant to travel a distance of 20 centuries. "Are you there?" he asked, when he saw a certain expression of satisfaction spread across his subject's face.

"I'm there."

"Yesterday, you analyzed the family, the fundamental basis of society," Hobson went on. "Today, would you like to interpret internal politics?"

"Let us take things in order," the savant replied—that locution must have been familiar to him in his courses at the Collège de France. "Let us tackle metaphysics. Politics are merely the consequence of the superstitious beliefs of peoples."

"Speak—and you, gentlemen, write."

On the Existence of God

"In creating human beings, God imprinted in their souls the notion of a superior principle, of which he is the original.

"At all times, among all peoples, there has been religion: 'The social bond is not easy to establish between human beings, who are so various, so free and so inconstant. To give them rules, to institute commandments and make obedience accept them, to make passion yield to reason and individual reason to public reason, assuredly requires something stronger than material force, more respectable than self-interest, surer than a philosophical theory, more immutable than a convention: something

61

that would be both at the bottom of every heart and hold empire over it.

"'That thing is a belief. There is nothing more powerful over the soul. A belief is the work of our mind, but we are not free to modify it at will. It is our creation, but we do not know that. It is human, but we think it Divine. It is an effect of our power, but it is stronger than us; it speaks to us continuously. Humans can tame their nature, but are enslaved by their thought.

"'Let us embrace with our gaze the road that humans have traveled. In the beginning, the family lived in isolation, and humans only knew domestic gods. Above the family formed the phratry, with its own god. Then came the tribe and the god of the tribe. Finally, the city arrived, and a god was conceived whose providence embraced the entire city. A hierarchy of belief, a hierarchy of association. The religious idea was, among the Ancients, the organizing breath of society.

"'The traditions of the Hindus, the Greeks and the Etruscans relate that the gods had revealed social laws to humans; beneath that legendary form there is a truth. Social laws were the work of the gods, but the gods, so powerful and so benevolent, were nothing but the beliefs themselves.

"'Now, an ancient belief commanded humans to honor their ancestors; the cult of the ancestors grouped the family around the altar. From there, the primary religion, came the first priests, the first idea of duty and the first morality. Then belief expanded, and association with it. As humans sensed that there were communal divinities, they came together in more extensive groups. The same rules, found and established within the family, applied successively to the phratry, the tribe and the city.'[10]

"Opinions of divinity therefore differed. Everyone imagined it according to the idea that he formed of it and gave it attributes so various that there were at first as many gods as families, as phratries, as tribes or as cities.

"Christianity confirmed the Arian doctrine and proclaimed the existence of one single God in three persons. Philosophers made him infinite or limited, universal or partial, material or immaterial, invisible or present—but all of them, save for a few exceptions who built a pedestal for their atheism, were in agreement as to his existence.

Whether that God, according to the locality, took the name of the Supreme Being, the Great Spirit, Jehovah, Allah, Jupiter, Zeus, Buddha, Brahma-Vishnu-Shiva, God; whether he was represented in three persons or one alone; whether he was unified or divided; whether he was honored under the appearances of the sun, the moon, water, fire, the earth, or even plants and animals, he was nonetheless God—which is to say, the unknown master that everything obeyed. Only the name and the form changed.

---

[10] The author includes a footnote crediting this quotation to Nome-Denis Fustel de Coulanges' *Cité antique*, Book III, Chapter IV. That text, first published in 1864, and translated into English as *The Ancient City*, was one of the most important of the period, attempting to build a theory of social evolution on the basis of historical data regarding the development of the Greek city states and the empires that absorbed them. It is on the basis of a similar theory, taking aboard many of Fustel's assertions, that the author of the present text is attempting to anticipate the future course of social evolution. A phratry is a subdivision of a tribe identified by the Athenians.

"All people feels the need to shelter beneath an invisible power, which they divines, which they sense, which they cannot explain, which reveals itself to them at every instant but never shows itself. Is not pretending to define that which escapes reason the height of human presumption? If God were to show himself in his real form, we would no longer be living in that dread of the unknown, which magnifies him in our eyes.

"'I do not know what put me in the world or what I am. I am in a terrible ignorance of everything. I only know what my body is, what my senses are, that my soul is the part of me that thinks what I say, which reflects upon everything and upon itself and does not know itself any more than the rest. I see the frightful spaces of the universe that enclose me, and I find myself attached to a corner of that vast expanse, without knowing why I am in this place rather than another, nor why the short time that is given to me to live, has been assigned to me at this point rather than another in the eternity that preceded me and that which will follow me. I see nothing but infinities everywhere, which enclose me like an atom, and like a shadow that lasts but an instant and never returns. All that I know is that I must soon die, but that I do not know what death is, any more than I can escape it.'[11]

"That perpetual uncertainty which is our destiny, that prospect of death which threatens us incessantly, which sometimes strikes us at the moment when we least expect it, the very impossibility of avoiding it, forces us to admit a supreme principle from which all humankind derives.

---

[11] The author's footnote credits this passage to article one of Pascal's *Pensées*, "Against the indifference of atheists."

"The limits within which our intelligence finds itself restrained, since infinity borders it on every side without it being able to fathom its extent, render our imperfection evident.

"The world, in spite of the clever sophisms of a few philosophers, cannot have made itself. 'Nothing comes from nothing,' says Lucretius. It follows logically that all the marvels that we see around us, distributed with such perfect regularity, which we admire without comprehending either the origin or he utility, are the work of that supreme principle. If humans had made themselves, they would understand the mystery of how they came into the world; they would understand their soul, their intelligence, their thought, their beginning and their end; in a word, they would comprehend themselves—and they do not. They cannot comprehend themselves, because they cannot both be cause and effect. In order for them to be the cause, they would have had to exist before being the effect, and if they had existed before that, they would have had no need to create themselves, since they would have had the quality of which they were claiming to be the author: existence.

"If humans had created the world, they would be able to explain its mechanism, its origin and its duration. They would know what is happening on thousands of planets, a new one of which, without them being aware of it, appears every day in the field of the telescope. They would know whether those planets are inhabited, like ours. But they know nothing; they merely reason from hypotheses that contradict one another. They are less than nothing in that unknown immensity.

"They cannot be the work of chance, any more than the world, because chance still supposes a Creator.

"It is therefore necessary that there is above us an uncreated being, which knows everything that we do not know, and which is all that we are not, which fills by itself that Infinity whose extent is hidden from the range of our reflection.

"Eternity! Infinity! Insoluble problems with which the audacious conceptions of thought collide. Ought not the very fact of our impotence and our negligibility to be sufficient to reveal the Creator?

"If humans have an intelligence too narrow to seek the proofs of the existence of God in the high regions of metaphysics, let them be content with the physical proofs they encounter every day in nature; let them be content with the sentiment innate within the soul, which furnishes the intuition via the organ of conscience. To invoke all those proofs one by one would be to fall into repetition; we have only to cast our eyes around to be convinced of it; and in any case, they carry little weight by comparison with metaphysical proofs.

"But I do not have to demonstrate here that which imposes itself, and always has imposed itself, on human reason; I am studying the mores, the laws and the beliefs of a society more advanced that ours; it is to that task that I ought to confine myself. I have only allowed myself to be drawn into this preliminary study in order to facilitate a transition between the ideas of our epoch and those of society in 2000 years.

"I'm looking for a temple, but I can't see any. Ah! Yes, I can see one—only one; an immense temple on the fronton of which I read, in letters of gold: TO THE SU-PREME BEING. Inside, nothing that denotes the practice of religious ceremonies. The walls are denuded of hangings. The architecture is severe and imposing: no altars, no statues, no ornaments, nothing that attracts the eye and captures the attention, to the detriment of the deity. The divinity alone is invisible and present, impalpable and real. One divines its presence, senses the perfume of sanctity that reigns in this place. It is truly great only when one reveals one's soul to it without the aid of any external apparatus.

"There are no priests living in idleness under the illusory pretext of the maintenance of worship. Humans do not have the right to withdraw from the circle of society, to decline the obligations of life. They are on this earth to fulfill their duties, to attain an objective. If they deny those duties and deny that objective, concentrating on their egoism, they become neutered beings; that is contrary to nature.

"This temple is open day and night. There is no fear of anyone stealing sacred objects; there are none. As for offices, there are none of those either. Everyone comes to pray to God when conscience instructs them to. Progress has got rid of our prejudices of exterior worship; all the people here bear their own worship in their hearts, adore their own particular Supreme Being as they conceive it, and render no other homage thereto but an honest life employed in labor. God demands no more.

"The religion of our day, especially the Catholic religion, is a medium of speculation like any other. Everything costs money: burials, births, marriages, dispensations . Merchants have established in the Churches; some hire out chairs, others sell candles, exercising their petty trades under the aegis of piety. Can one claim to be following the maxims of the Master in that fashion? Did Christ not cast the merchants out of the Temple? What can a candle do for a dead person? Can the offering of a relative or friend diminish their demerit, advance them on the road of Eternity? If the offerings of the living can redeem the sins of the dead, one could be a scoundrel in life, trusting in the generosity of those one leaves behind. Is it not the same with prayers? God would no longer be just if the supplications of the living could abridge the punishment of the dead. To counterbalance his wrath with the price of a certain number of candles, masses or indulgences would be too easy—and people survived only by poor or indifferent relatives, or none a all, would be subject to the full extent of their punishment, for lack of candles, masses and indulgences. On that basis, the rich would have the advantage over the poor of gaining heaven more rapidly, only having merited it by virtue of their money.

"The justice of God is the same for everyone. Is it not offensive to suppose, on the contrary, that it might be corruptible by presents, sensitive to prayers? All those puerilities diminish the Catholic religion and make it ridiculous; they bury it under a heap of contradictions.

"The Protestant religion, grafted on to the Catholic religion, has taken from it that which is good and left behind that which is defective. It has reestablished marriage for priests, arbitrarily abolished by Pope Gregory VII; it has made its temples, from which it has banished superfluous ornaments, places of meditation. There is no distinction of fortune there; the rich and the poor may sit down side by side; one does not pay for the time that one spends elevating one's soul to God. It is, in that sense, more advanced than the Catholic religion, but it is no less destined to perish as well, because both are born of human fantasy.

"The Creator has not imposed conventional rites on humans; he created them with the intuition of a Supreme Being but demanded no other worship than that they follow scrupulously the instinct of their conscience. If he had wanted to be adored under the form of some particular religion he would have shown himself visibly and dictated his will. Now, as he has surrounded himself with mystery, it is because he considers himself greater in remaining unknown.

"The primary duty of humans, on this earth, is to carry out the mission that God has confided to them. That mission consists of living by their labor, in order to earn a better existence solely by merit of duty accomplished; it is not difficult to be a good person at that price. A good person has only to follow the unique route mapped out by conscience, the interpreter of divine will. That mission also consists of transmitting the seed of generation of which the individual human is the depository; that is the worship most agreeable to God.

"Priests, in ridding themselves of that obligation, in devoting themselves to celibacy, are entering into open conflict with their Creator. Created themselves, by virtue of a divine principle, they refuse to obey the most sacred maxim of the gospel of which they are nevertheless the commentators. What purpose is there in their being in the world if their lives must be spent in futile practices, if they do not leave other beings after them to perpetuate the mystery of Creation? If their parents had thought like them, where would they be? Non-existent. It is, therefore, a false idea that they have of God in believing that the gift of their chastity is, in his eyes, a meritorious sacrifice. God did not create two sexes in order for people to reserve the homage of their distinctive attributes to him. If that were the case, the world would cease to be, for lack of generators.

"Priestly celibacy is thus condemned by the most elementary principles of reason. Their ministry is no less than the capacity that everyone has, to the same degree, to give thanks to God, without the assistance of a foreign intermediary. A human being is no less human for being a priest; as a human being, the consecration of human beings is impotent to dress him in the reflection of the divinity.

"It has been recognized, moreover, that continence irritates the inherent appetites of the human animal and sometimes excites priests to actions all the more monstrous because they are the result of long-suppressed desire. The sad examples of popes that history transmits to us and the annals of tribunals have made the abolition of that institution an urgent necessity.

"In the epoch I am describing to you, priests no longer exist—or, rather, everyone is his or her own priest. Religious ceremonies no longer waste precious time owed to more fruitful occupations; they no longer exist. God is content with the simple homage of human thought, at times when work leaves people the leisure to elevate themselves toward him.

"What does he make of the splendor and glitter of ornaments, the tedium of offices, the pomp of ceremonies? Is he not above the paltriness of vanity? To render him sensible to such puerilities is to diminish him; it is to make him in our image."

"And what idea do the people have of God?" asked Hobson.

"God," the savant continued, "is nowhere and everywhere; God is invisible and present; God is formless, devoid of appearance or volume, and he fills the world; God is infinitely good, infinitely powerful, infinitely everything; he is eternal, immaterial, universal; he is pure spirit.

"He has made use of matter to form humans, but, wishing to engrave within him an impression of the superior principle from which they derive, he has animated them with a parcel of his essence. There is nothing in the soul that indicates a mixture of different substances, nothing that seems molded of terrestrial clay, nothing that presents itself to us in the appearance of water, fire or earth. Those bodies, in fact, do not possess memory, intelligence or reflection; they do not have the faculties of remembering the past, embracing the present or anticipating the future: divine attributes, the origin of which can only go back to God.

"The soul is therefore perfectly distinct from that which falls upon the senses. In consequence, everything that lives, suffers and reflects is of divine essence, and necessarily eternal. Where is the soul? What is it? Where is yours? Where is mine? Who can say? Our intelligence does not extend that far. The soul cannot be seen. It is an eye that sees everything around it, but cannot see itself. Thus, it is unaware of its own form. But that is unimportant. It is aware of its wisdom, its memory, its movement: that alone is divine, that alone is eternal. It is futile to seek any further an appearance in which it hides and in which it resides. It exists; it is existence itself; that is all that we can know about it.

"The soul, within the carnal envelope, has lost its initial subtlety; there remains to it an intuition of the divine principle from which it emanates; it males vain efforts to raise itself up to that principle, to comprehend it, to see it; but the material prison in which it is enclosed thwarts its thrusts. Attached to the body, it cannot raise itself above matter; it obeys it and commands it at the same time; it can only become itself again, entirely purified of material contact, by means of the series of its incarnations. Eternal, like its original principle, it is a spark running through the centuries in order to regain its

71

point of departure: eternity. During that exile, however, it loses an exact notion of its nature.

"Does every person not hear, in the depths of conscience, a voice that cries: 'Limited spirit, imperfect being, I forbid you too cross the limit that I have imposed on your intelligence; I forbid you to penetrate the sanctuary reserved for me. Your soul will only enjoy my contemplation once delivered from its corporeal bonds. I give you the sentiment of Infinity and the sentiment of the Eternal, but I forbid you to plumb their depths. That is my essence; that is my prerogative.'

"Indeed, as far as our thought can reach, it encounters nothing but Infinity, always Infinity, more Infinity, the eternal immensity—and, in those fearful spaces, the infinite smallness of our being. The further it looks back into itself, the less it comprehends.

"How can we get out of that vicious circle? The idea of infinity implies the idea of God; the idea of God implies that of infinity, and reciprocally. It is necessary that God be infinite, to impose himself on his Creation; it is necessary that Infinity be divine, in order for it not to fall upon the senses. What is Infinity? What is God? Infinity is God, the one being the attribute of the other, similarly implying the idea of Eternity. If God were not eternal, it would be necessary for him to be created, for him to have had a beginning, for him to have an end; he would thus be reduced to our level; he would be derived himself from a superior principle, he would no longer be God. Why did he have no beginning? Why will he have no end? We are no more in a position to explain that than we are to explain Infinity, and Infinity imposes itself logically upon our thought. To limit Infinity would be to conceive of another Infinity, itself limited by another Infinity, and so on.

"Universality is another of the deity's attributes. If God were not nowhere and everywhere at the same time, would our conscience sense his presence? If he were occupied in judging the actions of one of us in particular, could he be, at the same time, the impartial judge of the least of our actions? His infinite justice would no longer be infallible, and, in order that it should be, as it must, it is necessary that he embraces everything at once; he is, therefore, infinite, eternal and universal.

"Insofar as infinite goodness is concerned, eternal punishment is repugnant to him. When made humans imperfect, it was not to punish them eternally for the weaknesses of their imperfection; by way of compensation, he endowed them with a certain measure of personal responsibility: the free will that permits them to choose between god and evil.

"Insofar as infinite justice is concerned, ought he to reserve the same destiny for the good and the evil? The simplest common sense answers in the negative. But the punishment he reserves for the wicked, by virtue of his infinite generosity, and the imperfection of the guilty party, cannot be eternal. Its duration is proportional to their sins. It is purely moral, not physical.

"Hell is merely a fiction invented by weak minds. The priests of all epochs and all religions have profited by it to take possession of the minds of peoples and hold them in a sort of superstitious stewardship. They have imagined gripping scenes that strike the imagination, and have appropriated to it the tendencies of their epoch.

"This is the description that Virgil gives us of Hell: 'Suddenly, Aeneas looks behind him, and sees to his left, under a rock, a vast fortress flanked by a triple wall. The Phlegeton, a rapid torrent, surrounds it with its flaming weaves, carrying rocky debris noisily. The enclosure is sealed by an immense door, sustained by massive diamond columns; no human force, nor even any divine force, can tear them from their foundations. An iron tower rises up into the clouds. Tisiphone is sitting on the threshold, dressed in a blood-stained robe whose folds she is lifting to her waist. She watches there, day and night, without ever closing her eyelids. Groaning voices escape from that place, the cruel whistling of whips and the frightful clanking of iron chains being dragged.'[12]

"That Hell is concordant with the idea the ancients had of the divinity. For them, the gods were heroes deified after death, legendary individuals who retained our appetites and vices. The represented them as continually at war with one another. Their own power was subject to laws to which they were bound to submit.

"Furthermore, their Hell was multiple in its tortures: 'I then saw Tityon, said the Sibyl, that monstrous nursling of the Earth, whose extended body covers nine arpents: an enormous vulture with a curved beak was tearing at his immortal liver and his entrails fecund in torments, digging therein to nourish itself, and residing eternally I the depths of his torso without giving any truce to his incessantly-reborn flesh. Shall I tell you about the Lapiths, Ixion and Pirithous? A frightful rock is suspended over them, which will fall, which is already falling upon their heads, threatening them eternally. In front of them shine sumptuous beds with golden feet, and before their lips, tables laden with luxurious foodstuffs befitting kings; but seated at their side is the most

---

[12] The author gives a reference to Book VI, lines 548-558 of the *Aeneid*. Tisiphone, usually but not always identified as one of the Furies, had a name identifying her as the avenger of murder

redoubtable of the Furies, who forbids them to reach out their hands, standing up and brandishing her torch and making her voice thunder. Some are rolling an enormous rock, others are attached to the spokes of a wheel what carries them in its rotations. There, forever, seated beneath the stone, is the unfortunate Theseus, and Phlegyas, raising his masculine voice in the shadow of Tartarus, testifying to the justice of the gods in crying incessantly to the dead instructed by his torture: *Learn from my example to respect justice and not to scorn the gods.*[13]

"The ancients thus went so far as to deify evil, and did not hesitate to place themselves under the protection of infernal gods. Their mythology, profoundly rooted in the mind, has survived their religion, and when Christianity triumphed over paganism it felt obliged to conserve these ancient beliefs and to erect the bases of its doctrine on the ruins of pagan superstition. Hence the old prejudice of Hell, implanted even in our era—with the difference, however, that the new religion, in unifying the divinity, also unified punishment.

"Time has reckoned with monuments and human beings, but prejudice remains, magnified by tradition. Christian priests, borrowing this image off Hell from antiquity, adapted it to the new doctrines they were propagating. In continually representing Hell to the eyes of credulous people, however, they do not suspect that they are diminishing God in the ideas of sane people.

---

[13] *Ibid.*, lines 575-627. Tityon was held to have raped Latona, the mother of Apollo. The Lapiths waged murderous war against the centaurs after a dispute arose at the wedding of Pirithous; Theseus aided them. Phlegyas set fire to a temple of Apollo as an act of vengeance.

Return good for evil, says the Gospel; but, taking the opposite direction to their sacred text, they attribute our faults to God, without leaving him our qualities. They make him vindictive while he commands us to forgive our peers."

"What is the destiny of humans after death, then?" asked Hobson.

"My head is heavy; I need to recover my strength," the savant replied. "Wake me up."

Hobson did as he was asked—but the reawakening was painful. Monsieur Landet was profoundly steeped in the subject he had just been studying. The magnetizer took a good ten minutes bringing him back to reality.

Finally, the savant opened his eyes. "Where am I?" he murmured.

"In the Café Anglais in front of a glass of sherry, which is only awaiting your pleasure."

"In the Café Anglais!" the savant repeated. Then he slapped his forehead. "Ah! I'm here! I've come back from so far away!"

The Incarnation of Souls

The following morning, at eleven o'clock, Monsieur Landet's domestic introduced Mr. Hobson into the savant's study.

The two friends exchanged a vigorous handshake in the American style and went into the dining-room, where a gourmet lunch had been laid out. Needless to say, the two stenographers were also there.

They chatted about the previous day's experiment, transporting themselves in the imagination into the night of centuries. They were lost in the limbo of the future to such an extent that Monsieur Landet, thinking that he was in the bosom of the reformed society he had glimpsed in the somnambulistic state, replied to his domestic, who was pouring out the Branne-Mouton: "You're very kind, Monsieur..." He was fidgeting in his chair, though. He was impatient and preoccupied.

From the dining-room they went back to the study.

Monsieur Landet drew the curtains to create a discreet half-light, settled himself in a soft Voltaire chair and held his hand out toward the magnetizer.

"Now, dear Master," he said, "release the fluid and let's depart for the higher regions of metaphysics." He had no sooner finished speaking than his eyes closed. The pressure of the magnetizer's will, combined with the savant's free disposition, had established between them what is known in magnetism as a sympathetic current.

Hobson gave him time to reach his destination and repeated the traditional phrase. "Are you there?"

"I'm there."

"We paused on the matter of human destiny after death."

"I'm impregnating myself with the beliefs I'm analyzing," the savant replied, and began: "God, in spite of his infinite bounty, cannot treat the virtuous and the wicked equally. It is necessary that his infinite bounty is in accord with his infinite justice. Thus, he condemns the wicked to a temporary pain, proportionate to their sins. That punishment consists of passing through a series of successive and compensatory incarnations, on the planet where he has lived, until the end of the world, the epoch in which they will finally be deemed worthy to share his blissful eternity and enjoy his contemplation."

"It is, then, a great felicity to enjoy the sight of God?" Hobson asked.

"It is the highest summit of felicity that the soul can attain," the savant went on. "God, enclosing within himself all the nuances of the universal infinity, suffices to fulfill the most extreme appetites of the soul, thus purified by the proof of existences.

"Humans, chained to matter, and delighting in vulgar pleasures, cannot have any exact idea of it, but my mind, disengaged from my body in the somnambulistic state, comes close to it without comprehending it."

"And how is this incarnation achieved?"

"The soul, freed from its material envelope, wanders in the Earth's zone of attraction—assuming the Earth to be the planet on which it is incarnated—and continues to be in fluidic communication with the people who are still connected with it by links of blood, affection or hatred, by reason of the cohesion that links souls together. Then, when the death of those individuals has broken the magnetic attachment that welded it to them, and the soul is thus disengaged from all human contact and none of those particularly known to it survive down here, all memory is extinguished within it; the past dissipates like a dream glimpsed in the somnambulistic state, and it is clad in a new body. In that new incarnation, bearing within it the seed of progress in an intuitive state, it recommences life at the beginning, but in a more advanced society, until, purified by a series of successive stages, it attains the degree of relative perfection that brings it closer to the eternal Infinity.

"These incarnations occur on the Earth—I am only occupied here with the Earth—and not between planets, as some modern philosophers claim. The soul, while being a simple substance, remains even after death within the Earth's zone of attraction by reason of the magnetic principle, which is exercised on simple substances as well as composite substances. And as the force of attraction emitted by the terrestrial nucleus is felt in a considerable proportion, it continues to be subject to it until relative perfection, toward which its various incarnations gradually bring it, delivers it from all external influence and transports it of its own accord into the eternal Infinity with which it is confused."

"How can these various incarnations through which it passes before arriving at perfection free it from all external influence?" Hobson interjected.

"The soul, as I have already said," the savant replied, "is subject to the same magnetic laws as matter— or, rather, to analogous ones. God or Infinity, whatever you care to call it, is the central nucleus of which it is an infinitesimal part and toward which it tends, but its imperfection, which subjects it to the terrestrial magnetic fluid, prevents it from aggregating therewith. Each new incarnation gradually strips it of the material tendencies that subject it to that terrestrial magnetic fluid and guides it to relative perfection. In consequence, the further it advances in the series of incarnations, the more it is isolated from material attraction, and the higher it rises toward the supreme goal. There comes a moment when, unburdened of the weight that held it captive, its crosses the frontier and launches itself toward the truth."

"The truth?" Hobson exclaimed.

"The truth," the savant went on. I shall explain the meaning of that abstract term. As I said before, God has created us with one objective: relative perfection. Take note that I say 'relative,' God alone realizing the absolute. Without that objective, we would have no reason for being. The only means of arriving at that relative perfection is the truth. The truth is the sum of all perfections, the supreme limit that fringes the eternal infinity.

Now, as the eternal infinity is God—if one takes the attribute for the possessor—on the day when the soul, entirely purified by the proof of incarnations attains that objective, it will enjoy blissful felicity in the contemplation of God. That will be the end of the world.

"This deduction follows from the fact that there is no effect without a cause, and that if we had been thrown upon the Earth to be abandoned to the caprice of our weaknesses, Creation would be the work of hazard. And everything, nature as well as our conscience, impresses us with the certainty of the existence of a Creator.

"I have fathomed the depths of the future, but I cannot make out the epoch in which the cataclysm will occur. One obstacle opposes the march of progress: lies."

"What do you mean by lies?"

"By lies, I mean everything that arises from human imperfection, with the free consent of human beings. And everything down here is lies: ambition, hatred, vanity, debauchery, cupidity, fraud. We are content in vice; we make it the object of our pleasures."

"Are we on the path of progress in the present century?"

"No, not yet. Human beings, thus far, have only employed the thrust of their intelligence to the profit of their egoism. They have only employed them to the refinement of material pleasures, to the satisfaction of their perishable being. With their souls, they are unconcerned, or, if they are concerned with them, it is only to enslave hem to their bestiality. Commerce, Industry, Finance appear to them as appropriate means to slake their thirst for lucre. By dint of aiming for wealth, they destroy mutual confidence. Envy is closely related to dupery. And fortune, divided between a small number of the privileged, has engendered corruption, debauchery, intrigue and their criminal cortege. Good people, in the strict sense of the word, have become ridiculous. Self-interest has engendered egoism. The Christian religion, in spite of its errors, has nevertheless invented the most beautiful of maxims: charity. But humans, launched too far forward in the current of the passions, are carried toward evil by the violence of the turbulence. They admire charity, but lack the energy to practice it."

"Is science not destined to bring us back to the right path?"

"On the contrary. It's science that has lost it. The more it multiplies its researches, the further it strays into the mysterious abysses of metaphysics; the more it tries to fathom that which surpasses its conceptions, and the prouder it becomes, the more it deifies itself, the more it denies the existence of its Creator.

"Philosophy, which would have been the most beautiful of sciences if it had been restricted to its own field of study, tends by its sophisms to make the world the fortuitous work of natural revolutions, which it explains by specious theories. So long as it was content with what nature furnished for its needs, it was happy. On the day when it created false pleasures, when it attempted to raise itself toward God, to comment on its own existence, it got lost. But God allows its mind to work; he laughs at its presumption and opposes a barrier to it on which it breaks: Infinity.

"Science, however, has not said its last word; it will make immense progress yet. To begin with, in the next few centuries from now, physical science will obtain a material preponderance that will exercise its empire on philosophy. That philosophy, based on the sovereignty of matter, cannot survive for long; it is in contradiction with the secret intuition of human beings. Theories, by dint of competing with one another, and becoming ingenious in the invention of new combinations, will collide with an inevitable shock and annihilate one another. Then error will dissipate as if by enchantment.

"Humans, frightened by the consequences of their presumption, alarmed by the harm that science will have caused them, will fall back on themselves; they will look around, compare themselves to that Infinity which thought has been fathoming for centuries without being able to find an end; they will contemplate those innumerable worlds gravitating in space, the existence of which science will have revealed, the fixed stars in the celestial vault being as many lamps illuminating worlds, as the sun is the central focal point of our system, blinding in its light. They will reflect on their immortal souls, imprisoned within perishable bodies, and see themselves face to face with their own oblivion. Vanquished, they will bow their heads.

"That revolution will only begin in the society to which I am transported, but many more centuries will pass before the truth fuses with Infinity."

"You condemn science, then?"

"Notice that I am making an abstraction from my own opinions here. I am penetrating the mind of the society that I am studying. The further science has been extended, the more avid humans have become for the hunt. Physical science has led them to deify matter. Applied to Industry, it has taught them to sacrifice the general interest to individual interest; it has caressed their weaknesses, initiated cunning and, by enriching the privileged few, has inaugurated poverty among the rest. The exact sciences, no less than the physical sciences, have contributed to the progress of Industry, which concentrates fortunes within a restricted group—but the most terrible of humankind's enemies is still metaphysical science; it leads it astray into a maze of erroneous speculations, flatters its pride, deceives its reason and proclaims it God.

"It is not that human intelligence ought to remain in a latent state. Humans were given intelligence in order that it should bear fruit, in steering them toward the study of nature, toward everything that falls upon their senses, toward everything that is within the range of their reflection, and finally toward themselves, according to Socrates' dictum: *Know thyself.* It should not violate that which its conscience, an infallible arbiter, recognizes as beyond its faculties, trespassing in the domain of the Creator. The struggle is unequal; it wastes its time there and its good instincts."

"You've only told me thus far about the end of the moral world. What about the end of the physical world—how should that be translated? One cannot happen without the other."

"To arrive at the end, it is necessary to return to the beginning. This is what out descendants imagine on that subject. In the beginning, before the planets and the stars occupied space, there were only suns in Infinity. A formidable cataclysm occurred; there was chaos. Those suns were shattered into millions of billons of fragments, which were disseminated in space and became as many fiery nuclei, around which vapors condensed, forming crusts by virtue of cooling. Hence the internal fire that burns at the center of the Earth and which, through the craters of volcanoes, secretes torrents of lava, the primal matter of new strata of land.

"Thus, every fixed star is a sun around which an entire planetary system gravitates, formed, like ours, from the debris of that sun.

"All these worlds are endowed with an attractive force emanating from their incandescent nuclei, which draws satellites in their wake, and retains them, as well as the souls distributed on their surfaces. But they gravitate around their suns, whose attractive force, as a central nucleus, possesses a seed of primal intensity so many times superior to each of them that it draws them into a perimeter proportional to the attractive power that they themselves exert. Thus, the most powerful are the most distant, and the weakest the closest.

"This is the reason for that: each planet, in describing its ellipse annually, or in a longer or shorter lapse of time, according to the distance that separates it from its sun, diminishes in volume, worn away by friction against its atmospheric layers, and loses its magnetic force by virtue of the gradual extinction of its central fire. Diminishing in volume and magnetic force, it first casts off its satellites, if it has any; the diminution of its own weight then brings it further and further into the zone of attraction of its sun. Its ellipse shrinking continually, as a direct result of its decrease in weight and in the intensity to its central fire, it ends up falling into the sun, which volatilizes it and absorbs it.

"That absorption, therefore, affects each planet successively, in proportion to the volume and the magnetic force that keeps it distant from the sun. It follows that the closer a planet is to the sun, the closer it is to its end. And as everything is regulated with a marvelous wisdom, the end of the physical world coincides with the end of the moral world; one is the consequence of the other. Thus, in conclusion, the absorption of souls by Infinity and the absorption of matter by the sun."

"At that culminating point, then, humans will have acquired the summit of relative perfection indispensable for their souls to fuse with Infinity?"

"Necessarily. Just as the planets return to their central nucleus, the sun, souls return to their central nucleus, Infinity, both having conserved the force to remain themselves, because the divine principle and the material principle in combination constituted the primal cause. Both were fragmented at the same time—but the divine principle rules over the material principle, as the soul rules the body.

"The inequality that separates beings of the same epoch is as insensible, in the whole, as the asperities on the skin of an orange or the mountain on the Earth's surface. Incarnations will level them out, and progress will melt souls into a perfect unity."

"But if souls must return to Infinity at the same time as planets return to the sun," Hobson objected, "you're reducing merit and demerit to negligibility. On that account, it's quite unnecessary to employ one's free will in being an honest man, since one will not be rewarded for it in the long run."

"Error!" replied the savant. "Souls enjoy down here the compensations of happiness, fortune and condition, according to their merits or demerits, while awaiting the end. Reward and punishment are purely terrestrial."

"What about all those worlds gravitating in space?" asked Hobson. "Are they subject to the same revolutions as the Earth? Do they recognize the same principles? Are they inhabited?"

"We don't know," the savant replied. "We only reason from hypotheses—but the hypotheses are conclusive. What would be the objective of their existence, if they only serve to ornament the immensity of space? Evidently, they are populated, as our world is by ourselves. Are their inhabitants of a species similar to ours? Are they more advanced than us? We don't know that either. Science has discovered the existence of these worlds and defined their nature, but it has not been able to penetrate the mysteries of their existence.

"However, one can easily conceive that their existence implies the idea of inhabitants, and that the stars around which they gravitate fulfill the office of suns in their regard."

"And what if you were to transport yourself to one of these planets, of your choice?" Hobson suggested.

"I can't."

"Why not?"

"Because once outside the terrestrial atmosphere I would asphyxiate for lack of air in free space."

"Try anyway!"

"What good would it do to tire myself out uselessly?"

"Try—I want you to."

And Hobson, bracing himself and directing his flamboyant eyes at the savant, overwhelmed him with the full weight of his will-power.

The savant, crushed by that fluidic pressure, cried out in an imploring voice: "Oh, you don't know the harm you're doing me."

"Obey, then!" said Hobson, imperiously.

"I obey," murmured Monsieur Landet—and, letting himself go, he abandoned himself to the impulsion of the magnetic current.

Suddenly, his face became livid, then red, and then purple; his lips trembled and his chest heaved; unintelligible words stuck in his throat; his arms extended in desperate efforts. He was suffocating.

Hobson realized too late the imprudence of his curiosity and rose to his feet, his eyes fixed and his muscles taut and his hands clenched. He deployed all his energy to reawaken his subject.

Monsieur Landet, however, was struggling against asphyxia. The distance to be crossed was too long for Hobson to be able to bring him back instantaneously into the terrestrial atmosphere.

Will-power crackled behind the magnetizer's forehead; his eyes emitted flashes; his hands streamed with the fluid that he was dispersing to earth; sweat beaded on his face—and in the meantime, nothing, nothing; the savant was still choking.

In the end, Hobson took a supreme decision; he lifted Monsieur Landet in his muscular arms and held him pressed against his body, in such a fashion that the molecules of his fluid penetrated his every pore.

It was a frightful thing to see, that struggle of two men, in which one was fighting death for the other.

Finally, the savant's respiration became more regular. When he was able to speak, he cried: "Take me away—take me away from this Infinity that is crushing me!"

It was only after a further quarter of an hour, during which the minutes seemed like centuries to the magnetizer, that Monsieur Landet reopened his eyes.

He stood up, and fell back into his armchair. He had fainted.

Chapter IV
INTERNAL POLITICS

Monsieur Landet paid dear for his temerity in having dared to rise toward free space and fathom the mysterious abysms of Infinity.

He was confined to bed for a weeks, and was prey to a kind of delirium that almost provoked a brain seizure. He talked about the absorption of worlds, the absorption of souls, incarnation, the end of the world, magnetic attraction. Then he named the planets one by one and fell back on to his pillow, murmuring: "Infinity! Always infinity!"

Evidently, he was still the victim of a magnetic influence, and Hobson, in using all the power of his will to snatch him back from suffocation in free space, had shaken the foundations of his reason.

Every day, the magnetizer, visibly anxious, came to obtain news of the savant.

Finally, the ideas in Monsieur Landet's head became coherent. His excitement eased and he fell into a profound sleep, which lasted no less than 48 hours.

When his domestic handed him the cards of the people who had come to enquire after his health, his first words were: "Let us take things in order"—a certain sign that the ideas were systematically arranged in the lobes of his brain.

Meanwhile, the physicians had formally forbidden him to involve himself with magnetism for a month. They had even had the barbarity to demand that it should not be mentioned in his presence during that lapse of time—otherwise, there was a danger of madness.

Hobson therefore avoided that topic of conversation in the invalid's presence, and whenever the latter, impatient to get astride his hobby-horse and dive into the tenebrous darkness of centuries to come, Hobson immediately hastened to call his attention to the progress of *Phylloxera*[14] in France—a subject that interested Monsieur Landet keenly in his capacity as the owner of a small vineyard on the hills of Beaujolais.

As distraction was recommended to him, he profited from it broadly, going to the theater, the Bois and racecourses, contrary to his habit; apart from that, he spent the greater number of his evenings at the home of the Marquise de Roche-Houdion.

One evening, when he was dining with her, a guest had the imprudence to talk about the impossibility of the Moon being inhabited, for want of an atmosphere. Monsieur Landet, as if impelled up by an invisible hand, launched into endless speculations about the utility of everything in the universe, making every effort to prove that the bodies clothing souls on planets are appropriate to the physical exigencies of their nature and that, although air is indispensable to the human organism, that does not mean that the inhabitants of other planets have

---

[14] *Phylloxera* is a genus of plant lice: a species imported to Europe from the Americas in the 1850s, to which Europeans vines had no resistance, began to devastate the French wine industry in the 1860s by destroying its root-stocks, cutting production by three-quarters by the mid 1880s. Resistant stocks had to be imported from America, on to which indigenous vines were grafted, but the problem was never conclusively solved.

the same needs as us, nor that their souls have envelopes identical to ours.

In spite of the desperate efforts of the Marquise, the savant was going on and on when a charitable neighbor, to create a diversion, asked him to fetch her something to drink.

Monsieur Landet, in the full flow of his oratory, looked at her in bewilderment. "What, Madame!" he cried. "You have conserved the habits of another world?"

An immense outburst of laughter greeted the savant's reply. The latter, believing it to be a deceptive echo, looked around in amazement. Then, falling from the height of his dreams, he said: "Oh! A thousand pardons, Madame. I thought I was on the Moon."

There was fear of a relapse, but fortunately, nothing happened. Apart from that incident, Monsieur Landet conscientiously kept silent for a month. When the last day had expired, he came into Hobson's study like a bolide.

"Finally!" he cried. "I have returned to you, dear Master." And he almost threw himself into the magnetizer's arms.

"One moment," said the later. "Not too fast. You know from experience, my dear Monsieur Landet, that there is a limit to human faculties."

"Alas!" sighed the savant. "I've wasted a month."

"No more imprudence, then."

"I swear to you…on your head."

"Thank you. I have only to be careful, then."

"When can we begin?"

"Soon. You're in a great hurry."

"I can no longer contain myself."

"Ah! If you excite yourself in advance, you'll spoil your lucidity and falsify your vision."

"What do you expect? A month of waiting, a month of starvation!"

"All right, I give in. Isolate yourself from any anticipatory thought—otherwise, the ideas of the day before will become confused with the ideas if the somnambulistic sleep."

So saying, Hobson stared at the savant and transpierced him with his gaze. That gaze sufficed to put him to sleep, by virtue of the habit that he and his subject had acquired.

"With what are you going to occupy yourself today?" he asked.

"Internal politics."

"No foreign thought is crossing your mind?"

"None. I'm lucid."

"Speak, then," said the magnetizer—and, addressing himself to the stenographers: "And you, gentlemen, write."

The Constitution

"I commenced the study of the world in 2000 years with the family, the basis of society," said the savant. "Then I talked about religion, the basis of human institutions. Today, I shall occupy myself with internal politics, born of the extension and division of families and the unification of the divinity.

"So long as the family was restricted to the narrow circle of its members, its internal organization served to direct it. It knew no other laws that those dictated to it by its daily needs, by the relationships between its members, by its simple and patriarchal life. On the day when the generations, in multiplying, ramify from the common branch, however, when the extension of the family makes its members unfamiliar to one another, a sanction more efficacious and positive than domestic right is required. Fixed limits are required on kinship. It is necessary to divide the mother-family into as many families as there are branches. From that division is born internal politics, the supreme tribunal around which all the families converge, organizing themselves under institutions elaborated in common, with a view to protecting them from one another.

"The first form of government adopted by humans corresponded with the instinct that he had of his independence. It was Republican, so far as we can judge from the monuments that remain to us from the earliest ages. The liberty of each individual was, however, subordinate to a superior will, to a directive will, as our free will is subordinate to God. At all times, humans have imposed a yoke upon themselves; either by virtue of sloth, or consciousness of their weakness, they have always bowed down before a master.

"That master, appointed by mutual confidence, was not long delayed in abusing his discretionary powers; he made use of them against those who had granted them to him, made them an instrument of his cupidity, his vanity and his passions; he overstepped his mandate and, finally, transformed into acquired property that which was only a temporary loan, by oppressing those he was supposed to support. He established inheritance. Inheritance! By virtue of what right? By virtue of the right of the strongest. Humans quickly fall into servitude; it is a need inherent in their nature to yield to the domination of the most audacious—always the influence of a superior will on an inferior one. Magnetism links souls to other souls; they obey the law of currents.

"Once inheritance was consecrated by human consent, its beneficiaries rooted themselves in the minds of peoples, by the intermediary of a so-called divine sanction. That gave rise to absolute power. The monarch became a sort of substitute, a kind of divine steward. That regime lasted for centuries, until the people, reawakened by the cry of indignant conscience, the voice of free will, by everything noble and generous sensed within, brought about a return to the past and, rising above the horrific spectacle of the crimes of an ambitious fist, broke their chains and raised their heads again.

"That revolution, suddenly effected with a great fracas, had been long in preparation in their minds. Wrath had been rumbling dully, and the masters, sensing the storm approaching, gradually made derisory concessions until the day when the wave, swollen to excess, overflowed.

"Humankind renews itself, like nature. Nations are superimposed on nations as terrains are superimposed on terrains, and these social convulsions are called revolutions. Internal revolutions are the work of healthy and energetic minds; external revolutions are the work of new and vigorous peoples.

"Thus, in antiquity, and especially at the commencement of the Christian Era, the Barbarians attacked the bastardized races of the Occident and exerted the chronic pressure that centuries bring over time: invasion.

"But the irresistible example of sloth, idleness and debauchery quickly insinuates itself into the heart of conquerors. The contagion spreads. Victors and vanquished, uniting in their fall, inevitably roll down the slope of decadence. Then comes a new invasion of Barbarians and a new race is extinguished by the impact.

"Was there not seen, in fallen Rome, proud Rome, the fatherland of heroes, a Nero clad in female garments, crowned with flowers, his face painted, his hair curled, dancing with courtesans in the smoking ruins of his capital—to admire what? The magical sight of a fire.

"When a people has reached the stage of being indifferent to such follies, it is finished.

"However, the Roman Empire was further sustained by the prestige of its former grandeur. The shadow of its past was respected—but the memory of men like Brutus, Fabricius and Marius was soon effaced in the night of forgetfulness. Wealth, power and the immensity of the empire taught Romans voluptuousness.

"Having nothing more to vanquish, their arm fell back, inactive for want of new conquests. They no longer thought of anything but enjoying the fruits of their triumphs. That is what doomed them.

"The Barbarians, who were watching the decadence attentively, launched themselves upon that effeminate people and, on founded a new empire the vestiges of the Roman Empire. Their generous blood vivified the vanquished, and from that interbreeding a new race was born. But that hybrid race did not take long to reject what was pure and healthy within it; it abandoned itself to the base instincts of the fallen race. Luxury, condemned momentarily, reappeared more dazzling than ever, dragging in its wake the procession of all the vices. Such is, in brief, the eternal history of nations. The highs and lows that have marked their different periods are due to the impact of invasions and the superimposition of social strata.

"The chronology of the first invasions is lost in the night of time. Monuments of those forgotten eras remain, however, to testify to the successive phases that those nations have passed through. Without going back to antediluvian epochs, only rare fossils of which remain to us, the Israelites, to begin with, implanted themselves in the land of Canaan by defeating the peoples who lived there before them. Victims themselves of the Roman invasion, they were dispersed throughout the entire world and, from the powerful people they had been, became a nomadic people, wandering in tribes from city to city sand town to town.

"In Egypt, the Pharaohs, or shepherd kings, overturned the 16th dynasty, and imposed themselves in its place.

"In the Occident, the Franks gradually penetrated all the way to the heart of Gaul, already Romanized by the campaigns of Julius Caesar, and succeeded in enslaving al the lands extending from the coast of Brittany to the Pyrenees, either directly or indirectly, instituting feudalism there. Their king was a suzerain to whom all the possessors of fiefs, great or small, owed liege-homage in the title of vassals. It was not until the departure of Louis XI that France fell under the immediate power of the sovereign.

"And it should be noted that the majority of invasions come from the north-east, relative to the invaded territory. Thus, the Visigoths fell upon Spain from the left bank of the Danube; the Vandals on Rome from the deserts of Scythia; the Huns on all of Europe from the icy steppes of the Caucasian regions; the Saxons on England from the Danish provinces, to give way to the Normans, themselves originally from the shores of the Baltic; the Franks on the Gallo-Roman lands from the forests of northern Germany; and the Tartars, finally, on the Chinese from the Kamchatka peninsula. The Turks, going from victory to victory, quit the heart of Asia, crossed the Archipelago and established themselves in Constantinople, the seat of the Greek Empire.

"The world, when it has reached a certain degree of civilization, is like a fruit eaten away within by a worm; it needs to purify itself by contact with barbarism, because that civilization, which ought to be solely concerned with the development of its intelligence, only addresses itself to its senses. It requires a shock; it requires a reaction. And interior revolutions are no less revelatory of a people numbed by excess than foreign revolutions. Civil war, condemned in principle, relieves it by its crimes, by its horrors. The sight of blood, of the blood of fellow citizens, stings its indignation, and when it rests, weary of carnage, its reason clears; the heart-rending spectacle of its dementia suddenly brings sobriety, and remorse causes long-suppressed good sentiments to germinate. But if it has shed blood, it has at least taken a step toward liberty.

"Yes, it is civilization that dooms great nations; it is also destined to raise them up again. The fault is in the application. The world is not sufficiently experienced to make appropriate use of it; it is a big baby, which it is prudent to keep in harness.

"Before arriving at the perfection that will be its end, it must pass through the various phases of existence. Having vegetated in infancy for a long time, it scarcely emerges from adolescence to enter into maturity; what for us is counted in decades is counted for civilization in centuries. The phases of society are regulated like the human life, proportional to the duration of their existence.

"Everything in nature obeys uniform laws, the simplicity of which we make a game of distorting; everything, on mature reflection, is intimately related and analogically concordant.

"Was it not civilization, in fact, that, by progressive refinement, delivered Media to the Persians, Greece to the Romans and Rome to the Barbarians?

"So long as a people is content with the facile and relaxed life that nature provides, it is strong and powerful. The day when it exaggerates its needs, the day when gives free rein to the fantasies of its imagination, it is a dead people; it has killed its liberty.

"In modern times, was it not the absolute monarchy that dragged France through the dirt progressively, to that terrible but fortunate reaction, the Revolution?

"I am following progress step by step, and I can see, before long, a sudden denouement, a second edition of the great Revolution. The world progresses in lurches. Although individual liberty has suddenly been infused into Europe, many people are still gnawing at the bit under the yoke of autocracy. A new revolution is necessary to confirm the first and level the rest of society.

"It will be announced by a formidable cataclysm; but it will not be partial, like the first, but universal. From that collision a reformed society will surge forth: that which I can see at this moment."

"But out of all the forms of government we have tried," Hobson interjected, "which is the one that ought to lead us to the objective?"

"The Republic," replied Monsieur Landet. "Can you doubt it? All the other forms of government only satisfy the interests of a minority. The Republic, by contrast, is the government of all by all, and that government is exercised by the intermediary of representatives, who, themselves, make and unmake the agents of power. Everyone collaborates in general action, everyone governs, everyone has a say in the matter, and that voice, transmitted by votes, is augmented by other voices, whose ensemble makes the machine of State function."

"So the government that we will have in 2000 years is a Republic?"

"Yes, a Republic, definitively constituted, after an interminable series of upsets occasioned by the ambition, cupidity and hatred of some. Oh, egoism is the deadliest enemy of humanity! It is a Republic, but not a lame Republic formed of the wreckage of fallen regimes, pulled in contrary directions by the competition of parties, disfigured by contradictions, privileges and injustices. It is a solid Republic based on the union of its citizens, on respect for the law, on individual liberty, on equality of rights, on the general interest and, above all, on universal suffrage.

"No more fits of intrigue and favor. Administrative responsibilities, so sought after in our day as rapid means of acquiring a fortune and honors, are positions of trust, accorded to the most deserving.

"That Republic is the image of a great Company, funded by shares, based on statutes elaborated by a board of directors and submitted for the approval of the general assembly. The citizens are the shareholders in that company, which is administered on their behalf by employees appointed by them. At the head of those employees is a managing director, equipped with discretionary powers, under the permanent control of a board of directors, itself appointed by the general assembly.

"The shareholders meet every year. The managing director justifies his actions to it and renders an account of the operations he has carried out, in concert with the board of directors. The general assembly, all-powerful, deliberates on the conduct of the managing director, the senior employees and the board of directors. The parallel is easy to see. The managing director is the President of the Republic; the senior employees are the ministers; the board of directors is the parliament and the general assembly public gatherings.

"Thus, the government comprises a passive President, active ministers, a responsible parliament and all-powerful public gatherings. Electoral assemblies are held every four years, at town halls, during ordinary assemblies, to proceed with the election of a representative; revisionary assemblies once a year, to assess the representative's conduct; and extraordinary assemblies in cases of urgency, to invalidate the representative if he has betrayed his mandate.

"The candidates submit programs to their electors. That program, once admitted, is carefully preserved in the archives of the town hall. It is a sort of profession of faith, which the elected representative is obliged to follow to the letter, under penalty of being relieved of his office at the annual assemblies.

"His initiative, attenuated by the imperative mandate, remains to him within the measure of the line of conduct he has mapped out, since the mandate is his own work, and since it is on the propositions it contains that the electors have accepted him.

"If the opinions advertized in the program are the strict expression of his thought, he only owes allegiance to himself; he has only to follow the politics he has indicated, having been put on his guard against the pull of passions.

"His will is, therefore, perfectly free between the limits he has set for himself. If he strays beyond them,

99

he is a man devoid of logic, stability and conviction, unworthy to represent the fraction of the country that has called on him to defend its interests. It is not on his own account that he governs but on the account of his electors. Party hatred, ambition and complaisance must be effaced before a unique objective: the mission to be fulfilled.

"The representative only speaks and acts by virtue of the instructions he has received; he is simply the delegate of his electors.

"In our day, universal suffrage is merely an illusion. Credulous people are dazzled by it, and appoint their representatives on the basis of their marvelous proclamations. As soon as they reach parliament, those representatives do not hesitate to renounce their principles. Party allegiance directs their slightest actions; cupidity and ambition are the objectives of their constant thought, and their electors, who believed what they said, are merely the stepping-stone of their pride. They have no other sanction but their conscience, and the country is condemned to support the punishment of its confidence, without appeal, for six years.

"With the imperative mandate, deception is no longer possible. It is a contract that binds the representative to the elector, as a lease binds the tenant to the proprietor. No more compromises that annul an election; no more tortuous maneuvers that are not clarified before the annual assemblies. Everything is above board. The electors follow their representatives step by step in the official bulletins. On the day his powers are reviewed, they revoke them or maintain them. The representative recognized as being in default on any point whatsoever is voted out, and a new candidate is elected.

"With such institutions, the people collaborate effectively in the mechanism of government. They have the upper hand over the ministers and the president, whose actions are examined on a daily basis by the parliament, since the management of the sovereign power is annually submitted to its control.

"The President is elected by universal suffrage, not by a majority of the representatives. His powers have a duration of four years. At the end of that time, his candidature is resubmitted to the vote, and the country, if there is occasion to do so, prolongs his powers for four further years or, if not, replaces him. Appointed at the same time as the parliament, he finishes in concert with it. His election, in order o be the exact expression of the will of the people, must be concordant with the election of the representatives. Both must march in step, supporting one another, both created by the needs of the moment.

"The issue of universal suffrage, the President can only be recalled by universal suffrage. In the case of discord or abuse of authority, parliament brings it to the attention of the reprobation of the country by means of an order of the day, which is pronounced by a plebiscite.

"There is, therefore, on the one hand, the executive power, represented by the President, the depository and guardian of the law, the link between the country and its delegates; on the other hand, there is the legislative power, represented by parliament, the center of discussion, where affairs elucidated by means of comparison, a permanent tribunal or the President's ministers explaining their politics and submitting them to the judgment of the country, which decides by means of the organ of its representatives; and finally, above all that, the constitutive and revisionary power represented by the public assemblies, the supreme tribunal, to which the representatives come annually to render their accounts.

"Such an internal organization thwarts the political rivalries that, in order to satisfy the interests of the smallest number, drag the masses into civil war. Concord reigns among all the citizens. It is they who decide in the last resort; in a word, they own the Republic, and it is not the Republic that owns them. Everyone makes use of his intelligence and muscle, everyone has a stake in the State; everyone is a judge in an infinitely small fraction, whose total constitutes the verdict.

"The President is only the statue of power. He does nothing by himself; his role is to represent the nation at the International Congress. The ministers govern in his name, but neither he nor they are responsible, parliament accepting or refusing them on the President's motion.

"The right to declare war, too serious a responsibility for one man, belongs in principle to the parliament, but that is merely held in reserve, since war has been abolished by the unanimous consent of peoples."

"War has been abolished?" Hobson interjected, sharply.

"War has been abolished and replaced by an International Congress. But I shall come back to that when the question of external politics arises. Let us take things in an orderly fashion.

"The right to declare war thus belongs to the parliament, which has not yet erased it from the book of the law. One day, as universal solidarity confirms the present constitution in the minds of peoples, a vote will declare the law unnecessary and repeal it. At present the world still takes precautions; it scarcely dares to believe in its happiness; it trembles at the memory of the past; the experience of anterior ages has educated its foresight.

"The President, as Monsieur Thiers has said in the *National*, speaking about King Louis-Philippe, 'reigns, but does not govern.' He has all the initiative, but he accomplishes nothing of his own purpose. He chooses his ministers, but does not impose them; the parliament accepts or refuses them. The theory of ministerial responsibility exposes the different powers to dangerous collisions that provoke public opinions and are often the signal for civil war. It permits the head of state to entrench himself behind a purely conventional irresponsibility and to make use of straw men to oppose the national will.

"The Republic being the government of the majority, it is essential that the leaders of the various administrative sections emerge from the bosom of that majority; otherwise, the oppositions produced between the constituted powers will leave affairs of State on sufferance.

"The responsibility of ministers is therefore considerably attenuated, not to say annulled, by the fact that they can only act after having submitted their plans to a parliamentary vote, as for simple proposals of law. It is, therefore, the parliament on which the real responsibility for their actions is incumbent, during their routine business. It is a clever means of maintaining them under the direct suffrage of the citizens.

"They participate nonetheless in an active manner in the needs of government, by their projects of innovation or reform, which they carry out when the balance of contrary opinions swings in their favor. From the impact of numerous intelligences, better results flow than from a single intelligence; error succumbs in the conflict, and whatever is good in every idea emerges in discussion, comes to the fore, and, in being aggregated, forms a complete whole.

"The ministers, proposed by the President and accepted by the majority, are subject to recall by that same majority; that goes without saying. The vote that has accepted them can also depose them in the same manner,

"Can you rejoice in the transformation that has taken place in society, as I do? Can you bear witness to the tranquility, the security, the cordial agreement that reigns among these unrecognizable people? The general interest, that grave social question which has discouraged our greatest modern statesmen, is so closely united with individual interests that everyone necessarily loves his country, that everyone makes themselves useful, that everyone profits from the common prosperity. And that is natural. What profound attachment can a citizen feel to a fatherland that consults him every six years, for form's sake? For a fatherland personified in an individual who buys his vote with mendacious promises and who, by an authoritarian gesture, annuls the veto of his voice? For a fatherland that allows itself to be abused by a handful of plotters and informs him, when he wakes up one morning, that a new tyrant has replaced the old?

"Has he been consulted? No. He is only consulted when it is too late, and his vote is obligatory. And it is on him that the expenses of that scandalous intrusion fall! What profound attachment can he feel to a fatherland that taxes his labor and his fatigue, to the profit of those privileged by a despot, who uses rigorous measures in his regard when injustice has provoked his indignation?

"Why should he open the way to honor and fortune to an unknown who, once in parliament, will laugh at his credulity? He, a free citizen, will dispose public fortune in favor of a smooth talker, and will continue to struggle against his poverty!

"To return to the popular assemblies, they are routinely held every four years, for legislative elections, and every year to review the actions carried out during the parliamentary session.

"The electoral assemblies take place at the town hall. The electors bring their votes, throw them into the urn, and the count is carried out in their presence. Nothing is secret. A committee appointed by them, composed of local notables, choose several candidates from among the most capable and introduces them to the electors. Once admitted as such, their maneuvers are scrupulously monitored; they are enclosed in cells dedicated to that usage during the entire duration of the election and the debates preceding the election. From their retreat they publish a political program, in which they set out their line of conduct, their projects, their appreciation of the affairs of the country in general and of their own district in particular. That profession of faith, attached to the wall of the town hall, becomes an imperative mandate, which is turned against them if they deviate from it by an iota.

"The candidate is, from then on, the slave of is program, each article of which is a weapon that a contrary maneuver suspends over his head. He is sincere whether he likes it or not. His ulterior motives, his underhanded calculations, are thwarted; he is condemned by his own actions, becoming his own pitiless adversary: *Verba volant, scripta manent.*[15]

"During this time, the president of the assembly organizes a public reading of his dossier, without any preamble or commentary. The electors then make their

---

[15] Words are fleeting; writing permanent.

decision and, the count having been made, the candidate, whether elected or not, is set free.

"In that manner, the elector knows his representative thoroughly; his entire life has been revealed to him, his intentions are guaranteed; he votes with a full awareness of the case.

"Only those who have been subject to an examination of elementary education are electors. It only requires that they know how to read and write and that they have a succinct notion of the history of their country and its parliamentary phases. Is it not of the highest importance that electors, before participating in the destiny of their country, should be aware of the ordeals that it has undergone since the era in which it was constituted? What serious weight can their votes carry in the balance of universal suffrage if they do not know its value? They will decide at hazard or according to a foreign influence, and foreign influences are always pernicious in such cases, being counseled by private interests.

"It is good that electors, before voting, meditate on what has gone before and discuss the probabilities of the future. It is good that they take account of the exact scope of their determination. Each single voice would be lost in the ensemble of the result obtained, but if the majority of the voters are ignorant, they run the risk of delivering their fatherland to anarchy, for want of the ability to appreciate its needs.

"Thus, for citizens to be admitted to participate in the election of a representative, it is necessary for them to present a diploma of elementary education. These diplomas are given to them at the age of 21, after an examination supervised by the mayor, assisted by deputies and the administrative officers of the district. From then on, they are citizens, entering in part to the national sovereignty.

"It follows from this that education is compulsory. Free public courses are held in the evenings at the town hall. Workers, returning from their labors, sometimes pause there to complete their primitive education; that is voluntary. As for children, they are sent to school at the age of seven, by courtesy of law as categorical as military law is today among us—conscription to study.

"Parliament, constituted on these bases, is the direct expression of the will of the country; all the representatives speak and act there according to the programs they have outlined. They propose, discuss and vote, in an invariable circle. It is up to them to reflect maturely before exposing their mandates. There is no secret ballot that would permit them to compromise their mandate under the anonymous cover of a yes or no thrown into the urn. On each voting record, beneath a printed yes or no, they write their names, in such a way that the following day's Official Bulletin is an echo of their words and actions. Their life is an open book; they no longer belong to themselves but to their electors.

"The revisionary assemblies meet every year at the town hall under the presidency of the mayor at the end of the parliamentary session, immediately after the closure of the general councils, in order that the representatives, who are also general councilors, can follow their politics through to the end, by discussing departmental decrees in the general council, along with the direct contributions, the number of which, fixed by parliament, remains to be divided between the contributors.

"The representative then appears before his electors, gives an account of his mission and defends himself against any grievances brought against him. Then the mayor, with the Official Bulletin in hand, assesses his votes and appeals to the electros, who confirm or invalidate him.

"Every article of the Constitution aims for the highest degree of individual liberty: everything for the people and by the people."

"Transport yourself into the bosom of the Parliament," ordered Hobson, whose curiosity was excited to the highest degree by the savant's strange double vision.

Monsieur Landet collected himself momentarily. "The session isn't open yet," he replied.

"When will it open?"

"At two o'clock."

"And what time is it?"

"Quarter to two."

"Where can you see that?"

"On your watch, in your pocket."

Hobson took his watch out of his fob pocket; it was, indeed, quarter to two. "While we wait for the hour to chime," he said to the savant, "have a rest."

"Something unusual is happening. The representatives are walking in the corridors, conversing with great agitation. The ministers are anxious. The session promises to be stormy."

Hobson squeezed the savant's hand. "Rest," he repeated. "You'll have need of new strength to follow the parliamentary debates of 2000 years hence attentively."

The savant seemed to yield to the magnetizer's advice, but the long relation he had just made had dried his throat. "I'm thirsty," he murmured.

Hobson prepared a cognac toddy and held it out to him.

Monsieur Landet seized the glass without hesitation, as if he were awake, and drained it in a single draught. Then he got up and walked to the window.

"Where are you going?" Hobson asked.

"To open the window—it's stifling in here."

"Don't do that—the fluid will escape from the room as the air is renewed. You'll lose the essence of your precious lucidity."

Monsieur Landet uttered a profound sigh, passed his hand over his brow and meekly came back to sit down. The immobility of death spread over his features. Not a muscle in his face quivered; his lowered eyelids seemed like a leaden cloak over his eyes. One might have thought that he was plunged into a lethargic sleep.

Hobson chatted with the stenographers, hastily riffling through the loose sheets of paper on which they had recorded the communication word for word.

"It's two o'clock!" the savant suddenly exclaimed, emerging from his prostration.

Hobson turned round; although accustomed to the prodigies accomplished under his empire, Monsieur Landet's lucidity astonished him, almost frightening him, especially after his audacious attempt to sent the savant into free space. He took out his watch.

"Two o'clock, indeed—you have a military precision."

The stenographers, eyes fixed on the wall clock, took up their posts again. The communication had never been so attractive; this time, it was a matter of a parliamentary session anticipated by 20 centuries.

Hobson sat down again facing the savant and took him by the hands, not without having darted an investigative glance at the stenographers, like the captain of a ship from his quarter-deck.

"The representatives are taking their places," Monsieur Landet began. "The benches are filing up; the president is going up to his armchair.

"A secretary is giving him the minutes of the last session to read. They're proceeding to ministerial reports.

"This isn't very interesting; I'll wait until it's over..."

After a pause, he resumed: "The president is shaking his hand-bell. Silence falls. He gets up. 'Messieurs' he says, 'an unexpected incident has occurred. The Minister of Finance has taken advantage of the parliamentary vacation to modify the law relating to the taxation of income, on his own authority, in spite of the opposition of the cabinet. I appeal to your loyalty and your patriotism to judge this affair with the strictest impartiality. The law is for you, gentlemen, use it—but don't exceed it. Moderation in all things is the secret of wisdom.'

"There is applause; the president rings his bell again to call for order.

"'I ask to speak!' exclaims the Minister of Finance.

"'The Minister of Finance has the floor.'

"The Minister launches himself toward the podium, an immense portfolio under his arm. He is very pale.

"I can't quite catch the first words of his speech. Emotion is paralyzing his voice. From to what I can grasp, a ministerial crisis is reaching its final phase. The minister's speech will decide the survival or the fall of the cabinet."

The savant paused. He listened attentively. Then he continued:

"I'll repeat what the minister says. 'By overstepping my entitlements, depriving me of your collaboration and breaking with the members of the cabinet, I thought to take upon myself the responsibility for a measure that you would approve, after having seen the results, but which you would have rejected had it been submitted to you in advance. The hostility that the ministry has shown me in the circumstances drove me to that solution, for the ministry, the issue of the majority, would have obtained the vote of that majority, and the theory that I would have set out before you, gentlemen, would have not sufficient force or you to grasp its equity. Only practice could furnish me with supporting proofs.

"'This is a matter of the equilibration of incomes. That equilibrium, rigorously impossible, offends justice when it is made by way of apportionment. The law assigns particular suppliers to every citizen, which he cannot quit without a court judgment; but the law, dividing production equally, ought not to annex the excess quantity of that production by levying upon it an exorbitant tax of 50%. The law cannot tax the disparity of intelligences as it taxes commercial products. Humans are endowed with more or less laborious natures; it is therefore not just that the more active should share the benefits of their excess of labor with those who restrict themselves to the strict measure of their obligations.

"'Now, this is what I have done. Instead of collecting annually half of the excess of income to the advantage of the state, thus preventing people from accumulating wealth. I published, on my own authority, a decree that imposes a progressive tax small enough to permit them to build capital, on the assumption that the primary raw material of industry and commerce is capital, and I fixed the enjoyment of that capital for a duration of 30

111

years, at the end of which the State becomes its owner. To facilitate that redemption, I have had a register of annuities drawn up my department's offices, from which, after the annual deductions of a review commission, the inscribed sums will emerge in turn, 30 years offer their inscription. I have based this on the system once employed with respect to railway shares. By this means, the capital belongs in principle to the State, and the temporary possessor only has a life interest in it. Every year, according to the determination of the Finance Commission, the State will deliver to anyone who possesses excess income a dividend of 4½% in exchange for the sum granted to the treasury. The difference of one tenth between 5%, which would be the normal rate of interest, and 4½%, which is the effective interest, constitutes, to the profit of the State, a tax of 10%, which progresses according to the sum deducted by the Finance Commission, which is converted into shares. That bond bears the date of the day on which it has been delivered and is immediately inscribed in numerical order on the list of annuities. When the 30 years is up, it will expire naturally. However, as the objective of this new measure is to encourage the development of commerce and industry by the circulation of capital, the bond is negotiable on the Bourse until it become valueless, not at the price on the day that it has been delivered, but at the price on the day when it is traded. That price is quoted to the nearest centime on a decreasing scale that gradually reduces it to zero on the expiration date.

"'In order to give that bond the confidence necessary to trade, the State will guarantee the reimbursement of the daily price quoted on the scale. If necessary, use can be made of a letter of exchange, then realizable in immediate cash, less the depreciation that a few days delay would cause. Its output is not restricted to a designated figure; it varies in proportion to the capital declared. It is continual.

"'That sort of public debt has the advantage over the old one of being redeemed by means of expiration and not by way of reimbursement. It permits the State to reduce taxes, as the entitlements exit from the register of annuities. I have ordered, to that effect, a general inventory of the revenue situation and an initial emission of redeemable entitlements. It is not, therefore, until 30 years from the ninth of the present month that the first entitlement will reach its expiration date.

"'I am not talking about hereditary capital; it is only stationary, since, by means of entitlements redeemable by expiration, it will return one day to the State. I have also left property in land out of the equation since, according to our Constitution, it is inalienable or alienable by mutation.

"'That everyone should be assured of a comfortable life, and that that assurance should be based in the formal prescriptions of the law is all well and good. It prevents the poverty that is only known to us through the remembrance of the barbarous times of history. But to remove the recompense of his labor from a hard-working man, no, gentlemen, that is not just; it is contrary to probity, offending the sentiment of moral satisfaction that is one of the advantages of a life usefully employed.

"'That every man has his daily bread is sufficient for him; if he desires superfluity, let him earn it! But the excess of his labor should not be distributed among those who have not shared in his fatigue. We shall all find our account in the annual dividends, the produce of which the State will devote to the needs of the general population, by the reduction of taxes.

"'Let the free citizen enjoy in peace, therefore, the fortune acquired by labor, outside of mutual obligations. Let his intelligence strive to activate progress by external commerce as well as by internal commerce. Although our duty is to aid one another, it is not to favor some with the fruits of the voluntary efforts of others. With such principles, we would remain stationary.'

"'We ask no more!' shouts a voice from the right. 'Are we not happy enough?'

"'We are—relatively,' the orator goes on. 'But ought we to savor a happiness contrary to justice?'

"'Justice is conventional!' cries another voice from the right.

"'No, gentlemen,' the minister continues, paying no heed to the interruption. 'No, I repeat once again, probity is opposed to it. The taxation of income, in the cause of redistribution, was established in an epoch in which society, emerging from a painful dream, demanded a solidly-based equality. Today, however, when equality is conclusively rooted, when our improved intelligence shows us its downside, it is up to us to decrease it. It no longer answers to the needs of the moment. Equality, by dint of being absolute, has become separate from justice, although one of these gentlemen'—he points to his right—'deems justice to be conventional. Intelligence is too fine a thing for us to risk allowing it to vegetate in inaction, by depriving it of incentives to fortune. We are not yet perfect, and life without an objective rapidly becomes tasteless. Inaction softens the vital forces of intelligence, and from that mental abasement the general interest suffers more than individual interest.

"'I have before my eyes the statistics of this month's commercial and industrial operations, as well as those of the sums garnered by the state. The appreciable difference that exists with the previous month's figures testifies in an evident manner in favor of the system that I have put into practice. I shall compare, gentlemen. In July, we made 120,218,000 francs in exports, as opposed to 74,000,496 francs in imports; industry furnished three inventions; internal commerce attained a figure of 17,000,320 francs in trade; income from all sources produced a surplus of 4,000,000 francs, redistributed by means of a deduction of ½% on every aspect of direct contributions. This month, we have made 182,417,039 francs in exports, against 38,000,000 francs in impost; industry has furnished 14 inventions, as many for the manufacture of textiles as for the simplification of machines. Internal commerce attained a figure of 13,000,000 francs in trade; the progressive tax on income produced 6,000,000 francs, redistributed by means of a deduction of ¾% on every aspect of direct contributions.

"'The progressive tax, as you can judge from these statistics, has poured into the State coffers two million more in a single month than the 50% tax; but that amelioration, appreciable as it may be, will only become glaring in 30 years' time, when the redemption of capital to the profit of the State will permit an annual deduction of 20% or 30% on every aspect of direct contribution, in addition to the results obtained by the progressive tax. The proportional redistribution will still take place every year, but the State will have capital at its disposal to give rise to enterprises that, if they required increases in taxes or borrowing, would be a new charge on individuals. In finance, the indirect path is always the most onerous. Better to head straight for the goal. That which profits the State profits individuals; the converse is not the case.

"'There, gentlemen, is the powerful motive that persuaded me to overstep the law. I have only taken action against equality in order to affirm that equality. It is a fault, I agree, but the results are there; they speak in my favor. It is now up to you to decide whether the law should be avenged, or whether the amelioration acquired ratifies its violation. Whatever your verdict may be, I accept it in advance.'

"The Minister descends from the podium, wiping the sweat trickling from his brow with his handkerchief. The right and the left maintain a glacial silence."

"What! There are still parties in a Republic solidified by unanimous consent?" Hobson put in. "And the denominations of right and left have survived the tempest of reaction?"

"Two camps are present," Monsieur Landet replied. "The Progressists and the Stationaries. According to the pattern of events, the majority varies between the two camps via the conjunction of the center. The Stationaries are timorous, anxious, prudent spirits who fear social upheavals due to progress; they represent the mass of landowners and agriculturalists, and correspond to our conservatives. The Progressists, as the word indicates, are the restless, bold, indefatigable spirits who pursue perfection relentlessly; they represent the intelligent and industrious masses and correspond to our advanced radicals. They are the ones who most often form the majority, apart from questions of liquidation, credit and current affairs, which are voted unanimously.

"The Minister under indictment is, of course, a Progressist minister, but the incident that has just occurred has turned the entire parliament against the Minister of Finance. The Progressists and the Stationaries both condemn him for different reasons. The Progressists reproach him for having broken the law in executing a reform that had not been voted by the parliament, even though he is a Progressist. The Stationaries accuse him of being revolutionary and are also critical of his initiative. Whichever way the minister turns, he is doomed. His own side, while recognizing the evident merit of his innovation, is abandoning him pitilessly. His crime is to have sinned formally. 'A vote! A vote of no confidence in the Ministry!' people are shouting on all sides.

"'I protest!' cries the Minister of the Interior, from his bench. 'The Ministry is not associated with the actions of one of its members, when those actions are made on his personal responsibility and have not been decided in Council.'

"'The Ministry is more than associated with the actions of each of its members; it is responsible for then,' replied a Stationary representative, getting to his feet. 'That's a principle. Principles stand; Ministries fall.'

"'Silence, gentlemen, silence!' cries the President in his turn, his voice dominating the tumult.

"'It's a cabinet matter!' the representative with principles goes on. 'I demand the floor.'

"'I demand it ahead of you,' says a Progressist. 'Before refuting it, permit me to follow the Minister of Finance's arguments and lend him my support.'

"The left and right look at one another in amazement. A representative is daring to defend what everyone is in agreement in condemning—something that even the Progressists, in spite of their thirst for reform, consider to be a crime!

"However, the parliamentary rules give every representative the right to take the floor, in any circumstances, provided that he then explains himself to the na-

117

tion at the annual assembly. The floor is, therefore, given to the Progressist.

"He goes up to the podium with a firm and assured tread. He is the leader of the extreme left. His speech might perhaps disrupt the majority.

"'Gentlemen,' he says. 'I have come to add to the Minister of Finance's speech what modesty forbade him to say. By expelling the Minister you would lose, in his person, a man whose talent, skill and experience are precious guarantees of the prosperity of the land. No one, during the course of his career, has been better able than him to administer the numerous personnel of the Treasury. No one has been better able to resolve financial questions. The system he has just described has been greeted with spectacular success. The figures speak for themselves.

"'But two parties divide this august assembly. One, satisfied with the present condition of the country, wants to impose a brake on the activity of our intelligence; the others—to which I belong—affirms that humans were made to improve themselves and that their intelligence in the subtle agent by means of which that will happen over time. Which of the two is right? Each one believes that it is. It is not for me to offer my appraisal here; I would be charged with partisanship. I shall therefore limit myself to what I believe to be logical.

"'These two parties, acting in accordance with contrary motives, have united to condemn an action that a member of one of them has taken it upon himself to execute, and which practice has justified.

"'I understand the prejudice of the right; it is following a principle. But you, gentlemen'—he turns to the left—'you, whose votes created this Ministry, who enclose the majority in your ranks—will you condemn a man whose only crime is to have anticipated your intentions, and an entire Ministry with him? The law has been broken, that's true—but after all, what is the law? Words.'"

At this point, Monsieur Landet paused.

"What's the matter?" asked Hobson. "Why have you stopped all of a sudden?"

"Because that audacious speech has unleashed the storm that has been rumbling since the beginning of the session," the savant said. "From every direction one hears nothing but shouting. 'Order! Order! To the assemblies! To the assemblies!'

"The President is shaking his bell in vain. The impassive orator confronts the tumult without flinching. A few representatives are advancing to the base of the podium, threatening him with their voices and gestures.

"Taking advantage of a momentary calm, the orator continues: 'Yes, gentlemen, words; I said it, and I repeat it.' Further tumult, more shouting. 'Words issued by vote and consecrated by usage, words that you erase as easily as you wrote them, words that are your work, but which you elevate to the status of a divinity. In deifying your work, you are deifying yourselves; in deifying yourselves you are forgetting that you are not infallible.'

"The President leans toward the podium and replies, severely: 'The law, Monsieur, represents the will of the nation, expressed by its representatives. Respect for the law is everyone's security. No one here will allow it to be insulted.'

"A thunder of bravos drowns out the President's voice.

"The representatives, electrified, are rushing the podium. They are tearing the impudent orator away from it, crying: 'To the vote! Put the Ministry to the vote!'"

Monsieur Landet paused again. He was waiting for the tempest to abate. Hobson, perceiving that the savant's head was leaning over his shoulder under the pressure of the fluid, relieved the pressure in order that he could continue to the end of the session.

"The representatives are writing their names on the voting papers," Monsieur Landet continued. "They're going to deposit them in the urn. The parliament is prey to a feverish agitation, but the right and the left are united with perfect accord. Only the ministers remain on their benches, bleak and depressed.

"It's the turn of the leader of the left to deposit his voting paper. The Chamber is noisy.

"'Gentlemen,' says the President, 'be the first to give an example of respect for the law, by respecting the individual.'

"Immediately, everyone falls silent, as if by enchantment. The representatives go up and down. There is a continual ebb and flow. The last one is casting his vote. The count is being made...

"...The President rises to his feet and says: 'Gentlemen, the Ministry is dismissed, by 722 votes to one.'

"At that moment, a Progressist climbs up to the podium, turns toward the leader and says: 'We'll meet again at the assemblies.'

"The criticized leader bows his head. He has been defeated by a crushing majority. The Ministry's fall is taking him down.

"They pass on, then, to a vote on the Minister of Finance's plan to create an annual payment of 4½%, redeemable in 30 years by expiration. It is adopted without any difficulty. Then the representatives retire noisily, unused to such incidents.

"Now wake me up—I'm exhausted."

He had opened his eyes already. He threw himself upon the sheets of stenography avidly, and read them rapidly.

"That's exactly what I dreamed about!" he cried, enthusiastically. "A sovereign parliament, a Ministry in stewardship, a passive President."

"Dreamed, you say?"

"Yes, dreamed—last night."

"That's because, for a month, you've only woken up incompletely. Under the empire of a magnetic torpor, you've anticipated the somnambulistic state."

"Bah!"

"I'm explaining your distraction, and the anxiety we've had regarding a brain seizure."

"Damnation!" said Monsieur Landet, singularly chilled. "Science is sublime, but life certainly has its charm!"

The Popular Assemblies

Monsieur Landet was only partly reassured when he parted company with the magnetizer. Who could tell whether the research on which he had embarked, with the aid of somnambulistic sleep, might eventually disturb his reason? Might his wretched carnal envelope, which he took pleasure in surrounding with the assiduous cares that only a perfect egoist could imagine, become confused with oblivion?

What savant is not a perfect egoist? Study, in concentrating his intellectual faculties of a unique and constant object, with which he lives, so to speak, in a communion of the soul, ends up absorbing him, to the point of infecting him with a monomania that summarizes all his enjoyments and leads him to delight only in himself.

Monsieur Landet, like all those who profess to possess strong minds, feared death more than anything else—although his speculations, cleverly deduced, had the gift of convincing his readers, they had not been succeeded in reassuring him with regard to human destiny after death.

What if, out of all the religions that humans have invented, he sometimes said to himself, *there is one that is true?* He went on, however, in a consolatory manner: *But there's no need to think about that; the moment hasn't yet arrived.*

Having returned home, still under the unfortunate impression of what Hobson had said, he occupied himself by having his secretary copy the stenographers' work. When that was done, he went over it minutely, licking it into shape and polishing it with an artistic caress. He was so satisfied by it that he completely forgot the danger he was in, and started meditating on the effect that his book would have in intellectual society.

Comforted by the whiff of glory that went to his head, he dined copiously, deigning to smile at some innocent wordplay by his secretary. Then he had himself taken to the Bois in order to dream at his ease, came home at about midnight and went to bed. He read the *Journal des Savants* distractedly for a while, and dropped off, to sleep the sleep of the just.

Ten o'clock was chiming on a clock in the neighborhood when he woke up the next day. He dressed himself in a trice, and went into his study.

He was expecting Hobson for lunch. What should he do until midday? Instinctively, he reread his secretary's work and was overtaken by an invincible drowsiness.

Hobson caught him struggling with that torpor. "Why, what's the matter?" he asked.

"Can you imagine, dear Master, that on re-reading the record of our last séance my head suddenly grew heavy? For an hour, now, I've been fighting to stay awake. I'm harassed, exhausted. It's as if my joints were disarticulated."

Hobson burst out laughing. "It's nothing, my dear savant, but a very common phenomenon, against which I forgot to forearm you. The attention that you put into re-reading that work has retraced in your mind the images presented to it during somnambulistic sleep, and that reading has produced the same effect on you as a magnetizer; you're subject to magnetic influence."

"Another unwelcome discovery," said the savant, slightly pale.

"Don't worry—there's no danger. I'll dispel the torpor; in five minutes, you'll be ten years younger."

"Oh, if only you had that secret," the savant sighed.

"You're very devoted to life, then?"

"I don't see that it's so disagreeable, for someone who has money, fame and honors, for someone who knows how to find pleasure wherever the turn of his mind takes him."

"You're talking as an egoist. Certainly, the person who is self-sufficient has no grounds to complain about life, unless physical infirmities render him a slave to malady, but anyone who has a heart, who finds his pleasure in that of others, who seeks happiness in love or friendship, experiences nothing but bitterness and disappointment—oh, people like that don't complain about the brevity of life!"

"That's because they don't reflect on the fable of 'The Frogs Who Wanted a King.'[16] By running after the unknown, one risks losing what one has; in uncertainty, 'it's better to have than to seek.'"

So saying, Monsieur Landet placidly stretched his legs and made a grimace.

"And I forgot to clear you!" exclaimed Hobson.

He made a few full-body passes over the savant. The latter, relieved of the burden that was weighing him down, got up, walked back and forth across the room, satisfied with his feeling of light.

"Well, shall we begin?" he said.

"Whenever you wish..."

"Following yesterday's incident in the Chamber," the savant eventually began, "a proclamation has been issued immediately convening the eleventh district of Paris to meet in assemblies in order to pass judgment on the conduct of the representative, in default of his mandate, who had lent the support of his words to an illegal maneuver.

"The session begins at one o'clock. The minister, elected by a provincial constituency, has returned there. Only the Progressist representative is at issue. Elected by the eleventh district, he belongs to that district.

"He goes up to the podium. Silence immediately falls. The people of Paris have learned to listen before they condemn.

"'Gentlemen,' says the accused—for he is one himself—'this extraordinary assembly, which is to decide my fate, is under a legal obligation. The spontaneity that led me to support the Minister of Finance has, I can see,

---

[16] Again, the citation is one of Aesop's fables, in which the dissatisfied frogs unwisely exchange King Log for King Stork.

alienated me from the confidence of my electors. What, however, has been my parliamentary conduct during the two years that I have defended their interests? Representing the Progressist party, I have followed the program of my mandate on all occasions.

"'Whenever, in the Chamber, there was a matter of an amelioration to introduce into the State, a proposed law in favor of the development of commerce and industry, I have been the first to lend all the strength my influence and my feeble eloquence thereto. Today, something new is happening. The Monsieur of Finance, taking advantage of the parliamentary vacation, took it upon himself to modify the tax on income.

"'I was in such total agreement with the Minister of Finance that, yielding to my first impulse, seeing nothing but the general interest, neglecting the form to see nothing but the fundamental, I spoke in favor of the Minister. That is my crime. By lending my support to an arbitrary action, I admit, I broke the law—but should intelligent and enlightened people allow themselves to be guided by the spirit of routine? Besides, the law, infringed as to the letter, was not in principle, since the attempt was rewarded with success and the approval of the majority crowned the result while censuring the execution. You all share my opinion, and yet you condemn me!

"'Did I have an active part in this action? No. I did nothing but support a friend once the deed was done...'

"'It is precisely that for which you are being reproached.' replies an anonymous voice.

"'I knew, gentlemen, in coming to this podium, that my cause was lost in advance. It is only out of deference to those who have honored me with their votes that I thought it my duty to explain my conduct. Today, I am expiating the sin of my frankness.'

"A faint murmur is heard in the crowd.

"An old man takes the orator's place. 'Gentlemen,' he says, 'I do not doubt the outcome of this debate for a moment. Victory will go to legality, I am convinced, although our representative has described it as routine. But before you render your verdict, I want to oppose my long experience to his impetuous fluency.

"'Where would we be without the law? What security would we have if an individual's caprice could modify it at will, at the cost of explaining himself later? The State, surrendered to hazard, would sail under the impulsion of temporary passions; changing direction along with its pilot, it would inevitably be wrecked by a false maneuver. Crime, that infamous stigma of human imperfection, would no longer be the same for all; there would be nuances, according to position, and the work of many centuries would collapse in a matter of years. No, gentlemen; in all things there has to be a sanction, and that sanction must be the same for everyone; that is what constitutes its force. Without checks, a State is no longer possible; there are only agglomerations of individuals obedient to their base instincts—for the base instincts always prevail over the good ones when impunity favors them.

"'The law is, therefore, a necessity of our vicious nature, a guarantee of our repose, a condition of our happiness. In order to be respected, it must be executed. If its execution does not reassure the confidence of the country, if its representatives are the first to overstep its bounds, trust—that source of public prosperity—dies, struck at its foundation.

"'A representative invested with your authority has dared to defend an illegal action in a parliamentary session; he has dared to saw that the law is only words; he has betrayed his mandate; he is unworthy to represent you.

"'What does the question of form matter, he has asked, given that the act itself was ratified? The question of form is everything, since the form is the law. Elaborated by your representatives, the law has been confirmed by your annual assemblies; it is therefore your work; it is therefore you. To encourage its infraction is to insult the principle of national sovereignty.

"'I am prepared to believe that our representative is only guilty of imprudence, but whoever speaks without giving his thought the necessary maturity is dangerous. Animated by the finest sentiments, he is capable of doing much harm. For the sake of public security, the march of business and society, an example must be made.'

"The notables deliberate between themselves and then invite the electors to decide by vote. The papers are distributed. Everyone deposits them in the urn, and the mayor, before the eyes of the entire audience, proceeds with the count.

"The representative is dismissed by a unanimous vote.

"The mayor then convenes a meeting of electors in a week's time to choose a new representative, after which the crowd disperses silently."

"But in submitting representatives to the control of the annual assembly of their electors for the review," Hobson objected, "and to the permanent control of that same assembly, convened in extraordinary session in case of a serious incident, their initiative is completely annihilated. Always feeling the sword of Damocles above their heads, caught in the mesh of their profession of faith, they dare not undertake anything important.

People are only capable of great work when they have a free hand, unhindered by any apprehension. Otherwise, it is servitude by abuse of liberty."

"Error!" riposted the savant. "The representatives' conduct is, indeed, limited by their mandate; everything they do, outside of that mandate, exposes them to the severity of their electors. That's true—but who is at fault? They are. Before accepting a candidature, let them broaden the frame of their program, let them ripen their plans, let them weigh the pros and cons, let them only put forward their strongest opinions.

"Once nominated, the route is quite simple, they only have to follow it within the latitude they have reserved for it. What you take for an obstacle is, on the contrary, an effective means of eliminating from candidature all those who see it as nothing but an objective of personal ambition. No more hypocritical proclamations, no more hidden agendas, no more ambiguous promises: a clear, concise reasoned program. If, in drawing it up, the candidate allows himself to be guided by conviction, he is sure never to deviate from it, and the annual assemblies become merely a legal formality for him. He has no reason to be afraid of extraordinary assemblies.

"Above all, the law must be precise. The few good dispositions a society shows to ameliorate itself will only be honest in so far as they are enforced. One of the numerous faults of our vicious nature is to seek subterfuges everywhere.

"The more I study these sage institutions, the more I see them as a precious lesson for modern society. But that which is so naturally adapted to a society matured by the 20 centuries that separates us from them is not applicable to ours. Destiny holds the thread of events in its hand, and only unreels it according to the order engraved in its immutable book.

"God has willed that his work, before acquiring the degree of perfection he has assigned to it, should pass through the slow purification of centuries, because the errors advertised by the different human generations form the experience of the following generations.

"Today, we are still in a state of ferment. The epoch we have just inaugurated is only just beginning to lay its foundations; 6000 years have brought us to this stage, some say; 2000 more will lead us to the new era I am glimpsing.

"Among other laws worthy of attention there is one that concerns the accumulation of administrative functions. Anyone, says the text of this law, who occupies a position in one of the administrative sections cannot occupy another in another section. He must devote himself entirely to that which is entrusted to him, and for which he receives recompense, according to a hierarchical grade. The accumulation of functions is therefore formally prohibited, given that in accepting several entails stealing time from one employment that is devoted to another and the salary thereof.

"It will be a long time before that useful reform will be introduced here. Governments have every interest in maintaining an institution that places them at the head of all the agencies directing the country. Administrative functions—I'm talking here about the most important— are accorded by grace and favor, rarely on merit; when they originate from a vote, they are due to intrigue and corruption. They are shared among those who are already overloaded by them, for the same reason that they are overloaded. Thus, a representative is, simultaneously, the mayor of his district, or sometimes a foreign ambassador; a senator is a general in command of an army division, or the governor of an overseas colony. Can the representative represent his electors, discuss their interests and participate in votes while he is safeguarding the interests of his country with the government to which he is accredited? Can he administer the district of which he is mayor while he is sitting in parliament? Can he be present everywhere at all times? Can he carry out conscientiously the various functions invested in him? It is evident that the time he devotes to one is prejudicial to the other, and yet he has one or several, according to the total number that have to be neglected. The senator who, in his capacity as a general, is in command of an army in the provinces, is too occupied with his general quarters to sit in the Senate; he only goes there at rare intervals. As for the governor of a distant colony, the distance he has to cover makes it a absolute impossibility.

"These are purely honorary responsibilities, which have no other result than to burden the budget with a quantity of useless salaries, to the profit of those who have least need of them. And an intelligent people tolerates being made a victim of the vanity of anyone who, by means of his importance, contributes to its prosperity or its ruination! For, in the final analysis, the first duty of a representative, before anything else, is to take the place of his electors in parliament. What is the purpose of the suffrage that appointed him? To award a vain title to a man whose negligence risks compromising not merely an entire district but also the entire country, since the absence of one vote might displace the majority? Today, it is a matter of lengthening the list of distinctions on a man's visiting card. It is the same with decorations; they attract one another. Merit counts for nothing, diplomatic considerations are their pretext; they are exchanged *en bloc*.

"It has happened that the absence of a representative has titled the balance of the majority to the opposite side and thus overturned the normal progress of affairs. You will object that the legislative, general and municipal elections are free. That's true—I'm not talking here about senatorial elections, whose electors are chosen from notable individuals—but the law ought to forearm citizens against intrigue, against their enthusiasms, against their sympathies. A man can only fruitfully give his intelligence to a task if that intelligence is not assailed by various preoccupations. Then again, it is not just that all dignities be conferred upon one person, when there is no lack of others for whom they would be a means of earning a living, first and foremost, and who would, in consequence, acquit themselves more conscientiously in their task.

"Let a representative by a general councilor in his département, no more. He has broadly studied the question of direct contributions in the Chamber; he knows the needs of the State better than anyone else; his advice might carry considerable weight in the General Council, with regard to the division of the tax burden between the département's contributors. He is also familiar with the government's projects; he has discussed them or heard them discussed. He also knows the statistics of the département he represents. He is therefore in a better position than anyone else to establish a calculation of taxation. Finally, that complementary function does not detract in any way from his functions as a representative, since the sessions of General Councils take place during parliamentary vacations.

"But that she should be mayor, no! That responsibility obliges a real presence, a perpetual vigilance. He can only do one of two things: go to the Chamber or administer his district. If he goes to the Chamber he leaves a deputy in his place, who then becomes the effective mayor. If he stays in his district, how can he justify the choice of his electors? He is a cogwheel lacking in the governmental machine, and his absence might cause an accident.

"The deputy's reason for being is to replace the mayor temporarily when the latter is ill or when superior reasons require him to be elsewhere; those are unexpected events that affect everyone. But always? That would be too easy. The deputy would have the difficulty, and the nominal mayor would have the honors and the appointments! The deputy, as his title indicates, is only a substitute; he replaces the mayor in extreme circumstances. From the moment that he replaces him in his functions throughout the year, why should he not have the title?

"Our descendants have put an end to this accumulation, but they have not closed access to administrative functions to those who exercise an honorable profession in private life. On the contrary; their collaboration is useful to the government. They bring to the Chamber the enlightenment they possess in their specialty. Representatives deliberate all questions in general; it is indispensable that nuclei of individuals competent in particular matters should be found among them—otherwise, they would be judging in ignorance of causes.

"The industrialist is consulted in matters of manufacture, the merchant for trade, the financier for the movement of capital. Advocates they all are, only being eligible on production of a diploma in law. To make laws, is it not necessary to be expert in jurisprudence? But any advocate who embraces a political career is obliged to take leave of his clientele, even though he only plays the role of consultant. The manufacturer, the merchant and the financier have their businesses managed. It is their property; they are free to confide it to a manager; if they leave it on sufferance, they alone are the responsible parties, and victims.

"As it is necessary for each administrative branch to be equally represented, functionaries are only permitted to seek to become representatives when they reach the age of retirement, fixed at 50 years. At that age, they still have all the lucidity of their faculties; matured by labor, they bring to their colleagues the solid knowledge and sound and sure judgment of experience—qualities indispensable to the direction of a nation.

"Only the army has no members in the Chamber, for the excellent reason that there is no army. I shall leave it until later to explain the means that have been devised for its replacement. Everything in due time.

"Only the ministers enjoy the privilege of fulfilling two administrative functions at once. It is necessary to say that those two functions are so intimately linked as to be integral. Chosen by a majority of the representatives, they nevertheless retain the role of representatives; during the exercise of their ministry, they may speak, if they have occasion to do so, in the name of their electors. Continually required to set out their plans before the Chamber, it is easy for them to take in hand the cause of their district while defending that of the government. Bound, moreover, by the imperative mandate they have accepted, they are obliged to submit to it, under penalty of being invalidated by the assemblies, in which they are judged as representatives."

"But there are functions awarded on merit," Hobson objected, "for example, that of a member of one of the various sections of the Institut, which are honorary titles rather than employments, and which do no harm to the exercise of a political responsibility."

"It is precisely for that reason that they are not included among administrative functions," the savant replied. "They are, as you say, distinctions afforded to those who, by study, have acquired a marked superiority in some specialty. They dedicate themselves to science, and are as useful, in enlightening the deliberations of the Chamber, as the experience of retired functionaries. They are not subject, therefore, to the ostracism that applies to the accumulation of administrative functions. What is meant by administrative functions is those which participate directly in the mechanism of government. Savants are never surplus to requirements when it is a matter of presiding over the destiny of a nation. A counterweight is required to the impetuosity and imagination of the young. In all things, equilibrium is the sole means of achieving precision.

"But I feel tired. My ideas are beginning to get confused, and I can no longer see the images designed in the fiery fog in which they present themselves to my mind distinctly. Wake me up. It's better to postpone the continuation to the next installment, as the feuilletonists say."

Hobson woke the savant.

"Well?" asked the latter, when he had collected himself slightly.

"Well," replied Hobson, "it's impossible to put on a more paradoxical show. You would be the first to complain if the reforms you have predicted were to be realized today."

"Really?"

"Yes—you've waxed lyrical about the suppression of the accumulation of administrative functions, but you are yourself a senator, a general councilor and a mayor.

"Oh, I can wax lyrical easily enough," Monsieur Landet replied. "We're no stick-in-the-muds in France. I work for posterity. On that account, I deserve it, without having the inconveniences."

Chapter V
SOPHISMS

Providence—Children—Egoism

That evening, Monsieur Landet went to the home of his old enemy—politically speaking—the Marquise de la Roche-Houdion. By the greatest good fortune, he found her alone in her small drawing-room, between a cup of tea and the *Revue des Deux Mondes*.

"What!" she exclaimed. "It's you, illustrious prophet! We never see you anymore. So you're always voyaging on the wings of the future, like witches on their broomsticks?"

"Joke as much as you like, dear friend," the savant replied, sitting down after kissing her hand. "I'll set up a rendezvous with you in 2000 years, to show you with your own eyes that my witchcraft has divined accurately."

"Two thousand years! That's a lot. And what will we be in that epoch?"

"Oh, I don't know that myself. It might be that you, the elegant Marquise de la Roche-Houdion, would be, in that epoch, merely a simple goose-girl, just as I, the grim Republican whom you have separated from his fellows in spite of his convictions, might be no more than a simple road-sweeper."

"Is that what you call an improvement?"

"Perhaps we'd be compensated for that lowly condition in being reborn morally improved."

"My dear Monsieur Landet, when you've run out of arguments you have a deplorable habit of losing your adversary in a maze of sophisms whose twists and turns only you know—and you're careful to keep the thread to yourself. Have the indulgence to descend to the level of my feeble intelligence."

"Then have the frankness to confess that it's a compliment you desire."

"Oh, these logicians! What about the end of the world? In what epoch do you place that?"

"My double vision hasn't extended as far as that, and I don't want to try to go any further. I'd lose what little mind I have left."

"Bah! Posterity will hold you to account."

"I certainly hope so—that's the least that it owes me. This escape to a better world, which my work will allow contemporary society to glimpse, ought to have a salutary effect on it. People will laugh at it to begin with—that's how serious things are greeted—then they'll take note of it, and the seeds that I shall have planted in every brain will produce their fruit. Perhaps it has been my mission to enlighten the world and help it to climb the slope of Progress!"

"And you believe, in good faith, everything that you say in somnambulistic sleep?"

"I'm astonished by that question, after the experiment that you witnessed."

"I don't deny the effect of magnetism—but I can't grant it the power to foresee that which has not happened, and which doesn't yet exist."

"But in that case, the revelation that I made here, in your presence, at your request…?"

"Was merely the effect of a hallucination, the mirage of your own ideas, Monsieur Landet—don't deceive yourself about that. Magnetism exerts a physical action on the human organism; that action provokes sleep—that much is evident—but in that sleep, it's the subject's most tenacious thoughts that cross his mind and are exposed to the light as in a dream."

"I don't want to debate with you, Marquise, a subject on which your opinion is obstinately fixed in a contradictory sense—that would drag on too long. I shall reserve my reply to the work that I am presently writing, in accordance with the stenographic record of my communications. I'm convinced that the solidity of my arguments will triumph over your prejudices, even if that work is not of the same kind as my treatise *On the End of Things*, which I perceive on your side-table, and whose pages have not yet been separated by your paper-knife.

The Marquise blushed slightly. "The fault is that of your penultimate work, which I haven't yet finished reading," she replied. "If you continue to put your works to my throat before leaving me time to digest their predecessors, you'll surely assassinate me. But let's resume our discussion. If we were of the same opinion, we'd end up finding one another dull. So you claim that society is on the road of Progress?"

"That's in the order of things. It's sufficient to compare the different ages of the world to be convinced. In giving us life, the Creator had an objective. Now, any objective, whatever it maybe, must suppose an amelioration. Common sense refuses to attribute caprices of God. In order to be infinitely perfect, his slightest thoughts and actions must be regulated with a mathematical precision, with a view to a utility that is hidden from us, or escapes us. He has an objective, I say, and that objective is to draw us gradually nearer to him in perfection, by the natural means that he has put at our disposal.

"For the same reason that every work emerging from his hands is perfectible to a certain degree, the work of God, which is perfection itself, must have the same property.

"Take, for example, a sculptor. At first, his statue is nothing but a formless block; he begins to shape it with sweeping strokes of his chisel, and then, as it takes form, he plies his implement prudently, lightly and delicately, for fear that a splinter detached too abruptly might injure the ideal that he is pursuing.

"Is it not the same with humankind? Thrown on to the Earth with an intuition of truth, beauty and justice, people know how far away they are from those goals, and if they persevere in the contrary path it isn't for want of knowing the cause. A formless block to begin with, humankind begins to shape itself, laboring, polishing, with a view to the objective that God has designed for it. It is both the block and the artisan, but it is only accomplishing its task by virtue of a divine impression.

"What is applicable to human life must be applicable to the existence of the world, both being in concordance. The world changes its surface as human beings change bodily; spring gives birth to fruits as generation gives birth to humans; summer matures them as the prime of life gives humans the plenitude of their strength; autumn causes them to fall and strips the trees of foliage, as old age makes humans decrepit; finally, winter, buries the earth beneath a mourning-cloak as death removes humans from life. Both have their seasons, both perish, but to be reborn again, the world the following spring, humankind in another epoch. And the mind of society is modified by the centuries, as the human mind is modified by age. The world and human beings are regulated in the same fashion.

"Would God justify the sentiment that innate intuition gives us of him if we were beings delivered at hazard, if no superior will had forearmed us against our weaknesses and were presiding over our destiny? That supreme will, by the action of which God is manifest, is what is conventionally called Providence."

"So you deny free will?"

"Far from denying it, I am providing evidence of it. Providence, although being the expression of divine will, is not an insurmountable barrier that God sets between our aspirations and their realization.

"The crimes committed every day are an indubitable proof that the human will knows no other restraint than its own resolution. The resistance it encounters in that struggle is nothing but the action of Providence, and conscience, that internal voice which tells us that we are doing good or evil, is the interpreter chosen by Providence to identify its weaknesses. Hence hesitation. According to temperaments, it concludes well or badly. Later, when evil is accomplished, conscience still makes its voice heard; it awakens remorse. It is still providence that gives people the hope of forgiveness, on the condition of repentance.

"Human will is therefore absolutely free to act according to its impressions; but it must take into account the slightest actions that bring it before the tribunal of the conscience, the vigilant guardian that Providence has delegated to it, in order to watch over it, to turn it away from reefs, indicating the right road and guiding it there if necessary.

"How can you imagine that, with such a mentor, enlightened by supernatural radiance, instructed by the experience of past centuries, human beings will not gradually strip away the unhealthy envelope with which the passions have surrounded them like a bark? Just as an apprentice acquires by practice the skill lacking in his first endeavors, humankind, the most perfectible endeavor of all, takes shape by means of intelligence, the divine parcel that transmit the sentiment of its mission."

"How is it, then, that instead of advancing, we're degenerating? How is it that our children are worse than us? The experience of past centuries, which you invoked just now, demonstrates that verity."

"You're not taking account, dear friend, of the fact that we haven't yet recovered from the rude shock of '89—that violent social commotion which, without transition, substituted the rule of human rights for an aristocratic regime. The epoch has not yet arrived when society, shaken at its base, will recover its normal equilibrium.

"War leaves traces that only future generations can succeed in erasing. The cataclysms of nature, which superimpose new terrain on old terrain and establish lines of demarcation between the different ages of the Earth, are only regularized over time.

"It is the same with children. Science, in an embryonic state in their minds, gradually follows their physical and moral development; it only extends fully when they are fully-grown.

"Nothing is accomplished in this world by the effort of our will alone. Will is only the superior agent that presides over action. Everything takes time. Time is the currency of destiny.

"Compare moral effects to physical effects; think about the interval that it will require for the new ideas that the great Revolution has thrown pell-mell into minds to emerge from chaos and coordinate with one another.

"The children born of the new era have absorbed the principle of liberty with their nurses' milk. They have grown up with that idea; they have become adults with the firm intention of enjoying its respect—and that sentiment of their personality has attenuated the sentiment of filial respect within them. The evil is not as great as you think. The parents have lost in terms of form, but they have gained in terms of affection, which is worth a hundred times more. Once, respect held sway; one loved one's father by virtue of duty, habit and necessity; one feared him as a master. Today, one listens to the voice of the heart. That natural impulse enlightens our impressions better than the deceptive appearances of prejudice. What good is vain ceremony and emphatic etiquette between a father and his child? Why raise children in constraint and terror? Should we not, on the contrary teach them to love their parents? Should we not, from the earliest infancy, allow them to follow the inclination of their sentiments? Affection need not be imposed; it is natural.

"The veterans of the 'good old times' complain bitterly about the cavalier attitudes of our children. They deplore the present system of education, which consists of spoiling them, giving in to their little whims, rendering their lives happy and easy from the beginning. 'Our fathers made men,' they say, 'but you are only making girls.' Error. Let us not bring up children in the school of adversity, by means of needless deprivations that they cannot understand; many of them are already victims when we strike them. Let us wait until they grow up to shape them for the struggles of life.

"Life is not long enough for us to hasten to sow thorns beneath the feet of children. Children, like old people, are too weak to support strife. Let us therefore smooth the path of existence, in order that they should not be horrified by it on the threshold. We know where that leads: to suicide. The men that we form progressively and naturally, are educated, practiced and laborious; they are not useless Hercules, like those you regret. What use is strength, when it is not guided by wisdom?"

"That's all very well in theory, my dear savant," the Marquise replied, "but look at the children of today, left to their caprices; the more they're given, the more they want. Their affection, of which you boast, is only addressed to those who give them treats or pleasures; it can only be captured via greed or self-interest. Their fathers and mothers are nothing compared to cakes or gold coins; all the generosity and caresses of the past are effaced before the temptation of the present. With your principles, my dear, you arrive at ingratitude."

"Your reasoning, my dear Marquise, applies to small children who are still on the path of formation—the heart and intelligence as well as the body. You demand a combination of qualities of them that is difficult to find in adulthood. Let time accomplish its work—I'm getting back to my pet subject. If the child forgets, the adult remembers. Don't ask children for a perfection that would cause them to die of meningitis."

"But don't all these faculties, which exist in them as seeds, at least require fertilization?"

"And it is rigor that you employ to that end. You educate them in the worst of all vices: hypocrisy. One does not love what one fears—or, at least, very rarely; that is only seen between lovers. A child's heart is neither as insensible nor as selfish as you asset; does not their first cry, when they fall and hurt themselves, appeal to their mother?"

"Because they need her."

"Oh, it you make that a question of self-interest, we'll go round in a vicious circle from which it will be impossible to find an exit. Self-interest is the dominant element in our character; it's mixed up in everything in this world. It enters into everyone's nature, in a more or less emphatic dose; it insinuates itself into the most well-tempered soul. And bizarrely enough, in wanting to take a stand in opposition to self-interest, one falls back into it; no matter where we try to flee, it presents itself to us in a new form.

"There is the self-interest of the heart, the self-interest of the mind, the self-interest of money, the self-interest of pleasure, the self-interest of devotion, and a hundred of other sorts of self-interest, which I don't have presently in mind. A good action is often dictated by a vulgar sentiment of egoism, which, analyzed minutely, uncovers a black spot. Is there a sentiment nobler, purer and more respectable than maternal love? And yet, maternal love does not escape the pitiless rule; it too is tainted with self-interest. For her child, a mother is capable of any devotion. That love is immense, merciful and blind, I grant you, but the mother, in loving her child thus, is counting on a reciprocal exchange of affection; she sows in order to harvest. She concentrates all her tenderness there, because it is from there that she obtains her greatest happiness.

"What is more egotistical than friendship? Do you have a friend, in the true sense of the word? You follow him everywhere, you involve yourself in his smallest affairs, at the risk of being indiscreet; you make his absences criminal, you're jealous of his other friendships, you want him to be solely occupied with you, never to leave you, that he be no one's friend but yours.

"What about love? It is the egoism of friendship taken to its highest expression, for love is passionate, and the more egotistical it is, the more tyrannical it is in consequence.

"What about courage? That sentiment, which provokes enthusiasm, which is, in appearance, so fine, so noble, so great, and which, examined profoundly, lays bare all the pettiness of ambition!

"Is it always for his fatherland that a soldier launches himself toward death? Is it not, very often, for a piece of ribbon to ornament his buttonhole, or for his commander to notice him and recommend him for promotion? Is not each daring deed an effort that hoists him toward the pinnacle?"

"No," the Marquise replied. "Under enemy fire, the soldier does not think of those vainglories. Has he even the time to covet them? The regimental drum carries him away; the powder intoxicates him; he does not know where he is going; he follows the others. And if, in the ardor of battle, a stray thought crosses his mind, it is the image of his mother, his wife or his children. He fights then to defend their fortune, their happiness—who knows?—perhaps their lives."

"Their unhappiness or death would make him suffer. He prefers to expose himself to more immediate suffering. Egoism, always egoism!"

"With such reasoning, you make virtue a monstrosity."

"Certainly—but you're the one who drove me to that pernicious logic. I'm extrapolating your principle—see where it leads."

"Debate is no longer possible with such weapons. We could continue until tomorrow morning without either of us winning. Let's leave these deceptive procedures to the diplomats; between ourselves, let's put our cards on the table. What do you expect? I belong to the old regime, myself, by right of birth; the prejudices of my father—if they are prejudices—are inherent in my nature, by virtue of blood. One can't argue with prejudices.

"You're of the revolutionary school, and, in a spirit of contradiction, you oppose yourself to our institutions. You're playing your role. We teach our children respect and submission; you teach them familiarity and insubordination. As you please—the future will decide between us. Liberty without limit, that's your maxim. Go on, keep going, and that liberty will explode in your hands. I'm more conciliatory than you; I admit the work of the Revolution; I combine its reforms with the law and traditional authority."

"Combinations are superfluous. Why confuse what is so simple? From the moment when people surpass that traditional authority, why impose it on them?"

"Yes, I know—the crown of your Utopian edifice is the Republic."

"Naturally. You judge by reference to the past and the present, without deducing the future upheavals of humankind; you judge with reference to what is no longer the case. Personally, I judge by reference to what is. For the moment, it's necessary to take account of the spirit of populations. What is suitable to some is contrary to others. Forms of government must adapt to temperaments. One people, born with the instinct of passivity, subjects itself to a monarchy; another, born with the instinct of liberty, breaks the yoke and establishes a Republic—it's a matter of inclination.

"And let's not confuse the word Republic with the word Anarchy! It's true that Anarchy is often a consequence of the Republic, but temporarily; it arises from the fact that minds fermenting for a long time have suddenly erupted under the pressure of passion. The possession of the liberty so much desired has intoxicated them; hatred has blinded them; a conflict has been produced, from which civil war has surged—but that anarchy is only accidental, and when the first lance is broken, calm is reestablished.

"For the Republic to bear its fruits, it needs to ripen; the Republic must be given time to establish itself on solid foundations, to take root in the hearts of its citizens; it has to let the impetuous rancor of parties flow. On that condition alone, the Republic will be fecund; it will become indispensable; it will impose itself. It is the refuge of all deceived peoples; it is the daughter of indignation. Demolish it, and it will return, more powerful still! The more it is persecuted, the stronger it becomes. Is not the proof that we call carry its seed within us in our personalities, and that the political quakes that shake the social strata drive us toward the same end?"

"All that's utopian!" replied the Marquise. "Since the world was created, it has only advanced in order to retreat again. Arts, letters and the sciences have made progress, that's incontestable—but that progress has worked to our detriment. The more the mind develops, the more the heart hardens. Can we find, in modern history, those sublime examples of virtue, devotion and courage of which we read on every page of ancient history?"

"And which probably never existed, save in the minds of writers. In our day, actions are in accordance with reflection. You see that as a bad thing; for myself, I see it as a great step toward the end of terrestrial ordeals."

Monsieur Landet rose to his feet in order to take his leave of the Marquise.

"You're leaving already?"

"It's midnight, my dear Marquise. This discussion has taken us well into the night without bringing forth any light."

"You'll come to dinner tomorrow?"

"Gladly."

"But on one condition."

"What?"

"That you bring your retinue."

"Ah! Marquise, you want a foretaste of the work before it's published."

"Isn't it me to whom you owe it? Wasn't I its first cause? It's agreed, then?"

"You know full well that I can refuse you nothing. But shh!—and above all, don't invite anyone else."

"It'll try..."

Monsieur Landet kissed the Marquise's delicate aristocratic hand, and went out.

Chapter VI
JUSTICE

"Summus jus, summa injuria"[17]

The Marquise kept her promise. She had not invited anyone else.

Immediately after dinner, Hobson put Monsieur Landet to sleep.

"Today," said the latter, "I shall deal with an exceedingly delicate aspect of the great social problem: Justice.

"Justice is an abstraction, which everyone fashions in his own way. The law varies, according to the country, temperaments, mores and prejudices. Prejudices, especially, exert the greatest influence on the mind of a people. 'One sees almost nothing of what is just or unjust that does not change its quality in changing climate. Three degrees of elevation toward the pole overturns all of jurisprudence. A meridian decides the truth. In a few years of possession, fundamental laws change. The law has its epochs. The entry of Saturn into Leo marks the origin of some crime. A fine justice that is bounded by a river! Truth this side of the Pyrenees, error beyond!'[18]

"Laws are subject to the transformations of epochs; they take on the imprint of contemporary ideas.

---

[17] "An excess of justice [leads to] an excess of injustice!" A Latin saying, cited by Cicero in *De Officiis*.

[18] The author's reference for this quotation is Pascal's *Pensées*, "De la justice," article IV. Garnier edition

"Among the ancients, crime was almost an honor, and vengeance was transmitted from generation to generation, like a sacred duty to be accomplished; justice was self-made. Today, it is the other way around; vengeance is reproved and punished by the law.

"In Sparta, there were schools of thievery, as there are schools for pickpockets in London today, with the difference that the former were authorized by the State and the latter hide from the police. Everyone knows the story of the young Spartan who, during a religious ceremony, preferred to allow his entrails to be devoured by a fox that he had stolen and hidden under his robe rather than reveal his larceny. A sad courage, that which consists in application to evil!

"Was there not a time when one could marry one's sister? It was the patriarchs themselves who first set an example of that union, considered culpable today. Ammon, the son of David, having conceived a grand passion for his sister Tamar, resolved to slake it. One day, when she came into his room to bring him food, he said: 'Come lie with me, my sister. And she answered him, Nay, my brother, do not force me; for no such thing ought to be done in Israel: do not thou this folly... Now, therefore, I pray thee, speak unto the king; for he will not withhold me from thee.'[19]

---

[19] The author's reference for this quotation is *II Kings* 8:2 ff. but that is incorrect; it is actually from *II Samuel* 13:11-13. I have given the version of the text contained in the King James Bible, as I have with the other quotations from scripture. The quotation is highly misleading, in any case; in fact, when Ammon rapes Tamar the incest horrifies the other members of his family and David is outraged.

"Thus, in the time of good King David, it was quite natural to marry one's sister. Today, however, social convention makes it incestuous. What crime is there in it, after all? The idea people attach to it.

"Marriage, in any case, is an entirely modern institution. Once, mutual consent was sufficient, and natural law accomplished its work. In India, fiancés came, hand in hand, to the bank of the Ganges, and there, facing the heavens, they each took their betrothal rings from the other's finger and threw it in the river; that was called marriage in the manner of the *Grand'hurwas*.[20]

"Better than that, among the Jews, when the wife called legitimate proved sterile, she presented one of her maidservants to her husband, in order that he might obtain a lineage and could thus perpetuate his family. Sarai, the wife of Abraham, being unable to have children by her husband, offered him one of her maidservants: 'And Sarai said unto Abram, Behold now, the Lord hath restrained me from bearing; I pray thee, go in unto my maid; it may be that I might obtain children by her. And Abram hearkened to the voice of Sarai. And Sarai, Abram's wife, took Hagar her maid, the Egyptian, after Abram had dwelt ten years in the land of Canaan.'[21]

[20] I have reproduced this term as the original text renders it. It might conceivably be a derivative of Garbhadanam, a term used in the context of Indian marriage ceremonies to refer to consummation, but it is more likely that the first part of the portmanteau word is simply the French for "great" and the second a contraction of "Ahuras," that being the plural of one of the ancient Aryan terms for a god.

[21] Again, the author gives an incorrect reference here, to *Genesis* 15:1 ff instead of *Genesis* 16: 2-3. Abram (who only starts calling himself Abraham subsequently) does indeed consent to the arrangement, but the Lord evidently does not, cursing Ha-

151

"Sarai had the conviction that she was behaving piously, and Abraham agreed in consequence, with the satisfaction of a duty accomplished. The centuries have overturned the manners illustrated; they have imposed new prejudices on humans. In our day under the terms of the law, Sarai would be neither more nor less than a common procuress, and Abraham, in accepting his wife's proposition, would be lending himself to an adultery all the more inadmissible because it was counseled and sanctioned by Sarai. And yet, the motive that caused Sarai to act was respectable. Examples of that sort abound in the Bible. The Jews thought that they were honoring the Lord in that way.

"Even immorality did not shock them, as can be judged by the following passage: 'Now King David was old and stricken in years; and they covered him with clothe but he gat no heat. Wherefore his servants said unto him, Let there be sought for my lord the king a young virgin; and let her stand before the king, and let her cherish him, and let her lie in thy bosom, that my lord the king may get heat. So they sought for a fair damsel throughout all the coasts of Israel, and found Abishag a Shunammite, and brought her to the king. And the damsel was very fair, and cherished the king, and ministered to him, but the king knew her not.'[22]

---

gar's son, Ishmael—although neither Hagar nor Ishmael has done anything wrong—and subsequently consenting to grant Sarai (then renamed Sarah) a son of her own, Isaac, in advance of the notorious Covenant.

[22] Yet again, the author gives an incorrect reference, to *Kings* 3: 1ff, rather than to *I Kings* 1: 2-4. The fact that he then goes on to insinuate, slyly, that the assertion of the scripture that no intercourse took place might not be reliable, together with the fact that he could have cited much more outrageous examples

"Without casting doubt on the problematic virginity of Abishag of Shunam, the act of seeking out a young woman, beautiful and virginal—virginal!—to 'warm' an old man chilled by age constitutes an act of monstrous depravity.

"For the Jews of those times, there was nothing immoral in that. If we regard the action as contrary to decency, it is because the centuries that have gone by since that epoch have modified our way of seeing. It's a question of appreciation, that's all.

"Among certain peoples of the Middle Ages, ancient hatreds between families were expunged and bloodshed halted by a marriage between the belligerent parties. Among others, and in Russia still at the present day, such a union was sacrilegious and it was said that the blood of the ancestors would fall on the children unto the 14th generation.

"In antiquity, a father had the right of life and death over his children. He killed his son at birth if he did not recognize him as his own. Today, the law attributes children born in marriage to the father, and forces him to give them his name whether he likes it or not. It thus renders him responsible for the fruits of adultery and exposes him to bear the burden of another man's child. That is a vice within our Code; but to make good laws, it is often necessary to sacrifice the exception to the rule.

"In Sparta, the government ordered children born with a deformity or a paltry constitution to be thrown from the summits of the Taygetus, considering them as improper as imperfect maneuvers in war.

---

of David's immorality had he so desired (the Bathsheba/Uriah incident, for example), strongly suggests that the sequence of "errors" is deliberate, occasioned by motives that are unclear.

"In Rome, the rights of a husband were unlimited. He condemned his wife to death if, while kissing her on the mouth, he perceived that she had drunk wine, a crime then unpardonable! Hence the Latin word *osculare*.[23] The husband was everything, the wife nothing. He was the sovereign judge in his house; civil law had nothing to say about his domestic affairs.

"The head of the family, he grouped around his heart the members who composed it, with the exclusion of his wife's parents; he held them under his jurisdiction, as chief, as judge, as priest. As father, he retained the right of guardianship over his children until death. After him, his eldest son, once having achieved his majority, inherited parental rights over his brothers. The laws reigning in the family, therefore, apart from a few that were generally accredited, were arbitrary. The husband and father possessed absolute power, more absolute than modern justice, since he condemned without appeal, without recourse to mercy.

"And the slaves? They were beasts of burden, objects, things that were bequeathed in wills, or given as gifts. They only had the physical appearance of men or women. They belonged to their master body and soul, who employed them as he wished, when he did not throw them to feed the lampreys that grew fat in his fishpond. Nero tested the effects of Locusta's poisons on them. And the Roman people, avid for human blood, sent them to face lions in the arena. Gladiators were counted in pairs, like animals. They were coupled,

---

[23] An esoteric joke. As well as "to kiss," the Latin verb in question can mean "to make a fuss." There is no trace of the double meaning in either French or English.

crossed and mated like animals in a stud-farm. That was the law.

"What seems to us to be revolting today was just in that epoch. Who knows whether, in future, humans, approaching their objective, will not have scruples about killing animals, not recognizing the right to take the lives of the beings that God has given to them? That would then be justice; we would be barbarians in their eyes. They would be content to live on the products of nature: bread, fruits and vegetables.

"To pass on to contemporary times, divorce, forbidden in France, is allowed in the greater part of the civilized world. What is punished here is licit elsewhere.

"In France, people are under the threat of the law; in England, they are under its protection. We are only permitted to have one wife; in Turkey, it is considered a good thing to have several. Where is the truth in this chaos of contradictions?

"'Larceny, incest, the murder of children and fathers, everything has its place among virtuous actions. Can there be anything more ludicrous than a man having the right to kill me because he lives overseas and his prince has a quarrel with mine, although I have none with him? Why are you killing me? What! Don't you live on the other side of the water? My friend, if you lived on this side, and I killed you, I would be a murderer, and it would be unjust to kill you like this, but since you live on the other side, I'm a good man and this is just.

"'Because of this confusion, some people have been led to say that justice is the authority of the legislator, others the prerogative of the sovereign, others still the present custom—and that is the most reliable. But according to that reasoning, nothing is just in itself; everything changes with time. Custom is the basis of all equity, by the sole reason that it is received; it is the mystical foundation of its authority.'[24]

"Justice therefore exists within us in the condition of an instinct; we have the notion of it, but we cannot circumscribe it within an invariable limit. That is one of the certain marks of our imperfection, along with the necessity of a Superior Being, who is the sole possessor of justice. It has the objective of discovering the truth. Now, as the truth is not of this world, it is a grave responsibility to disengage it from the tissue of errors with which it is enveloped. By dint of seeking it, we eventually denature it. *Summum jus, summa injuria.*

"Who can boast of being just? In the absence of striking evidence—and more!—justice, with all its procedures, is only based on probabilities. Pulled apart by contending advocates, who mount an assault of lies, it can only grope forwards. Which of the two is telling the truth? The cleverer often wins the case, and justice, blinded, but in good faith, pronounces on the basis of appearances. It is a power subject to manipulation, which one ought not to expose to the influence of speech; one risks falsifying it thus.

"The remedy, however, is quite simple. Our descendants have found it. Instead of complicating that which ought to emerge of its own accord, they have cut off the evil at its root, by eliminating the spirit of chicanery from the debates. No more advocates, no more public prosecutors. The accused remains, face to face with his judges. The work of justice is accomplished of its own accord. The facts are there. They speak sufficiently

---

[24] The author gives a reference to Pascal's *Pensées*, article XXIV, chapter IV.

for or against the accused. What good does it do, before the hearing, to charge him with a devastating indictment, or for him to pose as a victim in a hypocritical defense? Is there any need for so many fine phrases, to reveal what is or is not the case?

"A simple report is sufficient to guide the deliberations of the judges who interrogated the accused, confront him with his accomplices, if he has any, have witnesses deposed and, weighing the responses, establish an accurate account.

"Those who prosecute and defend by trade are equally reprehensible. They both act without conviction, one paid by the government, the other by anyone rich enough to buy the flexibility of his eloquence. Is it not shameful that men who enjoy a stainless reputation and who, outside of their functions, are honored and esteemed, should sell their conscience in this way?

"The defender is supposed to be convinced of his client's innocence, but in criminal matters where everything is against the accused, does he believe a word of what he says?

"I do not know whether the role of advocate or that of public prosecutor is the more odious. The public prosecutor is coldly inhuman in demanding the death penalty without good grounds. The advocate becomes his client's accomplice in taking his side against society. I would rather be the person who unmasks the crime, at the risk of being mistaken, than one who denies or excuses it in the presence of overwhelming evidence. And these two men, who play ball with the fate of the accused, are the best of friends on coming out of the hearing. They are doing their jobs.

"Is not the worse enemy of society the advocate who risks reintegrating into its bosom a malefactor

157

whom impunity will encourage to continue his dangerous exploits? What does he do? He earns his living, and for that, he argues for or against with the same facility. He adores tomorrow that which he overturned yesterday, benefiting from the harm he has done. When he takes up a good cause, it is hazard that had furnished it. Anything is good in order to make money. He will be neither more nor less esteemed in consequence; that is the way things are.

"In 3878 the title of advocate is nothing more than a certificate of study awarded to those who embrace a political career, as the title of bachelor of letters is awarded to those desirous of embarking on a liberal career. It is merely a diploma indispensable for standing as a candidate, just as the diploma of elementary education is for an elector.

"The standing magistracy, therefore, no longer exists; nothing remains but the seated magistracy, disengaged from and external influence, interrogating, judging and sentencing solely in the light of logic and conscience.

"There is no ornamented speech by an advocate to render a guilty person innocent, nor crushing indictment by a public prosecutor to make an innocent one guilty. Both fill an unnecessary role, repugnant to the austere rectitude of justice. The accused bears within him the evidence of his innocence or his culpability. It is the interrogation that gives rise to the probability; it is the confrontation of witnesses that shines a light on the truth.

"Take, for example, the affairs of the assize court, where the roles of advocate and public accuser are most prominent. With these two individuals eliminated, the judges are not under the influence of any bias before opening the discussion, nor any pressure afterwards. They establish extenuating circumstances themselves.

"In any case, there is no longer a head to dispute with society. The death penalty has been abolished for more than twelve centuries. It has been recognized that humans, being created, do not have the right to dispose of the lives of their fellows, created like them. Only the one who has given life has the right to take it away. In incarnating our souls he had designs of which we are ignorant; perhaps, in administering justice ourselves, we are spoiling them. Punishment is his prerogative, as well as mercy.

"Then again, is not a person driven by self-interest or any other passion obeying the irresistible power of instinct? What is instinct? Is it an acquired force, to which reflection, reason and study give birth within us, and develops with thought? If that were the case, we could rid ourselves of it with the same facility that we appropriated it. No, instinct is an unconscious force, a fatal deposit that nature has implanted in our soul when it was only in embryo, a deposit to which education gives the extension of a second nature. One succeeds is combating instinct, but never in stifling it."

"But you're falling into fatalism," the Marquise put in.

"Yes and no. Yes, if instinct, born within us, is the consequence of the vitiated blood that engendered us. Morality is then impotent to uproot it. It can shake it temporarily, but, like a staff thrown into water, it will soon reappear at the surface. It is inherent in the innate impressions of our soul, as vices of conformations are inherent in our physical configuration. The fault is not entirely that of the person who is its victim; it is, in large measure, that of his forebears, who yielded to evil penchants and, having assimilated them, have transmitted them by generation or education.

"No if, born of an honorable family and brought up with good principles, a person voluntarily allows his heart to be tainted by contact with bad society. A person whom hazard throws into that milieu before his ideas have had time to form, unable to weigh good and evil, might perhaps experience a good impulse. He will allow himself, it is true, to follow the bad examples he has been shown, but a light will shine in his blinded mind, he will remember vaguely the first impression engraved on his soul, and as soon as the evil is done, he will repent of it.

"He is, however, more guilty than the other. An effort of will would have sufficed to separate him from the current into which self-interest, pleasure or weakness had dragged him—whereas the unfortunate upon whom the deplorable weight of heredity weighs, combined with the bad lessons of education, sees evil merely as an ordinary line of conduct. A good impulse would seem ridiculous to him. Thus, he can be treated as predestined.

"Both of them are removed from society, to which they are harmful; they are sent to distant countries—but they are not removed from the number of the living. Who can tell whether their journey in this world is not the punishment of an anterior life? Who can tell whether the evil they have done might not have good consequences? Those are considerations that escape the limited conceptions of our intelligence. Everything in this world is so well-calculated, so well-arranged, that there is a danger at every step of disturbing the intentions of Providence. Everything has its reason for being; if a criminal exists, it is because he has an unknown utility; if not, why would he trouble our existence? Why would he strike an honest man rather than a scoundrel? Might it not be because that honest man is destined to end the ordeal of an unhappy life by his own hand? That would then be an evil for a good.

"Certainly, crime is condemned by all divine and human laws, but it is not the prerogative of humans, subject to so many weaknesses, to punish crime with crime. In any case, crime is no more excusable by personal sentiment than by legal reparation. Let us allow death to come; let us not summon it. Life is not very long, expiation will come, sooner or later. To repair an injustice, let us not commit a second.

"The role of the law, in cold-bloodedly avenging society, has something cynical about it, reminiscent of barbarian times. Unfortunately, the principle of talion is so inveterate in social beliefs that it will require another eight centuries to root it out. In that epoch, however, reaction operating within the human mind, people will have scruples about disposing of existences of which they are not the masters. They will reserve that concern to the Creator, the arbitrary sovereign of all things, who holds all destinies in his hands. His infinite justice is infallible. He will make use of it more surely, and in wiser measure, than we are able to do ourselves.

"That is not to say that a criminal should be treated in the same way as a good man—far from it. Given a criminal, with the full plenitude of his free will, God opposes to his actions those which his own plans have designed. If humans were merely unconscious machines obedient to a superior will, there're would be no merit in following the path of good in preference to that of evil, and God himself, having fashioned the criminal, would be the true criminal. God therefore allows nature to accomplish its work; he contents himself solely with directing it in its good and evil instinct without influencing it. He intends humans to learn perfection from imperfection; for that, it is necessary that they tolerate one another.

"I shall analyze the epoch to which I have been transported, according to the laws I see in force.

"No more remand prisons, no more solitary confinement.[25]

"The remand prison removed a man inopportunely from his family and his employment on the strength of a suspicion, to detriment of his dependents, who, during the time the remand last—sometimes for years—are deprived of their livelihood and fall abruptly from ease into poverty.

"In the case of his innocence, a not-guilty verdict returns him to his family and employment, but the tribunal does not take any account of the damage that his remand has done to his dependents. Justice is entirely penal, not remunerative; its infallibility is a dogma. Often, for that unfortunate, it means complete ruination. His business, suddenly interrupted, has lost its clientele.

"As for solitary confinement, it is essentially contrary to nature. We have the right to extract criminals from society, but we do not have the right to forbid them the use of speech. Enforced silence, physicians have established, idiotizes those on whom it is imposed after a certain period of time. Intelligence needs to expand its

---

[25] I have improvised somewhat in translating these institutions into modern terminology, especially in the second case, where the reference is to "*maisons centrales*" [literally, central houses]—prisons whose inmates were forbidden all communication, thus having the effect of permanent solitary confinement.

conceptions, and for that it makes use of speech. All development demands extension. By virtue of concentration and confinement, ideas in the brain become confused; they collide, mingling and forming a confused amalgam, a formless composite of a multitude of disjointed thoughts. The brain is so fatigued that it almost loses the faculty of thought; it lacks space; it is cluttered. It is necessary that thought be let out, like a spring surging from the ground, like a swollen river overflowing its banks, like compressed steam opening the safety-valve of a boiler, like lava spreading in fiery streams from the crater of a volcano.

"Let people be punished, but not turned into beasts. Let the body be attacked, but not the intelligence. Intelligence depends on the soul, and the soul depends on God.

"Let the body be attacked, I said, but not so that death ensues, because death involves the desertion of the soul, and it would then be the soul that would be affected.

"In solitary confinement, the condemned man reaches the point of no longer belonging to humankind. He is a machine, a thing, less than an animal; he has no instinctive reason.

"Solitary confinement has therefore been purely and simply suppressed, and remand prisons have been replaced by police surveillance. The accused continues his employment and remains in the midst of his family until justice decides his fate. The idea has been broached of compensation, but compensation has its inconveniences; it would only be allocated after the judgment, when the harm has already been done—which is to say, when time has run out. Then again, financial compensation might perhaps repair the material injury, but not the moral injury.

"In any case, crime, having decreased with progress, is a rare exception in this era, and the laws that punish it are only inscribed in the Code for form's sake.

"The death penalty has also been abolished, as I said. Human justice has been declared incompetent to pronounce such a grave sentence. There might be extenuating circumstances that escape its investigations. Its means of action are not sufficiently absolute for such a responsibility to be accepted.

"The criminal's entire punishment is exclusion from society. He is a poisonous plant, contact with which is dangerous. He is therefore separated from other people forever; his punishment is to be sent to a colony overseas.

"This law, applicable in 2000 years in consequence of the changes that have taken place in humans, would not be applicable in our day, when crime is too frequent an objection. Colonization would not be a sufficiently terrible prospect for the criminal, who, while counting on impunity, would still calculate the risks to be run. Death suddenly appears a pitiless possibility, before which he sometimes stops and recoils. It is, therefore, a security for present-day society; but that society, modified over time, will adopt a new constitution in conformity with its needs, its mores and its instincts.

"That is what the future has in store for us. The present is too young to change its face abruptly; it can only lay the foundations on which the future will be built. The world was not built in a day; it cannot be reformed overnight. It proceeds by means of shocks, which become more violent as it approaches its goal. That goal might be 3000, 4000 or 5000 years hence; my faculties do not permit me to penetrate that far into the future; judging by the symptoms I observe, it will not exceed that term, to which it is close, relative to the epoch of its creation.

"1789 marked the era of social convulsions; 1900 will consecrate the triumph of democracy; that is how, from one shock to the next, the world will reach its end.

"In matters of legislation, we are still in a rudimentary state. The present Code has not yet existed for 100 years, but for a nascent jurisprudence, what an immense step society has taken since '89!

"Now, we waste precious time with intricate dissertations, which confuse the mind instead of enlightening it, and debates run on in idle, often puerile, discussions. There is quibbling over form, but not fundamentals. All attention is concentrated on seeking weaknesses in the adversary's arguments. Laws are so contradictory that they may furnish each side with an argument that each believes, in good faith, to be irrefutable, to the extent that both are sometimes right, and the magistracy wrongs the less skillful in procedure. That is what comes from the precipitation with which laws are made one after another, without any thought of repealing the old— and the old are inevitably in direct contradiction with the new. Seeking clarification in the midst of such chaos, it is not the evidence that triumphs but the appearance.

"Lawsuits involving rights abound in examples of this kind. So many laws have been made in this area that the judgments of tribunals are always subject to dispute. The advocate of the civil party cites a law from some epoch on which he bases his argument; the public prosecutor opposes an anterior or posterior law that completely gives the lie to the law put forward by the advocate. What judge can boast of having been fair in such a case?

Each side has the law in its favor, and yet one of them must be in the wrong. Whoever is convicted in the first instance is acquitted on appeal, and vice versa. Justice varies according to the presentation of the case, the conscience of the judges and the skill of the advocates.

"The supreme court of appeal only rules on questions of procedure. If it recognizes that a case has not been correctly conducted in matters of form it sets aside the judgment and the work of several months must begin again, because one word has been written instead of another—puerilities that have nothing to do with the guilt or innocence of the accused. There is a distinction between the law and its interpretation.

"To avoid these pretexts for sophistry, in the society I am studying, an old law is repealed at the same time as a new one is promulgated, while specifying that contracts made before the publication of the said law remain under the jurisdiction of the old one. What has been done under the protection of one law cannot be undone under the protection of another. The new law only takes effect on the date of its publication.

"To obtain a clear and precise legislation, it has been reduced to its simplest expression. It has been disengaged from the mass of inconsequential embellishments that parliamentary assemblies increase every day. It has been stripped of the technical terms and arcane procedures that make it a mystery for the general public; it has been made accessible to everyone. It has conserved a special language necessary to the regularity of judiciary service, but that language is in conformity with everyday language and within the range of all those who have recourse to the law. This avoids the expense of specialist men of law, who are dispensable when one understands the glossary of the Code.

"People are self-sufficient, as far as possible. Why isolate people from what ought to be the support of their entire lives, the guarantee of their liberty? Why elevate to the rank of a science that which ought to shine by virtue of its simplicity? Is it necessary for someone to be a scientist to defend his interests or to have recourse to an advocate who will explain his case to him in a manner that he cannot grasp?

"There is no more need for juries, since the death penalty has been abolished. The responsibility of society is annulled, insofar as the life of one of its members is not at stake. Ordinary magistrates are responsible for the ordinary cases of the assize court. Besides, is the jury such a wise institution? It is connected to universal suffrage, in that the magistracy is drawn from the notable individuals of the district where the case arises, but do not those notable individuals, chosen by senior administrators, include party members, who follow the arguments with the prejudice of a political interest foreign to the fundamentals of the case?

"And, independently of that political inclination that directs their actions, are they sufficiently competent in judiciary matters? Some have studied law superficially, many are merchants, manufacturers and landlords; they give the advice dictated to them by broad common sense, but they are absolutely ignorant of procedure, which plays a very important role in the present judiciary system. They are therefore obliged to rely at every point on the experience and skill of the president, who interrogates the accused, confronts the witnesses and present the affair in the light that suits him. If the president happens to be a party member and some political allusion is hidden beneath the case he is instructing, he will exercise his influence on the jury; by virtue of specious arguments, he can extract a judgment in which the jury participates without knowing the true reason— because the law has been made into a science, and an arduous one, that is left entirely to specialists, and which, under the pretext of safeguarding social liberty one does not engage the responsibility of incompetent individuals.

"Justice is deferred to a sort of council of elders, to which no one is admitted but those justified by an honest, laborious and stainless life, and whose age guarantees their experience and judgment. They have lived, they have seen life, they have made comparisons. The moral correction of society is not the prerogative of youth.

"One cannot sit in judgment until the age of 50. The various functions that constitute the judiciary hierarchy are not acquired by way of advancement. A judge, from the day he becomes a judge, can immediately preside over trials if the vote of his colleagues designates that employment for him, but he is only the president for the duration of a session, and cedes his place to whoever the same colleagues choose to succeed him.

"In that way, no more ascendant responsibilities that make justice a stairway to honors. All judges are at the same level. They nominate their president themselves; they only designate a function. That ensures that justice is administered as a matter of conscience, not as a matter of career. Judges are paid a salary, because time is the currency of existence, but that salary is so small that it does not provide nourishment to cupidity. It is, moreover, the same for all, hierarchical powers only having as temporary duration.

"There are still notaries, solicitors and men of law of every sort, serving to advise those who, in spite of the efforts of the administration, do not want to take care of their interests themselves. The law does not impose them on the public as functionaries invested with an indispensable ministerial character; their collaboration is facultative and purely consultative; they are relegated to the rank of intermediaries. Everyone can be his own notary or solicitor; it is sufficient for a procedure to have the legal stamp of the town hall. What need is there, in fact, for that army of parasites whose collaboration becomes a servitude to all of life's actions? Are people not capable of dealing directly with the law, without an intermediary intent on maximizing expenses? What use is the town hall, then, if its authorization is not a sufficient control in the eyes of the tribunal? The town hall ought to be open to everyone, where everyone has authorization at their disposal free of charge.

"The responsibilities of notary and solicitor were created, in principle, to serve the acolytes of the law as a source of income and to come to the aid of the ignorant. Then stamp duty made vigilant auxiliaries of them, interested in drumming up custom. The State benefits more from that, in the sense that, if the public could dispense with men of law, they would provide less custom, and the man of law benefits from increasing that custom because, the more he pours into the coffers of the State, the more he receives in commission.

"You are familiar with the petty means that are employed nowadays to increase the client's expenses: interminable formulas, wide margins, blank spaces, elongated handwriting that is routinely confined to five words or 17 letters per line, and so on. The means are certainly sure, the use of legally-stamped paper having increased dramatically, but is truly puerile that, in a century like ours, people are subjected to such paltry exercises in speculation, which extend as far as the humble bureaucracy of the Treasury.

"Is the signature of the mayor not worth as much as that of a notary? Cannot a contract, of no matter what kind, have the same value drafted by an individual rather than an authorized clerk? Provided that it is comprehensible and precise, can that not fulfill the objectives of the law? The State has gained a little less, but the client, for whom no reduction of price is made according to his position, uses it within the strict limit of his needs.

"I compare our modern society with the one I have before my eyes: one eliminates from the administration everything that is not recognized as a general necessity; the other strives with all its might to multiply mechanisms, to imagine honorific employments, only figuring on paper, to distribute to four functionaries the work for which one would suffice, to levy excessive taxes on people with a view to luxurious constructions, festivals and enterprises that only profit one privileged class. That complicated apparatus hinders the functioning of the administration, weighing down is operations and cluttering up its projects.

"The work has therefore begun of simplifying it, on both a small and large scale. An exact account has been drawn up of the work of ministries, and, according to that scrupulously-calculated statistic, all useless auxiliaries have been expelled. With fewer branches, schemes and hierarchical grades, more rapid, clearer and more positive results have been obtained.

"By applying this system to constituted civil bodies such as notaries, solicitors, businessmen, agents of exchange, etc., immense service has been rendered to the public by ridding them of an insatiable octopus whose tentacles, constantly reaching out for it, had trapped it and was sucking out the best fruits of its labor.

"The State wants people, above all, to be self-sufficient, so that they can take part themselves in arguments regarding their interests, so that as free citizens, they can make full use of their rights, without being dependent on the demands of specialists for everything. Are there not other means of making a living than condemning people to being unable to carry out their affairs without the aid of a ministerial official?

"These are abuses of bureaucracy, which will disappear over time. At the present moment, people are too preoccupied with the whole to think about the details. When the Republic is solidly set on unshakable foundations, care will be taken to refine it; but I cannot see that until 1900, when a new upheaval of the social strata will superimpose democracy on aristocracy, in the same way that the convulsions of volcanic eruptions superimpose new terrains on primitive ones."

At this point Monsieur Landet, visibly exhausted, asked Hobson to wake him up.

Chapter VII
FINANCES

The Extremes Meet

The next session was devoted to finances.

"Today we shall touch on the ultimate exact science," said Monsieur Landet, "the one whose brutal precision creates the prosperity or ruination of peoples.

"Before getting to the era in which Finances will have reached their apogee, it is as well to undertake a retrospective review of their progress, since their birth.

"There is no point in talking about antiquity, when they did not exist in a regularized fashion, even less of the Middle Ages, when they were parceled out in landed property between feudal lords invested with absolute power.

"Louis XI, by incorporating feudalism to the crown, reunited the fascicles of public fortune and founded a kind of royal Treasury presenting the approximate appearances of a regular institution.

"His successors squandered the savings of that far-sighted king on fêtes, tourneys and romantic wars. The external campaigns in Italy under Charles VIII and Louis XI, and the internal campaign again the League under Henri II exhausted the wealth of France to such an extent that it required a sage and prudent monarch like Henri IV to fill up, by means of economies, the voids left in the State Treasury. From that epoch on, Finances began to take the form of a special administration. Under Louis

XII, Richelieu created superintendants charged with overseeing taxes and security royal wealth.

"Under Louis XIV, Colbert, a genius if ever there was one, organized the State Finances definitively and increased the exploitation of royal manufacture, agriculture, commerce and fisheries. His endeavor would have elevated France to heights inaccessible to other powers if Louis XIV, insatiable for pleasures, had not dug into that hard-won treasure with both hands, throwing it to his mistresses and the servile host of his courtiers. The shame and dolor preyed upon the minister; hindered in his noble career, he died—and Louis XIV, rid of an inconvenient controller, had no brake on his follies. When he could find no one else to pressurize, he demanded from war what he needed to feed the scandalous orgies of his reign. Iron, fire and pillage were all good to him. Like Nero, he offered his mistresses the grandiose panorama of the burning of the Palatinate.

"With peace concluded, he laid claim to a few profitable commercial cities, Strasbourg among them, by means of a secret commission, scorning human rights. And when the starving people came to the foot of his throne to expose the spectacle of their poverty, he extracted more millions from them to build Versailles.

"A shameful death removed him in the midst of general famine; his coffin was accompanied by curses— but historians exist shameless enough to call him a "great king." In my opinion, he was merely the petty king of a great century.

"I shall swiftly pass over Louis XV, whose long rein provokes disgust. It was a stampede, further complicated by the bankruptcy of Law,[26] who led France to an inevitable crisis whose consequences were borne by the luckless Louis XVI. And yet, if Louis XVI had not been so weak, if he had had the energy to reject the perfidious insinuations of his advisers, he would have been able to raise France from the abyss and change the face of the denouement. To do that, he had only to listen to Turgot, whose memorable letter has been handed down to posterity as the simplest and clearest summary of the science of Finances. I am extracting the following page therefrom:

"'Sire,

"'Your majesty has been kind enough to authorize me to submit to your eyes the engagement that he has made to himself to support me in the execution of the economical planning that is at all times, and today more than ever, an indispensable necessity. I would have liked to be able to explain the reflections suggested to me by the situation the finances are in, but time does not permit that, and I shall save a longer explanation until I have been able to obtain a more exact account. I shall limit myself at present, Sire, to remind you of these three promises:

"'No bankruptcy.

"'No increase in taxation.

"'No borrowing.

---

[26] The Edinburgh-born John Law (1671-1729) was appointed as France's Controller General of Finances under the Regency, before Louis XV came of age. He organized the French equivalent of the British and Dutch East India Companies, which failed conspicuously to duplicate the wealth generated by its rivals, and reorganized the French banking system in such a fashion that it suffered a spectacular collapse.

"'No bankruptcy, either admitted, or masked by forced reductions.

"'No increase in taxes, the reason being the situation of your people, and even more so in Your Majesty's heart.

"'No borrowing, because borrowing always diminishes available revenue; after some time, it necessitates either bankruptcy or increases in taxation. In times of peace, borrowing can only be permitted to liquidate old debts or to pay back other debts incurred at a more onerous rate of interest.

"'There is only one means to meet these three conditions, and that is to reduce expenditure to a lower level than that of income, and far enough below it to be able to save 20 million every year in order to pay off old debts. Otherwise, the first cannon-shot will force the State into bankruptcy.

"'It is therefore absolutely necessary for Your Majesty to demand that the directors of all sections to agree expenditure with the Minister of Finance. Without that, each department will run up debts, which will always be Your Majesty's debts, and the director of finance will not be able to recover the balance between expenditure and income.

"'Your Majesty knows that one of the greatest obstacles to the economy is the multitude of demands by which it is continually assailed, and which the excessive ease of his predecessors in granting them has unfortunately authorized.

"'It is necessary, sire, for you to arm yourself against your own generosity, and to consider where the money comes from that you distribute to your courtiers, and to compare the poverty of those from whom one is sometimes obliged to extract it with the most rigorous procedures with the situation of the people who are most entitled to receive your liberalities.

"'There are favors which it was believed possible to grant because they did not bear immediately upon the royal treasury. They include interests, commissions and privileges; they are the most dangerous and the most abusive. Any profit on impositions that is not absolutely necessary for their collection is a debt consecrated to the relief of contributors and the needs of the state.'[27]

"In rereading that heartfelt letter from a man who, alone in his epoch, had the noble frankness to tell the king the truth, does one not sense the prognostication of the events that would soon put an end to the disorders of the monarchy? Turgot came to power but did not stay there. Such an administrator was contrary to the ambition and cupidity of men like Maurepas, Calonne and Brienne.[28] He was defeated in the battle and retreated before the cabal. The task proposed was, in any case, if not impossible, at least gigantic; the court could not ad-

---

[27] The author includes a reference to Turgot, *Letter to the King from Compiègne*, August 24, 1774. Anne-Robert-Jacques Turgot's reforms, following the economic theories of the Physiocrats, would indeed have made a vast difference to France's finances had they been fully introduced. He was appointed controller general in August 1774 but was dismissed in 1776 and his brief introduction of free trade in corn abolished. He is now best-known as the first great elaborator of the philosophy of progress, of which M. Landet is such an enthusiastic supporter.

[28] Jean Maurepas was Louis XVI's prime minister. Charles-Alexandre de Calonne became controller general of finances, disastrously, in 1784 and was replaced in 1787 by the even more disastrous Étienne-Charles de Loménie Brienne.

just to the domestic economies of the excessively honest controller general.

"The Revolution expelled the unhealthy miasmas of the monarchy, and the Convention accomplished the superhuman work of pruning the dead wood of ravaged France within two years.[29]

"Finally, the Directoire laid the basis of the constitution to which we owe representative government and individual liberty.[30] France belonged to itself, after 18 centuries.

"Since then, within the system of direct and indirect taxation, Finances began to be organized according to serious and fixed rules. In spite of the wars of the First Empire and the sumptuous prodigality of the Second—I shall pass over in silence the Restoration and the July monarchy, which offered no distinctive character—they conserved a reasonable level, equilibrated by public debt. And when the disasters of 1870-71 arrived, France was rich enough to pay five billion francs for its liberty. Since then, commerce and industry have almost repaired the breach made in its Finances."

---

[29] The author inserts a footnote: "September 29, 1792 to August 23, 1795." This makes the text reference to "two years" slightly puzzling, but it is probably referring specifically to the Terror, which did indeed last less than two years within the three years of the Convention's rule. The Convention was actually set up on September 21, 1792 (the Republic was proclaimed the following day); the new constitution voted in on August 23, 1795 handed power over to the Directoire, but did not take effect until the end of October.

[30] The author adds a footnote repeating the date of the new constitution, August 23, but adds that it was "the so-called Year III Constitution," although it was actually promulgated in Year V of the new Revolutionary Calendar.

Here Monsieur Landet paused and collected himself for a few minutes. He had finished the history of State Finances and was penetrating into the future.

"Before arriving in the year 3878, I shall pause in the year 1959, the most distant epoch for the expiration of railway concessions. The companies, in issuing their shares, have made a contract with the State, under the terms of which they will only have an interest in and administration of their exploitation for a period of 99 years. When that period expires, the State, until then a silent partner in the exploitation, will acquire full ownership; the shares, expiring with the companies, will lapse.

"The creation of railway lines has been, for France and for Europe, a source of rapid fortune; everyone has profited from it, the shareholders as well as the customers. The necessity of circulation by virtue of progress in commerce and industry, constantly multiplying the number of networks, has forced the companies to borrow in order to undertake new works. They have, therefore, issued further shares.

"The exploitation of supplementary lines has increased the dividends of limited companies and the shared have increased in value proportionately. The shareholders, have grown accustomed to that productive placement, and have not taken into consideration the fact that the value will gradually decline as the expiry date of the concessions approaches.

"Like the capital shares, the secondary shares have been reimbursed at the price at which they were issued, but there is a difference between the two: the capital shareholder participates in the net benefits of exploitation before and after the reimbursement; the secondary shareholder, by contrast, only had a share in the money lent as a complimentary subsidy, with the chance of making a profit. Let us set the secondary shareholders aside; they are irrelevant.

"In exchange for the so-called capital share, reimbursed at the price of issue, in accordance with the depreciation indicated by the table of annuities, the company, wishing to recompense the shareholder for the results due to his money during the duration of its administration, issues him dividend shares.

"In 1959, a singular crisis arises. The majority of the shareholders, unaware of the terms of the contract linking the companies to the State, confuse the dividend shares with the capital shares, having considered the reimbursement of their entitlement as an unexpected bonus. Confident of their ever-increasing value on the Bourse, they have bought them back at the current price, without taking the wise precaution of carrying out that operation with savings from dividends received and thus reconstituting the supposed capital of the interest they enjoy.

"Basing their standard of living on their income, they have created needs in relation to a fictitious fortune; for fortune is relative, needs increasing by virtue of its extension. Habit makes the superfluous a necessity that becomes an integral part of nature. It is for that reason that it is necessary to prevent, as far as possible, the concentration of wealth in a few hands. The more one has, the more one wants to have. A man who lives happily with very little becomes unhappy with a hundred times what he possessed then; he becomes the slave of his fortune.

"Many people, as I said, not having set aside the dividends necessary to maintain their fortune at the level of interest that they would normally receive, are subject to partial ruination. That terrible shock is suffered by the heirs of the initial shareholders.

"Commerce, industry and business in general suffer the reverberations of that crisis. The gradual fall of the share price at the approach of the expiry date had given the signal for panic; their annulment has a devastating effect.

"Liquid fortunes depending, in large measure on that tradable and productive capital, are suddenly reduced by three quarters—I am talking here about those of the people lacking foresight. The absence of funds in the market brings operations to an abrupt halt.

"A turnaround changes the face of things. The State, in becoming the proprietor of the exploitation, finds itself at the head of a considerable stock-in-trade belonging to the shareholders. And as this stock-in-trade is indispensable to the regular functioning of the business, it is obliged to buy it from the shareholders, after evaluation. Now, the stock-in-trade of the Paris-Lyon-Méditerranée Company, estimated today at 2.5 billion francs, is worth 3.75 billion, by virtue of the supplementary networks added to the principal network. The shareholders, in exchange for their title of limited enjoyment, thus receive, in cash, a sum five times greater than the capital share at the moment of its creation. The benefit they receive is more than two thirds of the current price of the capital shares at the present moment—with the result that what had seemed to be a catastrophe is, on the contrary, a renewal of fortune.

The State finds itself rich by virtue of that gigantic haul, which translates into an annual income of between 950 million and a billion francs. To acquire the business's stock-in-trade, however, it is obliged to have recourse to a loan. That loan of 20 billion increases the public debt to the fabulous figure of 45 billion francs, which creates a deficit of 2.25 billion in interest payments per year, from tax receipts of every sort.

The State then commences the redemption of the debt; from the six billion brought in by taxes combined with the benefits of the exploitation of the railways, it reserves 2.25 billion to service the interest on the debt and a billion for its eventual redemption. After 45 years, therefore, it has repaid the debt in full."

"But instead of letting the capital saved every year lie dormant," Hobson objected, "it would be simpler to capitalize the interest, and as capitalized interest reform capital, it would only take the State 14 years to carry out the reimbursement—a saving in time and money."

"And by what means would it capitalize the interest?" Monsieur Landet replied. "It's on the taxpayers that the burden would fall. Now, as the taxpayers suffer it in some fashion, it's better to use the simplest means—which is to say, to buy back a billion shares every year. Better to burden them gradually and take longer to reach the term than to strike them hard to get there more rapidly, in conditions fatal to public prosperity.

"Without that new loan of 20 billion, 19 years would suffice to extinguish the 25 billions already existing.

"The reimbursement of the public debt leads to a crisis even graver than the first. The capitalists, recovering possession of their money, no longer know what to do with it; they cannot reconcile themselves to leave it inactive in their coffers, but have insufficient confidence to invest it in industrial or commercial shares. No longer finding in France the facility of a safe placement, they convert it into foreign income. And the State, in extinguishing an obligation that absorbs a little more than a third of its income, loses three-quarters of that same income in the capital that assured it.

"Prosperity emigrates with the money. Everything is paralyzed in its flight. Industry no longer functions; it lacks its primary raw material, the money that furnishes it with its machines, it fuel, its elements of fabrication. The workers can no longer earn a living. Commerce is restricted, as its guarantees slip away. Agriculture can no longer find an outlet for its produce; it is neglected; the more it hesitates to produce, the less it earns. Discouragement becomes widespread. What point is there in working hard if one does not have a solid foundation of savings for the future that can make the excess income of the present bear fruit and ensure the tranquility of old age? Work requires an encouragement of its efforts, a recompense for its fatigue.

"People take account of the peril. It is recognized that the public debt, while being a burden on the taxpayers, on whom its interest weighs, brings in even more than it costs. It is so inveterately established in social habits that it ought to continue to exist anyway, because it generates capital that can be invested in great enterprises, which enrich collective life.

"They hasten, therefore, to reconstitute the debt to its previous level. The State invites the citizens to bring back the funds invested abroad, to restore them to circulation in their own country. The capitalists are not deaf to this appeal. Immediately, money flows into the coffers; income bonds are issued in exchange; and prosperity is reborn under the impulsion of that sovereign motor.

"But the State changes tactics. Instead of paying off the debt, it lets it stand, limiting itself to equilibrating it with the compensation of the benefit of exploitation of the railways. It no longer burdens the taxpayers to more than a minimal degree; it falls almost entirely on the receipts of indirect contributions. What point is there, anyway, in paying it off? To buy dear that which was sold cheap, in order to sell it again? The contemporary rationale for amortization is that it aims, as its name indicates, if not for the extinction, at least for the diminution of the debt—and yet its maintenance has created a utopia.

"'It is an unnecessary, deceptive and dispensable measure' says Monsieur Dupuynode, 'which, instead of reducing the debt, has served to augment it, constantly and everywhere, thanks to the illusions it creates. What, in fact, does this work of the Danaïdes—amortizing when one never ceases to borrow—signify? Is it not a ludicrous commerce, that which consists of buying back old bonds dearly, at the same time as one is obliged to issue new bonds, which one sells at a low price?'[31]

"Public debt is necessary, as in the present, and I will even say in the future, given the attitude of society. Cursed be the day when it was invented! Now that it is implanted among us, however, let us not seek to uproot it, but submit to it; it is a counterweight to the prosperity of business. When humans are sufficiently mature to get rid of society's stockholders as a useless fraction enjoying unjust prerogatives, we shall be able to think of

---

[31] As noted in the introduction, the author gives no reference here, but the quote is from Gustave Dupuynode's *Études d'économie politique sur la proprieté territoriale* (1843), a significant contribution to Physiocrat economics. The Danaides were the 50 daughters of Danaus, who murdered the 50 sons of Aegyptus; their punishment in the afterlife was to collect water using sieves.

money merely as an agent of transaction, not an element of wealth.

"Gold and silver are means of exchange that far-sighted nature reveals in its bosom within reach of our hands; humans have made an idol of it because of the pleasures it procures them, but that is not true wealth. True wealth is, first of all, agriculture, the primary source that furnishes us with the indispensable, and secondly, industry and commerce, which, with the aid of the calculations of intelligence, give us the necessary and the superfluous. But the superfluous passes too often for the necessary, to the point that, in the vainglory of self-love, people prefer to deprive themselves of useful things in order to procure that which flatters the imagination and attracts the gaze. All that is a mirage! The example is set by the upper classes, and the poorer classes, wanting to compete with them, ruin themselves in the unequal game.

"Work is the only capital that is not liable to the fluctuations of politics. It produces returns in the measure of the zeal that one puts into it, while money is centralized in hands that have not earned a centime of what it would need to take possession of it in that proportion.

"Rationally, money ought only to serve to calculate an amount of capital, not to be one. It only has real value insofar as it rests on something other than itself. Why is France so rich in spite of its debt and Turkey so poor? Because France possesses a true capital: agriculture, industry and commerce developed to the highest degree, while Turkey possesses nothing. It is a nation in lethargy, deprived of all moral and physical activity, a petrified nation.

"Thus, although people can make money, real fortune—fortune itself—is labor. Labor makes money bear

184

fruit. Without labor no fortune is possible. Money is only virtual capital.

"I am going a further forward, and I can see another revolution brewing, toward the year 3500.

"The people, avid for liberty and equality, are suppressing public debt yet again and imposing, on income of every sort, and exorbitant tax of 50% when those incomes surpass a figure fixed by the law. This time, however, there is no fear that capitalists will invest their money abroad; the world has established a universal confederation, and the measure in question has been agreed by the International Congress. The people profit from it, to be sure, but lose in another sense. Commerce and industry are hampered in their thrust as capital escapes them, and without capital—which is to say, without a guarantee—there can be no initiative.

"That state of affairs lasts 450 years, until, in 3878, as we have seen, the Minister of Finance takes advantage of the parliamentary vacation to create, on his own authority, a new bond paying 4½%, amortizable over 30 years by virtue of expiration.

"That wise measure allows capital to remain in the same hands long enough to bear fruit; it suddenly revives commerce and industry.

"It is as well to pause on that law and to detail its advantages, which the minister only sketched out on the podium.

"Here, then, public debt is reconstituted in such a way as to reconcile all interests. So long as it existed in the form of a loan, it was a bad thing, because, weighing upon the taxpayers for the periodic service of interest payments, it was onerous to the masses and only profitable to a minority. When it becomes a gradually-expiring life-interest it is a good thing, because, while favoring the minority, it does not burden the masses.

"Interest is levied either on the capital itself or on the movement of that capital, which, after a determined lapse of time, reverts to the masses and, in consequence, enriches them. In addition, as the Minister emphasized during his explanation, between 5%, which is the usual rate of interest, and the 4½% that is the interest prescribed by the law, there is a difference of one tenth, to the profit of the State. That difference becomes a progressive tax, augmenting by reason of the magnitude of the sums invested and the number of bonds issued in exchange. It permits the State to offer immediate relief to taxpayers, while awaiting the distant expiry of the first amortizations.

"As that bond is designed to represent capital in commerce and industry, it is necessary that it has a fixed and invariable value which is entirely independent on fluctuations in business. At the same time, that value has to be guaranteed by the State; otherwise, it would only be fictitious and conventional; it would lack the principal element of circulation: confidence. A scale of decrease has therefore been established, in which the price of the bond, to a base of 100 francs, is calculated to the nearest centime, every day, from the date of its issue to that of its expiry, 30 years thereafter. And the State guarantees the reimbursement at the daily price indicated on the scale of decrease—with the result that merchants and manufacturers operate in accordance within certain rules and do not abuse the value of the paper they have in their hands.

"In case of reimbursement, the State immediately becomes the owner of the bond, which is immediately annulled—but it does not lose by this premature reimbursement since the interest paid before then has been raised either on the capital itself or on the movement of the capital, and it only reimburses the bond at the price on the day when it is presented to the Treasury.

"Thus, in commerce and in industry, the bond is considered more as a letter of exchange than as an interest-bearing instrument. It is endorsed and passed on in payment, but it is convertible into cash not at the price on the day when it was put into circulation but at the price on the day when it falls due, surrendering the difference to compensate the prejudice incurred, the right to draw the dividend for the current trimester being reserved."

"But if the State guarantees the reimbursement of the bond at the price on the scale of decrease," Hobson objected, "it's easy to reconstitute the capital immediately by selling back the bond a fortnight after it has been issued."

"What seems to you to be a benefit would be a loss," Monsieur Landet replied. "Because the State takes ten per cent of the interest in advance, one would lose 20% on the second placement, including the initial 10%, 30% on the third, including the loss on the first and second, and so on, every year, when the Finance Commission collects the taxes on behalf of the State. Thus, assuming that the recipient resells his bond to that State at the conversion rate, he would be paying 30 times ten percent, or 300 francs—which is to say, twice the value of the capital. There is, as you see, every advantage in leaving the capital in the State coffers, receiving the interest that it yields and making use of it in business, without having recourse to reimbursement, for when the State reimburses, it retains the dividend for the current trimester."

"To avoid this 'conscription' of income, however," Hobson objected, again, "individuals have only to move their money abroad."

"Impossible," the savant retorted. "The laws voted by each nation are immediately transmitted to the International Congress, which employs prohibitive measures."

"It's easy, however, for merchant or manufacturers only to record a part of their business in his books."

"The books of the people with whom he had traded would contradict his; the Finance Commission would perceive it and open an enquiry, which would result in a severe penalty. To deceive the surveillance of the State requires perfect agreement, and fraud is unmasked sooner or later."

"Since there nothing else they can do, what if everyone spends his income as it comes in?"

"The State sees nothing inconvenient in that—on the contrary. The more everyone spends, the more immediately reverts to the masses. But the merchant and the manufacturer would lose too much by it to risk doing that. They will still prefer to exchange their money for a bond that discounts the present and ensures the future for them."

"What about the old and the infirm?"

"Let us take things in order. I'm getting to them.

"In the assemblies, an amendment to the law has been introduced on the motion of an elector. The assemblies, as a revisionary power, enjoy the role that the Senate plays today. They can meet and vote an amendment, which they instruct their representative to put before parliament.

"As I said, an amendment has been introduced in the following terms: 'In consideration of the age that renders old people incapable of earning a living, when the income he has is insufficient to ensure his existence; and in consideration of a malady or infirmity that might put someone in the same situation of physical incapacity as the old person:

"'Article One: at 60, the age fixed for retirement, the old person will be taken at the State's expense into a special hospice.

"'Article Two: Every individual recognized as infirm by medical judgment will be placed, until death, in a retirement home.'

"No limit has been fixed to the issue of income bonds. A limit is only necessary when the debt constitutes a loan; but when it is presented in the form of a temporary entitlement, it can increase, without any inconvenience, in proportion to the prosperity of business. It does not burden anyone; it is, instead, a benefit to everyone, since it reverts to the social body at the end of the legal term and the ten per cent tax is in immediate effect before then. The issue thus takes place in direct proportion to the affluence of capital.

"The public debt, thus modified, is a savings bank in which the worker deposits the excess of his labor. As that excess is only levied beyond the bounds of necessity, he is free to capitalize the interest on the sum invested in the Treasury and thus to reconstitute the capital, with the aim of providing for a comfortable old age or leaving his children a fortune that they can conserve by the same economic means, while paying their tribute to the fatherland.

"The law, in any case, determines a sufficient level of ease. It fixes a maximum income of 6000 francs for everyone, the surplus becoming the property of the Treasury under the conditions that we have previously studied. The worker can thus, without privation, leave the interest he receives intact.

"At present, a serious question is on everyone's mind. Is inheritance just or unjust?

"I espy two philosophers who are discussing this very subject under the portico of a school of political economy. They can appreciate the questions of their own time better than I can. I shall give them the floor.

"'People are never content with their lot,' said the first interlocutor. 'That axiom dates from the remotest antiquity. Will it always be necessarily true? You are free, you live without anxiety, you are happy, and that is not enough? What more do you want? History tells us that in barbaric times our forefathers blindly obeyed the caprices of a sovereign, that a cataclysm suddenly turned France upside down, that Europe felt the reverberation, and that, from that boiling over of minds suppressed by 18 centuries of slavery, the constitutional regime was born. In a few years, the face of the world changed abruptly; a new social stratum was superimposed on the old; liberty was then glimpsed. Attempts were made to reconcile it with royalty, but the wreckage of the authoritarian principle, having escaped the disaster, floated to the surface of the constitutional regime. There was a collision between the powers, and the debris of monarchy, known as divine right, foundered on a reef—in 1830, if I'm not mistaken.

"'For the fallen monarchy, the custom-bound people substituted a mixed monarchy, which mutilated universal suffrage. However, the instinct of liberty seethed within them; a new explosion burst forth, and the victorious Republic surged forth for a second time from the rubble of that bastard monarchy. An ambitious man, however, after being appointed as its President, seized all power and, in a bold move, resuscitated the empire inaugurated by a certain Napoléon I after the first revolution. The Empire, an essentially military government, led the people to the beat of drums. War fed its insatiable cupidity until, lurching from one disaster to the next, it collapsed with a great noise. For the third time, the Republic appeared, serene and radiant. With time and patience, it repaired the damage done by the preceding regimes and, in spite of the attempts to restore the monarchy that shook its foundations, it survived, because it has imposed itself on the French heart. From that memorable day onwards, liberty emerged from the clouds that had veiled it; it gradually insinuated itself into the mechanism of government.

"'Twenty centuries have gone by since then. Today, we have acquired the sum total of the liberty to which one can aspire, without it becoming a threat to liberty itself. An excess of liberty is bordering on absolutism. Each step that one takes forward is a step backwards. It is time to stop, believe me; otherwise, by virtue of striving for that abstraction, which is one of the infinite attributes of the Creator, and by dint of attempting to realize that which belongs to eternity, we shall sin by the opposite excess.

"'There is a limit at which the greatest good becomes confused with the greatest evil to the point of fusion. That is the law of extremes—and truth does not reside in extremes; it resides in just compromise. Everything in this mortal world is relative, everything is perishable. Extremes suppose infinity; infinity only belongs to perfection. Now, the extremes that humans can conceive are necessarily limited, like the intelligence that conceives them, like the body to which the deposit of that intelligence has been confided, like the planet to which the deposit of that body has been confided and on which it moves, and like the planetary system, in which that planet gravitates. Infinity is God.

"'There comes a point at which the extremes forged by the human imagination, in drawing apart, collide with an insurmountable obstacle, beyond which God reigns as master. Forced either to retrace their steps or to skirt the boundary of the obstacle in its extension, they turn in a vicious circle and end up at the same point, where they combine. That's why extremes meet.'

"'On what do you base your reasoning in order to maintain that the conceptions of intelligence obey the laws of circumference rather than proceeding in a straight line?' the second interlocutor replies.

"'I proceed by analogy and compare immaterial things with material ones. Look around you. The Earth we inhabit is a sphere gravitating in space. Its rotational movement is accomplished, as the word indicates, by tracing a circumference, as is its orbital movement around the sun. The planets and stars visible to the naked eye or through a telescope all affect a spherical form; and the word *sphere* means cubic circumference. The movement of the planets around the sun is accomplished in the same conditions as that of the Earth. The vault of the sky covers us like half of a globe whose other half appear at the antipodes. The horizon surrounds us like a vast circumference of which we are the center. In no matter which direction we direct or gaze, we see nothing but spheres and circumferences.

"'Is it not the same with thought?

"'The brain gives rise to it; it emerges, launches forward, grows by virtue of the other thoughts it encounters in its path; then it folds back upon itself and returns to its point of departure in order to combine itself with those that it has recruited in its trajectory.

"'It progresses initially toward induction, and then returns to its first expression in the firm of deduction. Induction and deduction are necessarily linked; their intimate relationship brings them together. Invincible, as thought gains substance in associating the ideas swarming around it, it tends to return toward the initial idea. That is a phenomenon which it is sufficient to look out for to be observed. But its trajectory is not accomplished in a straight line. The ideas that are accumulated by induction are of a different order from those accumulated by deduction.

"'What is life? A circumference that extracts us from nothingness to bring us back to nothingness. From the cradle, humans are headed towards the grave, but their short existence is divided into two distinct periods: a period of progress and a period of decline. They only acquire the plenitude of their faculties in the middle of their career. Before then, they are insufficiently mature; after then they are wearing out. Weakness numbs the body, reason thickens, memory languishes; they become children again, and death grips them as birth gave then life, feeble in body and mind.

"'There are precocious natures that are in advance of their age: those which are not destined for a long career, of which abridger it voluntarily by forcing the growth of their intellectual faculties; there are also those to whom physical forces do not afford the time to reach old age; death strikes them suddenly, either by accident or disorganization of the vital system—but those are exceptions.

"'Finally, if it is permissible to compare immaterial things with material ones, the soul emerges from Infinity to return to Infinity. It accompanies the body through the phases of life, suffers with it and perishes with it, but survives it and recovers a new envelope on the Earth, until, from one incarnation to the next, it returns to its point of departure: Infinity. A parcel of eternity, it returns to its element.'

"'And what proves to you that the phenomenon does not operate in a straight line, like the flux and reflux that comes and goes in the same groove? What proves to you that the just compromise is not an apogee from which one redescends by the same path as one climbed?'

"'The phenomena that advertise the coming and going. They present analogous points but are fundamentally different. At the beginning of life, the soul, to employ Locke's image, is a *tabula rasa* on which education traces the first notions of all things. Fashioned by daily contact with other souls, it reaches maturity; then it weakens and fades with the body, all the while conserving the imprint that experience has left upon it. Thus, in the first phase, it opens itself up to life; in the second, it closes itself off therefrom.

"'The body itself grows and develops, until that development, having no further scope, wears it out and consumes it; it is like a young bush that grows under the ascendant action of its sap, until that sap, for want of an outlet, is diverted into the branches and finally dries up and subverts itself.'

"'I admit the hypothesis. The arguments with which you support it seem satisfactory to me—but what proves that liberty has attained the appropriate level at which it ought to be fixed?'

"'That appropriate level is not sufficiently definite for it to be permissible to set a limit on it. Humans need to be wise enough to appreciate the point at which the balance does not offend the symmetry of his judgment too obviously. By dint of seeking absolute precision, sensitivity to compensation is denatured. Since we are imperfect beings, let us not entertain the foolish ambition to achieve perfection. Let us remain within the sphere of our petty faults. The best means of attenuating them is to tolerate them mutually. Good politics does not cut, it conciliates.

"'Of what can you complain? You all collaborate in the functioning of the machine of State. The ensemble of your voices constitutes national sovereignty. Your representatives, by their mandate, are directly subject to your jurisdiction. Ministers are chosen by a majority of those same representatives. The President is only the figurehead of power. In the final analysis, it is you who govern, you who are everything Would you like everyone to have an active part in power? How could one be heard in such a formidable conflict? That would be anarchy, and anarchy, as history has proven, is civil war. There exists on that subject a fable by a certain La Fontaine, who was one of the literary glories of the twentieth century: 'The Old Man and his Children':

"My dear children," he said, speaking to his sons,
"See if you can break these bundled branches;
I'll explain the knot that ties them together."
The eldest, having taken them, made every effort,
And returned them, saying: "I'll give them to the
strongest."
A second succeeded him and assumed the posture,
But in vain. A younger one also made the attempt.
They all wasted their time; the bundle resisted;
Those branches bound together no one could break.

"Weaklings," said the father. "I'll have to show you

What my strength can do in such an encounter."

They thought he was joking; they smiled, but wrongly;

He separated the branches, and broke them with ease.

"You see," he continued, "the effect of unity.

Join together, my children, let love unite you."

While his illness lasted, he said nothing more.

Finally, feeling near to the end of his days:

"My dear children," he said, "I'm joining our ancestors;

Farewell; promise me to live as brothers;

That I might obtain that grace as I die."

Each of the three sons assured him, weeping.

He took their hands and died. And the three brothers

Found great prosperity, but their affairs became tangled.

A creditor claimed seizure; a neighbor brought suit.

At first our trio got out of the difficulty.

But friendship waned as success became rarer.

Blood had joined them; self-interest separated them.

Ambition and envy, along with consultants,

Regarding inheritance, arrived at the same time.

They divided things up, contesting and cheating.

The judge condemned them on a hundred points

The creditors and neighbors immediately returned,

Some claiming error, others a default.

The disunited brothers had contrary opinions.

One wanted to settle, another to do nothing.

They all lost their wealth and wanted too late

To take advantage of the branches bundled and torn apart.[32]

"'Is not the State is merely an assembly of bundles whose unity gives it strength? Separate them, and you experience a force of resistance against each one that would defy all your efforts because each one merely consists of a few sticks. Untie the knot the binds each bundle, though, and the weakest hand can break the sticks separately like a piece of straw.

"'The bundle of the State is the majority of the representatives, whose assembly constitutes power. The secondary bundles are the electors, whose assembly forms a representative. Break up the majority, and each representative, although greatly weakened, will still be strong by virtue of the electors he represents. Break up the electors, and you will have anarchy. Individually, they are nothing; collectively, they are everything.

"'To grant a wider extension to our political rights would lead to confusion, discord and carnage. Fortunately, that is not our way.

"'Let us pass on to our financial system. It safeguards property in land, the primary resource of our needs, by declaring it inalienable or alienable by mutation. It equilibrates as much as possible the provenance of our incomes and the ease with which we acquire them, by subjecting them to proportional taxation. It

_____

[32] The author gives a reference to La Fontaine *Fables*, Book IV, Fable XXI, but does not specify the edition to which he is referring. The fable itself dates back much further; La Fontaine only modified it and put it into verse; I have provided a literal translation without making any attempt to retain the rhyme-scheme or scansion.

husbands the indirect contributions, relieves direct contributions and balances commercial operations. It assures us a comfortable easy existence sheltered from need, imposing on us reciprocal obligations of commerce.

"'It makes itself the bank of our savings, which return to it 30 years after the day when they are deposited in the Treasury, leaving us time to capitalize the interest that it pays us every year and thus to recompose the capital of which it becomes the owner at the end of that interval.

"'That wise precaution does not deprive a hard-working man of the profits he accumulates, and yet it prevents their excessive accumulation. His heirs enjoy his privilege, on condition that they subject themselves to the same economies as him.

"'What more can you want?'

"'I want inheritance to be completely abolished, as unjust and immoral. By what right do children enjoy the privileges due to the work and intelligence of their parents? What right does an idler have enjoy a more agreeable life than a laborer?'

"'By what right does the mass of society enjoy, directly or indirectly, the inheritance of one of its members? What right has a stranger to profit from benefits to which he has not made any contribution of fatigue, to the disadvantage of those who are linked to the deceased by the closes of ties? On that argument, neither one has any right to it—but the children come before the stranger; that's the law of nature.

"'At any rate, there is a limit to the extension of the fortune. The capital reverts to the State after 30 years. The citizen, if he wants to maintain his fortune at the same level, must reinvest his interest during that period.

In that way, the concentration of wealth is impossible; the more one amasses, the more reverts to everyone.

"'Penalize idle capital, by all means. It is dormant, and only benefits one person. But respect active capital. It works, it produces, it circulates and benefits everyone.

"'Fortune, applied to commerce and industry, fragments in the same measure that it accumulates. It comes in by one door and goes out by another. Everyone seizes a fraction of it as it passes by. As for leveling it out in a fixed, invariable, positive manner, that's materially impossible. It would only take one day, one hour, one minute, to become confused, and for the census to begin again. After all, money is displaced by the needs of the moment. In every commercial or manufacturing operation, it is necessary in a more or less abundant quantity. To divide its traffic equally is to muzzle its activity. To muzzle its activity is to kill the life-force of a nation, Better, on the contrary, to favor activity, which involves intelligence and stimulates progress.

"'Otherwise, one annihilates private initiative, and the annihilation of private initiative is decline. People are afraid, hesitant, reluctant. Effort is not encouraged, success offers no opportunity for recompense; people work without appetite, without hope, without an objective; they become machines. One does exactly what one must nothing more.

"'Do you think the mass of society would be any richer if the State took possession of all capital? No. The State could not make a profit from it because it would distribute it to salaried employees, who would not be interested in business. And that is one of the defects of our nature; we only devote ourselves entirely to work to the extent that it is in our interests to do so.

"'Work, in order to bear fruit, requires independence. If you paralyze it or pressurize it loses its alimentation: hope. I said, penalize idle capital; I repeat it, but penalize it with a certain restriction. Let those who have earned it enjoy it. Don't deprive their children entire. Who knows whether nature has accorded them enough strength to merit ease by way of labor?

"'The more I examine our financial system, the more I find it conciliatory, rational and far-sighted. It compensates, but does not cut. Idle capital returns sooner or later to the social mass; it can only be amassed up to a certain limit. Active capital is shared out proportionately.

"'There has always been inheritance; it is necessarily so. Without dealing it a brutal blow, there are many other means of attenuating it. We possess those means; don't demand anymore; otherwise, submitted to one another's control everyone would become a tyrant, and the greatest liberty would consist of not being free. It would be worse than monarchy.

"'Which, in fact, is the more tyrannical: the autocracy that crushes its subjects under the yoke of absolute power; or the sovereign people that, by dint of equalizing its rights, its resources and its intelligence pressurizes every individual in every way all the time, imposing a reciprocal despotism, so that no one dares take a step forward for fear of catching his neighbor's eye? The two are the same, for their effects are identical; the extremes have met. There is only a nuance of nomenclature; instead of being named king or emperor, it calls itself the nation. Absolute liberty is servitude.'"

"Those two interlocutors," Monsieur Landet continued, "comprise a Stationary and a Progressive. The

Stationary has given us a rapid glimpse if the finances of his epoch. I shall continue his line of argument.

"Thus, the abolition of inheritance is under discussion. Should it be decreed? No—the interest of citizens is too tightly bound together for the thread of their practical life to be voluntarily broken. Let us abandon that chimera and pass on to positive laws.

"Property in land is inalienable or alienable by mutation; it is transmitted from father to son. As regards new buildings demanded by the multiplication of the population, it is carried out at state expense, which cedes them to owners in return for an annual repayment equal to the rate of interest, so as to reconstitute the capital expended in 20 years. The payment can be made in full, if the buyer possesses sufficient cash savings to make the disbursement in its entirety, but the State does not cede his claim until he has established that he does not already own another plot; that would be contrary to the objective of the law, which, setting a limit to property in land, attempts to inhibit the extension of capital no matter what form it might take.

"The concentration of capital becomes a source of poverty for generations to come. Those who acquire it only return a portion of it to circulation. Those who convert it into immovable property enjoy a personal income of which the commonweal does not share. It follows that the agglomeration of cash or immovable property in a few hands gradually depletes the social body, which languishes alongside a latent wealth that it cannot reach. That is what one sees today in England: either fortune or poverty, both to an excessive degree; no middle way.

"Fortune beyond our needs is unjust and immoral. The superfluity is built on the necessity of the have-nots. It falls to those who do the least work, by means of those who do the most—I'm speaking here about modern society.

"Our descendants, in order to obviate this inconvenience, have devised a system of compensation that I shall explain shortly, with regard to direct taxation.

"Capital is continually displaced, passing from hand to hand by virtue of transactions. That displacement is the source of public fortune, but in the incessant comings and goings it sometimes remains, in large measure, with those whose prestige is sufficiently powerful to retain it. Money attracts money.

"The balance of compensations is the only remedy that can be applied to maintain equilibrium, but that remedy, handled with care, ought not to aim at the capital itself, but on its results.

"To return to property in land, every citizen being an owner, since it is inalienable, repairs are made at the expense of individuals, if their quota of direct contributions testifies to their income, at state expense in the opposite circumstance. Direct contributions, in order to establish their quota, are also based on the statistics of each citizen's affairs.

"A Special Commission, emanating from the Ministry of Finance, is responsible for that verification; it works with the account books, which it compels and compares. That census takes place every year.

"Idleness is, therefore, severely proscribed. Everyone works for a living, People work according to their tastes, but they work, and the State, as I said before when talking about the family, assigns everyone a supplier from which he cannot depart without an important reason assessed and judged by the tribunal. In that way, everyone is sheltered from poverty. Mutual aid operates within a fixed and secure framework.

"Life, freed from material preoccupations of success is, in consequence, peaceful, happy and regulated. There is nothing to be desired.

"Everyone is at approximately the same level. So much the better for people who, by virtue of a surplus of intelligence or labor, are able to gain further ease; they have earned it; they owe it to themselves. They profit by it; that is fair; but their children, if they do not have the intelligence to save a part of the interest after their death, will fall in accordance with the prescription within 30 years.

"The concentration of capital in the hands of the State, by virtue of the system of public debt, does not deprive anyone, but nevertheless serves the general interest.

"The State no longer acquires capital by way of loans under the entitlement of obligation; it acquires it by way of property, under the entitlement of law. That which, before 1959, was a measure of prosperity, would be a monstrosity in 3878. Other times, other mores. Laws follow the current of customs, and the thread that binds them always has as its point of origin the society that provokes them.

"That moral transformation has not taken place without effort, without conflict, without revolutions. It could only be imposed after a series of painful but decisive battles. Gradually, the public debt has been amortized, as I said before, with the produce of taxes and railway receipts. Immediately thereafter, however, the State, overturning the legislation, took possession of half the capital by levying a tax of 50% on its income. It was only long afterwards that the Minister of Finance replaced that 50% tax by the income bond expiring after 30 years.

"There were murmurs, there were debates, there were battles, but the victory has remained with the reformers. The further democracy goes, the more ground it gains. Liberty, Equality and Fraternity, vain words today, will one day be a reality.

"Direct taxation has acquired a greater extension as it has also been imposed on businesses on the bass of the figures collected by the Finance Commission.

"As in our day, direct contributions voted by parliament are shared out by general councils between the taxpayers, but property in land being almost equally divided, by virtue of the law that paralyzes its development within a certain limit, the tax quota is established primarily in proportion to the incomes specified in business accounts. A Commission of Enquiry verifies it every year, and calculates the tax due based on its calculation of conversion.

"That quota, up to a minimum, permits taxpayers only pay a relative price for enterprises owned by the state, such as railways, steamships and telegraphs—in sum, everything constituting circulation and transport.

"Direct contributions therefore have two principal branches: property taxes, which the State estimates fairly before collection, and commercial taxes, which are subject to variations in business and almost reenter the domain of indirect contributions, since they do not fall upon the taxpayer immediately.

"Property taxes always produce the same result because the property, however parceled out it might be, whether it belongs to one or several individuals, is subject to the same tax as a whole. That tax is divided by the general councils into as many parts as there are private properties; it is only a question of fractions.

"The indirect contributions that, in our day, are such a great help to a government in distress after a ruinous war, by virtue of the enormous duties that they levy on raw materials, only attack objects of secondary necessity or superfluity, such as playing cards, tobacco, coffee, chocolate and tea. Flour, pepper, salt, sugar, wine and other alcoholic beverages—everything, in a word, that enters into everyday human consumption, is exempt from import duties.

"In our day, wars, competition between parties and social revolutions are such a drain on State finances that we have been reduced to demanding from people more than they can give, and the derisory liberty that is mirrored in the imagination consists of striking the poor with the same taxes as the rich. The former pay as dearly as the latter, and thus pay more dearly.

"Thus, a cask of wine bought for 85 francs outside the walls pays, for the right of entry, 30 centimes a liter, and even if the wine is only worth 20 centimes a liter, the cask must nevertheless pay 30 centimes a liter. The duty is not based on quality but on quantity. So the rich, who can afford a cask of fine wine worth 70 francs a liter, only pay 30 centimes a liter. For the duty to be fair, it would be necessary for it to be in accord with the quality of the material on which it is imposed, or that it should not exist at all.

According to that erroneous calculation, the rich drink wine at a relatively cheaper price than the poor, and the fruit of the labor of poor increases the government's reserve to the sole end of constructing so-called public monuments, to which their mediocre resources do not allow them access. Everything for the rich, nothing for the poor—and yet, everything by means of the poor.

"But let us to return to the society of 2000 years hence.

"The first reform that it brought in was the alleviation of indirect taxation. In fact, indirect taxation paralyze commerce and industry by opposing exaggerated taxes to their development: a poor speculation because, slowing down labor itself infallibly weaken the most obvious State revenues.

"Then again, indirect taxation, not being addressed in the same way as direct taxation, weighs indiscriminately upon on the poor and the rich, whereas direct contributions are assessed according to exact calculations of effective property.

"The true secret of finances is not to direct them at the social body; it is, on the contrary, to establish a proportion between incomes, to equilibrate the means of existence by a system of compensation. Only direct contributions furnish that system of compensation, because they alone are targeted as to where they fall, by contrast with indirect contributions.

"There are complaints about the demands of the people; there is astonishment with regard to their murmurs; their rebellions are punished. Let us tackle the evil at its birth; let us begin by not rendering material life impossible for the poor by bleeding them dry while the rich might give without sacrifice; or, let us augment their salaries in proportion.

"Indirect taxation is, however, indispensable to some degree in a constitutional State. There are petty taxes that can reduce the needs of the government without hindering the poor classes. The constitution that I am analyzing has not excluded them entirely, and the greatest benefits it obtains from them come from the customs duties levied on items of secondary necessity; but it makes no differentiation in taxation between imports and exports, because, when exchange is not equally weighed, when importation is not in proportion to exportation, a quantity of money flows out of a country unequal to that which flows in. It is necessary, in order to equilibrate a country's finances, that the revenue brought in by exports should be equal to that which leaves by way of imports. Free trade is the only way to obtain that solution."

Chapter VIII
AGRICULTURE, INDUSTRY
AND COMMERCE

Agriculture—Agricultural Associations

"The foremost of all the goods that the Creator has given to humans in bringing them out of nothingness is the earth.

"The earth is the primary source that supplies the needs of human beings. It offers to bring within reach cereals, fruits and vegetables for their nourishment, water to quench their thirst, wood to shelter them and warm limbs numbed by cold, and the foliage of those woodlands to protect them against the ardor of the sun.

"In addition, the Creator has populated the world with an infinity of animal species, some of which furnish them with wool for them to weave and make clothes, others hides in order that they might make shoes, and nearly all of them flesh, to fortify them with solid nourishment and complete the excessively light diet of bread, vegetables and fruits.

"Thus, in the earliest times, the soil was sufficient for essential human needs; their intelligence had not yet invented the marvels that are the preoccupations of their entire existence. They only had to reach down in order to gather, and only had to gather in order to live.

"As they multiplied, however, humans founded cities. Their intelligence, activated by emulation, devised refinements. They abandoned the simple and facile life of the fields for the hazardous and stressful life of cities.

"Since that day, the indispensable has been neglected: the indispensable, which ought to have been the object of our assiduous concerns, because rural life fortifies the body whereas urban life weakens it, and also because the natural richness of the soil does not yield all of its treasures for want of arms to exploit them. Commerce and industry take possession of the laborers; it has been forgotten that it is the land that encloses in its bosom the raw materials that are the bases of industry.

"Before studying the means of utilizing them, ought one not seek to multiplying them, to purify them and to perfect them?

"Humans, animals and vegetables are perpetuated by procreation. Who knows whether minerals do not harbor a spark of vitality within them that is hidden from the investigations of science?

"How is it that, independently of volcanic eruptions, the nature of terrains varies with the centuries? If the formation of minerals is not produced by procreation—as I believe—then it is the result of the combination of chemical elements that encounter one another in the bowels of the Earth.

"Thus, after having observes the nature of the soil in different epochs, and the phenomena that have signaled each modification, humans ought to apply themselves to provoking the formation of metals artificially and preparing ground with a view to that production, aiding nature in its work.

"Soil becomes weary and exhausted when it is not alimented. As a woman in the pains of childbirth requires a charitable hand to abridge her pain by facilitating the birth, the earth requires humans to employ their arms to fecundate the seeds enclosed in its entrails. Left to itself, it is true, it will produce, because it encloses the elements of generation within it, but that neglected production does not take long to become paltry and unhealthy, until it declines completely. On the other hand, fertilize it, water it and care for it, and it will respond to your efforts. The more you cultivate it, the more it will profit.

"It is an error to think that the soil is a capital inferior to other placements. Today, it only yields 2 or 2½%, because the cities absorb three-quarters of the workforce, but it can produce more. It is all a matter of fertilization.

"The earth is so forsaken that, if one brought it back to agriculture it would require to less than ten years for it to be able to compete with commerce and industry. In a word, it would be necessary to return it to health. After ten years of hard labor and assiduous care, however, it is evident that it would yield 5, perhaps 6%.

"The Egyptians, in the remotest antiquity, recognized the importance of agriculture more than we do; it was the basis of their political economy. It is worth adding that they possessed a powerful agent of fertilization that we do not have: the Nile. The regular flooding of that river contributed greatly to fortify in an astonishing manner the country over which it poured the overflow of its waters.

"In our day, Rumania, southern Russia and China draw the major part of their income from agriculture. The greatest fortunes of these countries are in land, and their owners know full well how to make it bring in 4½ or even 5%. That certainly does not match the yield of commercial interests, but it is higher than that of industrial or financial shares, whose dividends dazzle to begin with but often leave nothing in hand but a piece of paper, good for nothing but lighting the fire. The earth is a real capital, visible and palpable, represented by itself and not by an illusion.

"But enough talk of times past and present; let us occupy ourselves with the world of 2000 years hence."

Here the savant collected himself for a few minutes—the time to cross 20 centuries.

"Why!" he cried. "Fourier was not as utopian as he was thought to be during his lifetime, and even after his death; the future has proved his theories right. His plan for agricultural associations has been realized.

"In attributing the invention of the association to Fourier I am robbing another author of his legitimate due. Fourier was only the activating nerve. It was Plato who first set out the plan in his treatise on *The Republic*, in which he brought out the advantages of the commonalty of goods and the division of labor according to individual aptitudes. But the theory strayed a little further alone the path of fantasy. Having ingeniously analyzed the division of labor and entered into the smallest details of the association, he concluded with the commonalty of women and children. This is what he said: 'I propose that the wives of our warriors should be common to all, that none of them live specifically with any one of them, that the children should be communal, and that the latter should not know their parents, nor the parents their children.'[33]

"The virtuous Socrates must have addressed one of those reprimands to Plato of which he possessed the secret when he read that scheme for paternity in society.[34]

---

[33] The author gives a reference to Plato's *Republic* Book V.

[34] The argument in question is, in fact, attributed to Socrates in the dialogue; the real Socrates could not have raised any objection, because he was dead before the *Republic* was written.

In making women a capital, at the mercy of an indeterminate social reckoning, he ignored the therapeutics which demonstrate that, in that kind of association, every member of society destroys the work of his colleague. Thus, in wanting to lodge his ideal Republic too securely, he risked undermining its foundations. No children, no Republic."

Monsieur Landet smiled. "But I'm straying from my subject," he said. "You might say me what Racine wrote in the *Plaideurs*: 'Advocate, get to the Deluge.'

"The association has thus become the basis of agricultural exploitation. It is now a matter of going back to its establishment and explaining its institutions. I shall take one of these societies as an example.

"Starting from the principles that a collection of specialties forms a complete whole; that one obtains better results on a large scale than a small one; and that participation in benefits is a stimulant to the activity of labor; a few individuals organized themselves into a regular society to which each of them made an initial subscription. The partners were based in a productive commune, and the society members were shareholders in their work. With their capital, the society bought adjacent lands, in a region that as neither too dry nor too damp, surrounded by other lands that it reserved the right to acquire later, with funds deposited annually in a savings bank.

"Then they built comfortable, well-ventilated and spacious accommodations for the society members and their families as well as their livestock and equipment. Finally, they proceeded, by election, to the choice of the members appointed to run the nascent colony. These members, supported by an administrative council, were nominated for as many years as it pleased the society to assign to their term, but the latter retained the power to reelect them, or dismiss them in the case of poor administration.

"As soon as the society was organized according to the statutes elaborated by the administrative council and ratified by the general assembly of society members, the colony began to function. It divided up the labor, according to each person's specialty, in such a way that the combined specialties fit together to form a perfect whole. Everyone was given work appropriate to their aptitudes, whether for agricultural labor or for service within the colony.

"These first phases were long, difficult and beset by difficulties of every sort. The society, courageously pursuing its endeavor, had to struggle against the awkward dispositions of a terrain whose yield did not repay the interest on the capital. Then it had recourse to loans, which, while facilitating the means of action, but a burden on the common funds whose redemption would take a long time. Finally, by dint of perseverance, labor and care, the soil was enriched. The seeds buried in the furrows engendered an abundance of produce whose superior quality doubled its value.

"From then on the association was on the path to prosperity. The debts were reduced, to short-term loans paid off on an annual basis and the society members began to receive dividends proportional to their shares. The savings fund grew by a third of the net benefits, permitting the association to buy, as needed, more terrain situated on the perimeter of its farmland.

"The families, thus grouped, live happily. They enjoy a relative wellbeing, and an assurance of future security, for themselves and for their children, who enter into direct participation in the association after them. They are habituated to the active and intelligent life that the association has made for them.

"Love of community is profoundly rooted in human hearts; fraternity has cemented the effect of cohabitation. Good instincts, no longer having to combat envy or poverty, are fully developed. All the members apply themselves as best they can to the task that the prosperity of the colony requires of them; they are working for themselves, since they benefit from it, in proportion to their fatigue and there share in the subscription of the colony.

"Let us pass on now to the colony's constitution.

"At the head of the association is a managing director, assisted by two deputies and an administrative council, all dependent on the suffrage of the members.

"The income is divided into three parts: the interest derivative of the capital, the dividends providing net benefits and the reserve put into the savings fund.

"Every year, and inventory of the financial year is compiled, and once the interest payments and payments to the savings fund have been deducted, the remaining third is divided between the society members proportionately to the work they have done and the number of their shares.

"The society members have no need to buy the necessities of life externally; the association furnishes them with clothing, footwear, bed linen and so on. As for meals, they are held in common, in one or several rooms, depending on the size of the colony.

"The society members cannot leave the colony without surrendering their shares to it. They do not admit strangers once the initial work is complete, limiting their number to the founders or the founders' families. In case of the total extinction of a family, the vacant share reverts to the association.

"The statutes fix a maximum of 30,000 francs and a minimum of 5000 francs for the contribution of each society member. The State imposes that clause on the association to prevent capitalists from speculating; by way of compensation, however, it has exempted it from the control of the Finance Commission with respect to the conversion into bonds of the excess of prescribed incomes, deeming that in this case, the capitalization is not to the profit of an individual but that of an entire society. And as its aim, in penalizing the excess of private capital, is to break up fortunes as much as possible, to redistribute them to on a wide scale, the association shares its views. Before the adoption of the reform proposed by the Minister of Finance, the association was similarly exempted from the previous law that imposed a tax of 50% on the excess of its revenues.

"The association is also free of mutual obligations of commerce external to the colony. They are restricted to the circle of the association itself, which furnishes its members with the objects of primary necessity and fabricates, with the products of exploitation, that which nature does not provide in its entirety—clothing, bed linen, shoes, furniture, etc. As for objects of secondary necessity, the colonists can acquire them in the city, or wherever they please. Such purchases are entirely facultative; they no longer have the character of a legal obligation.

"The State, in encouraging the agricultural associations and the industrial associations that I shall mention in due course, wants to develop by this means a spirit of unity and to equalize conditions and fortunes by way of fraternity. It has made them into free communes, which it liberates from all imposition, in order to inspire citizens with an appetite for labor and patriarchal life, liberated from all preoccupation. In a word, it is aiming to render itself unnecessary, or at least only to conserve a central arbitrage, to group around it a nursery of small states independent from one another, relating to it as it is related to the International Congress.

"In order to reach this goal it treats private fortunes with a rigor that is perhaps in contradiction with individual liberty. This precise purpose of this rigor is to bring out the moral and material advantages of social cohesion.

"When the time comes that each association encloses within itself all the material aliments of existence, and cities will have become cities of workers, governing themselves with institutions adapted to their needs, society will form a single immense machine whose innumerable cogwheels will spin, apparently in opposite directions but in reality in perfect accord; the State will no longer be anything but the central axle of that machine.

"From then on, taxation will become local; it will fall within the purview of associations. The State, whose role will be reduced to that of a surveillance commission and a supreme court, will only draw exactly what is needed for the exercise of functions that are purely moral, no longer effective.

"That is where enlightened minds want to lead society. I do not know where they will arrive there, but I assume so, to judge by the progress realized since our epoch. The association, logically, ought to ramify and substitute itself for the egotistical regime of 'every man for himself.'

"As I said on the subject of the family, society began with the family and will end with it. The association is the only means of dividing society into rational cate-

gories, cemented by reciprocal needs and common interest."

Industry: Industrial Associations

After pausing for a few minutes, Monsieur Landet
went on:

"Let us now deal with of industrial associations.

"They are of two sorts: dependent and independent.
Dependent associations are those which, not having been
founded with common capital, belong to the State, which
is both their employer and their sleeping partner. Independent associations are those which, having been
founded with common capital, belong entirely to themselves. The former are State factories, the latter the factories of a constituted society."

"You're not talking about companies founded on
shares?" said Hobson.

"There are none."

"What?"

"No, there are none. It has been realized that industrial enterprises created for the profit of shareholders
outside the exploitation concentrate public fortune in the
hands of a few privileged individuals, not by virtue of
their intelligence or their personal labor but by virtue of
the quantity of money they put into the business and the
sum of the work they extract from the workers. It was
not just, in fact, that people outside an enterprise shared
in it benefits without having done their share of the
work."

"So the State takes possession of all monopolies."

"Yes. The State attracts to itself, as to a common
center, everything that only profits those who have done
nothing to merit it, to the prejudice of those who devote

their time and effort thereto. It wants to equilibrate the balance of compensations as much as possible, in attributing the fruits of labor to the same people from whom they are acquired. It takes possession of all monopolies in order to divide between the workers the reward that it judges to be unjustly diverted to the shareholders."

"By dint of claiming to affirm individual liberty, one finishes up annihilating it; one falls into absolutism. The State becomes an impersonal power, uniting all prerogatives, all monopolies. Separately, the citizens are nothing; property is generalized to the point at which it no longer has any individual existence; it belongs to everyone and no one; private initiative is stabbed in the heart."

Monsieur Landet smiled sardonically. "Oh, you really are a product of your century!" he said. "The State becomes an impersonal power, it is true; that general interest sacrifices individual liberty to it, I also admit; but, exchanging liberty for liberty, is it not preferable that it is the State—which is to say, the social body—that takes possession of the ensemble of property rather than a few individuals already favored by fortune? 'That which profits the State profits individuals; the converse is not the case,' the Finance Minister said at the podium.

"Enterprises mounted on shares, I repeat, profit a few shareholders whose work makes no contribution to them—people who, already rich, have no further need to increase their fortunes. Before the shareholders, the administrators take the lion's share, in the secrecy of closed board meetings. The public, in view of whom these enterprises have supposedly been put into operation, pay more dearly for the products, by the amount that swells the dividends of the shareholders, when the contrary ought to be the case. The more the utility these enterprises makes itself felt, the more success they enjoy, and the more dearly the administrators, in accord with the shareholders, make the customers pay. In brief, they raise their prices when their profits impose a duty on them to reduce them.

"And the workman who has been the effective cause of this prosperity? No one thinks about him. He is a cog in the machine, who much furnish a determined sum of work per day. If he does more, so much the better for the shareholders and administrators; if he does not reach his target, he is sacked, and that is that. He is the one who makes the dividends increase, but he is not included in the distribution. The shareholders enjoy an income in tranquility, which is like a rolling snowball, without any cost of effort.

"The workers sustain all the fatigue and the most meager wages, the shareholders have none of the fatigue and all the benefits."

"Oh! You're making an apology for socialism!"

"Certainly."

"You know what its consequences are, though?"

"Better than anyone; I have been the victim of it in 1848 and 1871. In 1848 a bullet fired from a barricade broke my left arm; in 1871 my town house, near the Conseil d'État was burned down. In encouraging its doctrine I'm neglecting my personal interest; I'm not envisaging that which has been, but that which ought to be, that which will be in 2000 years. Personally, I have powerful motives for hating it, but I support it even so, because it is good, just and natural."

"You're pursuing an ideal. All that is good, just and natural is often in contradiction with practicality."

"Today, yes, because those who want to take liberty to excess are the first to use tyrannical reprisals when they have the upper hand. All regimes are like that. Has not the red terror always been followed by the white terror?[35] So, you would like one social class to have all the privileges, all the honors, all the enjoyments, by right of birth, and the other to have all the fatigue, all the insults and all the poverty by virtue of fate? No, that can only by temporary; it's contrary to morality."

"Then you foresee the triumph of socialism?"

"Complete, dazzling and definitive."

"I'd be curious to know how it has emerged victorious from the centuries-long struggle that it has sustained against the old institutions."

"Oh, in a very simple manner: by conciliation. Those who had not, weary of being the mere instruments of those who had, went on strike. They refused to work any longer for the advantage of their employers, shareholders or private masters, if the latter did not allow them to share in the profits, after inventory."

"And you find that quite natural?"

"It's logical."

"Everything, however, requires a director."

"And what can the director do without the worker? One is the brain, the other the hand. The hand can do nothing without the brain, the brain without the hand. The director is the soul, the workers the body; they obey a directive will as the body obeys the impression of the

---

[35] The "white terror," as opposed to the "red terror," initially referred to the anti-Jacobin backlash of 1795, in which many Revolutionaries were massacred in the French provinces, in supposed revenge for the Convention's Terror. The phrase was then carried forward to refer to other such backlashes in 1799, after Napoléon's overthrow of the Directoire, and 1815, after his fall.

soul. Deprived of the body, the soul can no longer act; nothing remains but a corpse. Let us invert the comparison; imagine a healthy soul in a paralyzed body; it might experience external impressions and want to act, but it is impotent to move an inert mass. The soul is as necessary to the body as the body is to the soul. That necessity is so obvious that the materialist school confounds the two."

"The soul is more necessary than the body, since it is the essence of life."

"What is life without action, without movement, without practical utility? I'll choose another example, taking for an item of comparison a steam engine. All its wheels, gears and belts move by virtue of the primary impulsion transmitted by the drive-shaft. Suppress the drive-shaft; the wheels creased to turn, the gears to mesh, the belts to relay. The machine stops; it no longer has a soul. Change tactics; remove a wheel—just one—from the assembly; in spite of the primary impulsion transmitted by the drive-shaft, you will only obtain a partial result, without determinant effect. The wheel that you have removed commands another, and so on. And that series of connected mechanisms ends up with a complete action. That complete action gives a result that each component, taken separately, could not obtain. Thus, the drive-shaft can do nothing without the wheels, the wheels nothing without the drive-shaft. They are indispensable to one another. Such is the theory of the association.

"I have had recourse to that parable to bring out the necessity first of conciliation, then of association.

"Those who had not therefore said to those who have: 'You are the stomach, we are the limbs; you cannot function without us, we cannot function without you.

You are the mind, we are the hand. You bring money, we bring labor; money is nothing without labor, labor is nothing without money. United, we can do anything; separated, we can do nothing. Until now, your money has found in us agents of fecundity; our poverty has found in you a means of making a living. Our collaboration has made you rich and left us poor. The moment has come to level the conditions. You have every interest in hearing us. Let us not cut; let us conciliate. Since you, who possess, have need of us and we, who do not possess, have need of you, let us associate in work in which we collaborate. That will be a stimulant to our activity, a recompense for our fatigue. You will profit from it more than us, by the increase in profits that the prospect of our individual interest will realize for you as well as us.'

"The shareholders and employers resisted. The workers were obstinate in their cause, Finally, justice was done to their claim. There was a proportional adjustment of the level of their salaries to the sum of their labor. Spurred on by their own interests, they redoubled their zeal and increased the profits to the point at which, when divided up, the shareholders or employers found a further advantage therein.

"Then enterprises mounted by means of shares were extended so far that the State was troubled by it. Seeing them as rival powers, growing every day, it decreed the annulment of shares of every sort and reimbursed their owners at the issue price. Consequently, the exploitation of the enterprises seized reverted to the State. It maintained the association of workers and placed a managing director at their head, also associated, but in proportion to the responsibility of his functions. The workers' share was immediately increased by three quarters of that which had previously been reserved for the shareholders and administrators—a share that represented half the net profits."

"But since the State has nationalized industrial enterprises," Hobson objected, "what use, on the Bourse, is the annuity of 4½% created by the Finance Minister supposedly to favor the development of commerce and industry?"

"It serves to facilitate the transactions between manufacturers and merchants. The decree that monopolizes enterprises mounted by shares does not affect enterprises mounted at individual expense, but it only admits, in establishing a trading company, the association of people participating directly in the enterprise and it limits that trading company to three names. The conscription of income, combined with the association of the workforce, is sufficient guarantee that an employer cannot acquire a disproportionate fortune.

"I shall pass on now to independent associations.

"Independent associations are those that do not derive from the State, but belong to themselves. They are founded with communal capital. The society members are workers in the enterprise. They realize a true association; they are established on the same basis as agricultural associations and, like them, are examples if the conscription of income. There is, however, one detail to note: the ensemble of associations of the same party forms a corporation.

"Every corporation exhibits its products annually at the National Palace, before a jury composed of members elected by each corporation. The jury, having invited the public to write comments in a ledger open at the door of the National Palace, awards a prize to the corporation whose product surpasses the rest and combines three qualities: elegance, solidity and economy.

"The goal of these corporations is the improvement of the practical arts by the spirit of competition.

"Is it not to corporations that we owe those marvels of good taste, in architecture, furniture, costume, sculpture and painting, which, before the great Revolution, marked each century with an original style: the Byzantine, the Gothic, the Romantic, the Renaissance, the Louis XIII, Louis XIV, Louis XV and Louis XVI styles? All those styles were the consequence of the popular turn of mind. Some were severe, others graceful, but the severe succeeded the graceful without abrupt transition; each had its distinctive character. And how well those works were designed, executed and polished! How well they withstood the insults of time. The reason is that once, independently of the spirit of corporation, people were not as dogged in their haste; they invested time in their work, with a view to solidity and real beauty, whereas today, people are only concerned with appearances, and everything is done at 'full steam.' Fragility is built in, under the pretext of promoting commerce.

"That reminds me of a conversation I had one day with a rich *parvenu* at the annual dinner of the Society of French Agriculturalists at the Café Riche.

"'Personally,' he said to me, sententiously, 'I want a sovereign.'

"'Oh? Why?'

"'To promote commerce.'

"'You think that a sovereign is indispensable to nourish labor?'

"'Yes, the Empire is the proof of it. A sovereign is surrounded by a court relentless in its expenditure; he holds ball, receptions, gala feasts, and all the money that comes in by the door goes out by the window.'

"'Under the pretext of stimulating the circulation of capital, then, it's necessary to attribute 36 million francs to a single individual, in order that he might rack his brains to imagine large-scale enjoyments whose expenses would suffice for the upkeep of a large number of families?'

"'There speaks an intransigent! Come on, you can't grant me one poor little sovereign—a king, an emperor, a sultan or whatever?'

"'A fetish!'

"'A fetish, if you like, provided that it represents a sovereign.'

"'You cling absolutely to your sovereign, to serve as a sieve for taxpayers' money. You cling to him, not because of the utility that he might have but for the superior reason that he is called *the sovereign*?'

"'Well, yes—it does no harm to anyone, and would give me pleasure.'

"Let us close the parentheses and return to the exhibitions.

"The annual exhibitions of different bodies of industry thus take place in the same location. The ensemble of corporations puts on a complete exhibition of everything new that the industry has produced during the year.

"One of these exhibitions is taking place now. The crowds are flocking into it, avid to keep up with the course of progress. I'm going in with it.

"A fantastic spectacle! The most difficult problems of modern science have been resolved; their solution is childishly simple. Here there are locomotives moved, not by steam but by electricity, by solar heat and by compressed air. There are dirigible balloons equipped for long voyages. Further on there are submarine vessels

225

maneuvering, bizarrely enough, under the pressure of a jet of water—the element vanquished by the element. And the visitors are passing back and forth without manifesting the slightest sign of astonishment. Electricity plays the greatest role in all those inventions. It is appropriated to everything: lighting, locomotion, manufacture; there are batteries, wires and coils everywhere; currents are flowing in all directions.

"In sum, everything that our nursling scientists deem chimerical is displayed before the eyes of the crowd. Oh, I regret not being a mathematician, so that I might describe the mechanisms that drive all these machines, but since infancy I've manifested an invincible horror of algebra, geometry, mechanics and all those arcana. If nature abhors a vacuum, can I not have a horror of numbers? It's the law of antipathies. Magnetism, always magnetism! That comes back to your domain, Monsieur Hobson.

"How I would like to have overcome that antipathy! What I can see is so fabulous, that, for want of a minute description, no one would believe me. I'll content myself with admiring it, without being able to explain it."

"So steam has had its day?"

"Steam? Oh, you're causing me to fall from the height at which I'm flying. Steam? But that's the ABC of science. It requires costly combustibles, whereas sunlight, compressed air and natural electricity cost nothing. The true objective of industry is to do much with little; it has gone further still—is does much with nothing."

Monsieur Landet had never been gripped by that feverish gaiety before. Hobson looked at him anxiously.

"Electricity! Electricity!" the savant continued. "It's you who are the spark of life; I feel it in the contagious tremor that is agitating me. Thus the essence of the soul is discovered. One can fabricate it. Oh, if only I could analyze the composition of that elixir! My God! My God! To see all these marvels and not be able to comprehend them!"

Monsieur Landet took his head in both hands and squeezed it angrily. Hobson, alarmed by that overexcitement, made as if to wake him up.

"No, no—let me be!" cried the savant. "I want to enjoy this intoxicating contemplation, remain in this magical milieu; I want to live this life, I want to die in my illusion."

Hobson got to his feet and directed his eyes at the savant. "Wake up!" he commanded.

"No, no—I don't want to!"

"Wake up! I order you to."

The savant uttered a sigh and seemed to yield to the magnetizer's will.

A few minutes later, he was awake, striding back and forth in the apartment as if he had quicksilver in his veins.

"Well, what's the matter with me?" he suddenly demanded of Hobson.

"Consult the stenography," the latter replied, "and you'll see."

Monsieur Landet threw himself on the sheets of paper.

When he had finished reading, he exclaimed: "Fabulous! Fabulous! Fabulous! The transmission of electric currents across 20 centuries!"

Commerce: Mutual Obligations, Commercial Freedom, Free Trade and Protection

Hobson tried to oblige Monsieur Landet to rest for a few days. The feverish fit by which the latter had been gripped at the end of the last séance caused him to fear a brain hemorrhage. But Monsieur Landet pressed him so insistently that he withdrew the order. The world—so the savant said—was waiting impatiently for the results of their experiments...

"We're going to talk about commerce. 'The art of mutual deception'—that's the best definition of it that one can give in our epoch.

"Today, the exchange of products is an element of wealth; it skirts the extreme limit at which good faith becomes confused with fraud.

"The great art of the tradesman consists of depreciating the other person's products and giving value to his own; to supply poorer merchandise and make it appear better; to seduce by price and deceive in quality; to attract, to dazzle, to captivate the client with promises, claims and articles defying all competition, on which he is surer to make a loss, but the price of which he will raise when the reputation of his business is secure—in brief, to toy with the credulity of the public.

"It is not the best and most solid products that have the greatest chance of success; it is those which flatter the gaze and whose ostentation implies a value higher than they have in reality.

"The shopkeeper who can capture clients quickly by appealing to their vanity makes a considerable fortune. He knows the human species and addresses himself to its vices. That which is of good quality, solid and well-made passes unnoticed, because it has no effect.

"Conscience, in business, is a hindrance to the prosperity of the retailer; the public is not grateful for it. The great means of attraction is publicity: posters on walls, advertisements in the newspapers, leaflets handed out on street corners, illustrated brochures, chromolithographic images—in sum, everything that attracts attention.

"One finds therein the description of extraordinary articles at fabulous cheap prices. One allows oneself to be tempted, one investigates out of curiosity, one ends up buying—then, one is soon disagreeably surprised to perceive that what had so much appearance is utterly worthless. A bargain buy is always expensive.

"The big clothing stores have another system. At the opening of every season, they advertise articles of superior quality that they are selling at a loss. Women flock in, avid to take advantage of such an opportunity, but they do not get away with a single acquisition. They are pursued, bombarded and pestered by the sales staff, who offer them gloves, cravats, umbrellas, reciting the conventional claptrap. They allow themselves to be carried away, and they make purchases. Then the head of the department appears like a *deus ex machina*, a smile on his lips, a heartfelt expression and wisps of hair over his forehead. He unfurls a roll of cloth of indecisive shade, pompously emphasizing its suppleness, its shine and its color.

"'But it's faded, Monsieur.'

"'Exactly, Madame, that's exactly what provides its cachet, it's the very latest thing, the fashionable shade, the...feel it for yourself Madame, it's all wool. It can serve every purpose: to make curtains, a dress, a tablecloth; it's hard-wearing, it can g into the laundry without shrinking. An extraordinary opportunity—take advantage of it, Madame; we won't have any left tomorrow.'

"The unfortunate victim yields to the eloquence of the department head's performance. 'Is that all you need,

Madame?' the indefatigable drone resumes. 'We've just got in some superb vases from Japan; we're selling them at 18 francs, cost price, instead of 25. Would you like to see them? Looking costs nothing. Take the elevator at the end of the corridor to the second floor; you'll find a branch of the tramway that will take you to the porcelain department. Madame...'

"The department head sketches a bow and vanishes.

"The lady in question goes home laden with trinkets. That evening, a friend comes to take tea. 'Oh, what have you bought today?' cries the friend, at the sight of the packages heaped on the furniture.

"'Yes, I haven't had time to unpack it all. Go on, unpack them yourself and tell me whether I have good taste.'

"The friend unties the string and tears off the brown paper. The first thing presented to her eyes is the fine cloth. 'What are you going to make with that outdated Havana cashmere, a lining?"

"'Lining!'

"'Well, yes, it's no good for anything else—it's faded.'

"'So much the better! What? Don't you now that faded shades are all the rage this year?'

"The friend, whose husband is a cloth-merchant, bursts out laughing. 'Oh, my dear, there's faded and faded—this is ten years old; someone's sold you a pup!'

"A few days later, a further disappointment for the over-credulous lady. It's her day for receiving visitors. Enter another friend, whose husband manufactures porcelain. After the usual compliments, she exclaims: 'Oh, how can you put that imitation Japanese vase next to that genuine Dresden clock?'

"'Imitation! But that's authentic, direct from Japan—I bought those two vases at   's store.'

"The friend picks one of the vases up and examines it. 'My poor friend,' she says, 'this Japanese porcelain has come all the way from the Rue Paradis-Poisonnière. I recognize the trademark—it's my husband who manufactured it.'

"'Oh!'

"In addition to these minor inconveniences of speculation, there are others more serious, which have terrible consequences for small traders. Clothing stores have expanded so rapidly recently that they have been transformed into veritable merchant towns, through which one circulates in elevators and tramways. They centralize a number of products belonging to different specialties: household items, furniture, saddlery, gardening tools, jewelry, clocks, bronzes, children's toys, Chinoiserie. books, etc. They are thus absorbing the customary clientele of small traders, and, by means of the price reductions permitted by a considerable volume of trade, rendering competition impossible.

"In order to attract and take possession of clients more surely, the owner of one of these stores has installed an art gallery, a reading room and a buffet in which cakes and refreshments are distributed gratuitously. All that is lacking is a flirtation room to shelter lovers on rainy ways. Many people go there out of curiosity, many out of greed, but of that number, some pause at the shelves and, seduced by the honeyed language of the salespersons, do not go home with empty hands. Thus, the generosity of the owner is not without positive results.

"The customers find it easier to buy everything they need from the same place at a better price and they are right, saving time and money—but the small trader finds his shop becoming deserted over time. The volume of his business does not permit him to compete with the exceptional prices of the big stores, to make up for low margins in terms of quantity, and even if he could, the members of the public would still prefer to go where they are attracted by the fever of distraction, the enchantment of the visual display.

"It is, however, necessary that everyone should live, and for that, it is necessary to respect the integrity of every body of trade. The encroachments of department stores are an attack on individual liberty, by an abuse of liberty. This commercial centralization with end up becoming and a monopoly, which will impose itself by means of prohibitive prices, and, if there is to be a monopoly, a State monopoly is better than a private monopoly. Liberty sometimes consists of limiting the extension of liberty, because an excess of liberty gives some tyrannical power over others.

"There is one simple means of halting the progress of commercial centralization. The large stores employ prohibitive prices, so let the states impose prohibitive taxes on them; make them pay a duty for every specialty other than clothing, narrowly defined. Competition will then be equalized and the supplementary duties, added to general expenses, will raise the department stores' prices to the point at which they will either go out of business or revert to their original specialty and keep to it rigorously.

"What makes them so powerful today is that they regain in quantity the losses incurred in detail, when they willingly sacrifice a few articles in order to attract visitors. When the detail is separately taxed, however, they will no longer be able to write it off against quantity. They will die, submerged by a colossal deficit.

"We're approaching that denouement. Small traders are languishing, bankruptcies being declared on all sides; the ferment is increasing and a crisis is inevitable. It will burst forth.

"The State will then get involved; it will erect barriers against the rising tide and, to ensure free trade, it will be protectionist.

"If I'm talking about this matter at length, it is in order that the comparison with the future will be more striking."

Monsieur Landet collected himself for a few minutes, and then continued.

"By contrast with our epoch, commerce in 3878 has for its motto: 'The art of mutual obligation.' Its objective is to enable everyone to live and enjoy the profits of trade, not to enrich itself. If fortune favors it, it is over and beyond mutual obligations."

"What are mutual obligations?" asked Hobson.

"I touched on the subject briefly while talking about the family," replied Monsieur Landet, "but this necessitates a detailed explanation.

"The objective of commerce, as I said a little while ago, is to enable everyone to live, not to enrich itself. A material difficulty raised an obstacle to that thesis for a long time: the equal distribution of exchange.

"Our descendants have gone straight to the target; they have resolved the problem by means of a law. In all circumstances, only laws are capable of furnishing positive results. This law assigns a particular supplier to each citizen, who cannot be changed without the judgment of a tribunal. Thus it assigns him a baker, a butcher, a greengrocer, a dairy supplier, a tailor, a shirt-maker, a bootmaker, and so on. The baker, the butcher, the green-grocer, the dairy supplier, the tailor, the shirt-maker, the bootmaker and the rest are subject to the same obligations of exchange. They must serve their regular clientele first and can only develop their commerce further when they have answered the needs of that clientele.

"This division of mutual obligations is made by the municipal councils, as the division of direct contributions between the taxpayers is made by the general councils. The municipal councils, by fixing the limit of their mutual obligations for the citizens of their district, know in advance the annual volume of trade that each one has and the personal benefit resulting therefrom.

"In this way, every trader has the assurance of a comfortable existence, that assurance being guaranteed by the State.

"But the law has anticipated the possibility of a supplier discharging his obligations badly by delivering poor merchandise. In that case, it permits the injured citizen to go to the tribunal, in order to be liberated from the obligation linking him to that supplier and to have another designated within the district.

"Commerce is thus returned to its true expression. Its traffic is equilibrated in such a way as to provide everyone with a living and not to concentrate wealth in the same hands. Having discharged its mutual obligations, it can enlarge the frame of its operations; free trade smoothes its path."

"Ah! Free trade!" exclaimed Hobson.

"Yes. Napoléon I was inspired with vision when, from the height of his rock on Saint Helena, seeking to fathom the depths of the future, he cried: "We must fall back henceforth on the free navigation of the seas and the entire freedom of universal trade."[36]

"Free trade has prevailed over protectionism; that was a natural consequence of the triumph of liberty.

"No more barriers which, in the form of prohibitive taxes, stopped imported goods at the frontiers of empires, reserving the internal market to indigenous produce. No more treaties that favor the products of one nation in preference to those of another. No more customs duties at the gates of cities that double or triple the price of commodities before they are put into circulation and isolate cities from rural areas by an exaggerated system of protection, and which, in the bosom of the same country, penalize indigenous products with exorbitant taxation and slow down consumption. A free market open to foreign competition, without distinction of nationality.

"The admission for foreign competition is a spur to activity and stimulates self-respect. The protectionist system, which consists of repulsion by crushing taxes and customs tariffs, harms indigenes more than it is useful to them. A single country cannot enclose all raw materials in its bosom. Each one has its specialty of production, according to the nature of its soil and its climate. Southern Russia and Rumania produce wheat, England and Belgium coal; Spain produces mercury and copper, Germany iron, Greece silver, California gold, and so on. It is, therefore, necessary that these counties exchange

---

[36] The author gives a reference to *Mémorial de Sainte-Hélène*, Conversation of June 12, 1816, which he credits to Michel Chevalier, presumably the name of a publisher. The conversations in question—which ran to six volumes—were compiled and published by Emanuel Las Cases

the superabundance of their production with one another, to equilibrate universal consumption.

"Since each needs the others in the same proportion, however, it is necessary to remedy these inequalities of production by freedom of trade; if not, assuming that each country uses the same mode of prohibition, famine will destroy a part of the population in one place, while lack of combustibles there will impede the means of locomotion and manufacture in another and thus slow down internal trade; elsewhere, the absence of silver with force the State to issue banknotes, the number of which, surpassing the effective capital that they ought to represent, will lead to bankruptcy. Those are the fatal consequences that protectionism brings with it.

"Internal production is therefore insufficient to the needs of indigenes, who have recourse to imports to make up their deficiencies, as they have recourse to exports to disperse the excess of their production. Now, the taxes imposed on imported foreign merchandise at the frontier force the retailer to raise the price of the merchandise by the extent to the duty that the State has imposed. That duty is sometimes more than the value of the merchandise. The retailer necessarily passes that on to the customer and only the State profits from the rise in price. It is not the foreigner, in view of whom these customs duties are imposed, who bears the cost; it is the indigene, whose interests the State is claiming to protect.

"And the State, which is the only one to profit from it, would gain even more if it halved the tariffs. Three times as much would be consumed and the additional consumption would produce a third as much again.

"Protectionists hide behind the vain pretext that they are reserving the internal market in excluding foreign produce by prohibitive taxes. The truth is that they see these taxes as a benefit to the State, and that that benefit comes back to them one way or another. It is generally governors who are protectionists, having been supporters of free trade before coming to power, just as conservatives become conservatives as soon as they have possessions, having been Republicans when they had none.

"Traders have no advantage in being protectionist. They cannot be content to deal in indigenous products. To respond to the demands of their customers, they need to mingle them with exotic products, and the levy that these products pay to the State at the frontier forces them in order to make a profit on them, to sell them at a price surpassing both the purchase price and the customs duty, sometimes triple their value. The result of this is that the client consumes as little as possible. If, on the other hand, the merchandise were free of duty, the client would consume more, and the State would still benefit from it in one form or another.

"In sum, protection paralyzes progress in every respect. It slows down trade, and prevents manufacturers from taking advantage of the best conditions of localization and manufacture and improving their products. It tends to perpetuate obsolete methods by permitting the sale of indigenous products cheaper than foreign ones. It isolates people. It is a national blockade.

"Free trade, on the other hand, based on the principle of universal solidarity, opens up vast scope for progress. It stimulates the self-respect of nations by competition, and drives improvement by comparison; it develops trade and facilitates means of transport by way of fairly-balanced prices; it cements the fraternity of peoples, which it leads directly toward their objective: relative perfection.

"Since the freedom of commerce has been universally proclaimed and sanctioned by the International Congress, Industry has invented marvels and public wealth has increased by virtue the free circulation of products. Feverish activity is manifest everywhere. The railways are scarcely sufficient to transport merchandise. Ships plow the seas in every direction, their holds laden with specialties from the five continents. They go through straits without any tolls impeding their progress; they come into port under full sail and unload their cargoes without the customs imposing disproportionate taxes on them before knowing whether or not they will be sold.

"Free trade, by eliminating contraband, has vanquished the worst enemy of commerce, fraud, and revived its best agent, mutual confidence."

Chapter IX
EXTERNAL POLITICS

The International Congress

Monsieur Landet was beginning to experience a certain fatigue in the wake of the somnambulistic sleep. This fatigue made itself manifest in a general numbness of all his limbs and a mental torpor that weakened his intellectual faculties.

Hobson did not think they should take the experiments any further; he invoked his responsibility, and did not want to put the savant's reason—and perhaps his life—in any more peril.

Monsieur Landet, fanatically avid for the unknown, triumphed over the magnetizer's scruples, by assuring him that the next séance would be the last.

He said saved external politics until the end because external politics was, within the whole, that which he had examined in particular, because it was the bond of linking nations together...

"All that blood! All that blood! All that blood!" cried Monsieur Landet, as soon as the séance began, making a gesture of horror. "Europe is transformed into an immense battlefield. The countries present a desolate appearance. I see nothing on all sides but massacres, ruins, conflagrations. The plains are covered in white bones. Plague, a consequence of this human butchery, extends its ravages from province to province, its murderous miasmas borne on the wind. Death! Death! The image of death is everywhere; the rivers carry cadavers, their waters are tainted with red gleams, pools of blood dapple the soil. Birds of prey come, flapping their wings, to feast at the hideous banquet. Behold the degree of dementia to which the passions have led humankind.

"Such engines of destruction have been invented that war has been rendered impossible henceforth. We have reached the point of killing one another without seeing or hearing one another, at several leagues' distance, laying mines, blowing up entire downs, launching bombs that kill thousands of men at a stroke when they explode. What am I saying? These bombs disturb the layers of the atmosphere, provoke earthquakes, divert rivers in their courses and bring down blocks of stone from the summits of mountains.

"Electric sparks set fire to powder at a distance of 2000 leagues and from Paris, by means of submarine cables, blow up a squadron of ships at sea or a district in America. One step further on that fatal path, and all the parts of the terrestrial crust will be breached.

"Finally, a European conflict has taken place. The nations, forming coalitions against one another, have met in a gigantic battle, the last of all.

"All that blood! All that blood! All that blood!

"The battalions disappearing in clouds of powder; shells weighing 60,000 kilograms and slabs of rock launched by balistas are crossing paths in the air; regiments are falling upon regiments, the dead are heaped up on the dead.

"And when arms weary of scything down this human harvest, when no more powder remains to charge the cannons, when the balistas refuse to slide on their springs, set on fire by friction, it stops.

"The spectacle of their folly suddenly sobers up the opposing sides. One of them takes the initiative of conciliation; it sends a negotiator to the enemy camp.

"'Brothers,' says the latter, 'I've been sent by my side to propose that we put an end to this bloody conflict. We've given the purest blood of our youth to it. When we go back to our homes, victors or vanquished, we'll find mourning and misery there. No more strong arms to cultivate the earth of aliment commerce and industry; no one is left but old men, women and children. Twenty years will scarcely suffice to repair the damage done in one day of delirium. Industry is mortally wounded; no one thinks about manufacturing any longer, being solely occupied in destruction. Commerce is suspended; labor no longer finds an outlet for its products. What am I saying? There are no more laborers, there are only soldiers. The small quantity of merchandise circulating between nations is seized in transit. No one has any respect for anything any longer. Family, property, the most sacred things of all, are at the mercy of the victor. Rational justice has been overturned; there is but one right now, the right of might. Progress, by dint of civilization, is taking us back to savagery! And why? To avenge the injured self-respect of a sovereign! To protect diplomatic interests by alliance! Shall we suffer that men to whom we are strangers continue to sacrifice us to their individual quarrels?

"'No, Brothers, let us shake hands before these cadavers. We were not made to kill one another. Death belongs to God. Our duty is to fraternize, to unite ourselves in universal solidarity.'

"The two camps shook hands, and war was abolished, by the unanimous decision of the nations. Then, the belligerent parties immediately constituted an International Congress, and decided that differences between nations would be judged by that tribunal.

"The International Congress is composed of delegates of all the nations, under the direction of a president elected by the delegates. Each nation has four delegates, under the presidency of the Head of State. Thus, the congress is a sort of international parliament in which the debates end in a vote; each delegation is a commission representing a nation.

"The Congress is the central government of the Universal Confederation. It regulates the relationships of nations with one another. The laws particular to each State are transmitted to it; it refers them to the authorities and opposes them with its veto if that veto is considered necessary to the universal interest.

"In brief, all the States are grouped around the International Congress as, in America, the States of the Union are around the Congress in Washington. The Congress possesses a neutral territory called the Territory of Congress, on which is built the International Palace. The delegates of the States meet there regularly, every year, to discuss current affairs, and extraordinarily when there is cause.

"Beside the International Palace is the Universal Exhibition Hall, to which people come every five years to exhibit their products and communicate their inventions. The objective of these quinquennial exhibitions is to accelerate the march of progress by bringing people up to date with innovations in every part of the world.

"Already stimulated by their annual exhibitions, they make improvements, in view of the Universal Exhibition, and further improvements thereafter..."

Chapter X
EPILOGUE

"Sic Itur ad Astra"[37]

At that point, Monsieur Landet stopped. His lips moved, but no sound came out.

Hobson made a few sweeping passes over him and woke him up, but he could not get anything out of him but unintelligible muttering. The savant had completely lost his memory. Frightened by this mental lethargy, he had him taken back to his own house. Not being able to dissipate the torpor, he sent for a physician and informed the Marquise de la Roche-Houdion.

When the Marquise came into the savant's room, she found him in bed, his expression bleak and downcast, his arms limp, his eyes staring and bewildered, his lips pated and his face red.

He did not recognize her.

"It's me, my friend," she said. "Me, your old enemy. Speak, answer me I beg you."

No reply.

Finally, the doctor arrived. He was brought to the invalid. After having examined him, he shook his head.

"Well?" said the Marquise and the magnetizer, simultaneously.

---

[37] The full line from book IX of Virgil's *Aeneid* from which this exhortation is extracted is *Macte animo! generose puer, sic itur ad astra.* Its approximate translation is "Buck up, child! This is the way to the stars."

"Monsieur Landet won't last the night," he replied. "A brain seizure has just become manifest. This torpor is the prelude to a delirium that is bound to carry the invalid away."

"How much longer will this lethargy last, Doctor?" the Marquis asked.

"Two hours, Madame."

Hobson and the Marquise waited, without saying a word. They were distressed. A long-standing friendship, one of those profound friendships based on esteem, that can exist between a man and an equally superior woman, united the savant and the Marquise. Mr. Hobson, although he had not known the savant very long, experienced a sympathy for him instilled by working together and reciprocal trust. Magnetism had contributed a great deal to giving that sentiment an appearance of irresistible attachment. How Hobson regretted, now, having yielded to the savant's insistence!

From time to time, the doctor put his ear to the savant's chest.

Suddenly, as if he had been activated by a spring, Monsieur Landet sat up straight and waved his arms. His eyes were animated by a spark of vitality and he cried: "My manuscript! My manuscript! I want my manuscript!"

His manuscript was placed in his hands.

"Ah! I can die now that my political testament is complete. I can die, consoled by my posthumous glory; I am leaving the world a constitution."

His hands clenched upon the manuscript; his eyes were bloodshot.

"Stop—stop the electric current! Can't you see that it's killing me? Ah, it's animal electricity! That's true—I forgot!

"Oh, the fever's devouring me, I have fire in my veins! Water! Water!

"Lift the weight that's pressing on my head! My ideas are getting confused—they're swarming, seething; my brain's going to explode! Oh, that weight! Always that weight, crushing me like a stone block!

"Let me be, for mercy's sake! Don't torment me!

"No, I haven't betrayed my mandate; no, I haven't rebelled against the suffrage of my electors. You say that I took the floor to defend the Finance Minister. That wasn't me, you're mistaken. What! You're taking my income and giving me a piece of paper in exchange! But you'll ruin me! Give me back my money! I don't want that!

"Finally, free trade stimulates the activity of peoples. Merchants pass frontiers free of duties. No more flags establishing different tariffs between nationalities. Ships cleave the seas under the protectorate of the Universal Confederation. Liberty! Liberty! Liberty!

"All that blood before getting there! Oh, it sickens me to see it! Take that horrible vision away! I'm suffering! I'm suffering! I can feel the grip of death!

"Dying! While glory awaits me beyond the tomb. What shall I become beyond this life? I shall wander in space, awaiting my return to Earth in a new body. And when will that series of incarnations end? When?

"But what's that fixed dot advancing toward me? It's growing, growing, spreading out like a patch of oil; it's dazzling me, it's blinding me. Ah! It's the sun!

"Into what turbulence am I being drawn? I've got vertigo. The Earth is worn away by the friction of its atmospheric layers; its orbit is shrinking. It's getting nearer and nearer to the sun. It's falling into its sphere of attraction, it's making contact. Ah! It's volatilizing it and absorbing it.

"And the soul! My soul! Free! Free! Free of terrestrial attraction, it's returning to Infinity. Infinity! Infinity! Infinity…!"

He fell back on to his pillow, murmuring that word, which expired on his lips.

The doctor approached, placed one hand on his chest and held a mirror to his lips with the other.

Hobson and the Marquise did not say a word, but their gazes interrogated the doctor.

Slowly, the latter said: "He's dead."

SF & FANTASY

Henri Allorge. *The Great Cataclysm*
Guy d'Armen. *Doc Ardan: The City of Gold and Lepers*
G.-J. Arnaud. *The Ice Company*
Cyprien Bérard. *The Vampire Lord Ruthwen*
Aloysius Bertrand. *Gaspard de la Nuit*
Richard Bessière. *The Gardens of the Apocalypse*
Albert Bleunard. *Ever Smaller*
Félix Bodin. *The Novel of the Future*
Alphonse Brown. *City of Glass*
André Caroff. *The Terror of Madame Atomos; Miss Atomos; The Return of Madame Atomos*
Félicien Champsaur. *The Human Arrow*
Didier de Chousy. *Ignis*
Captain Danrit. *Undersea Odyssey*
C. I. Defontenay. *Star (Psi Cassiopeia)*
Charles Derennes. *The People of the Pole*
Georges Dodds (anthologist). *The Missing Link*
Harry Dickson. *The Heir of Dracula*
Jules Dornay. *Lord Ruthven Begins*
Sâr Dubnotal *vs. Jack the Ripper*
Alexandre Dumas. *The Return of Lord Ruthven*
Renée Dunan. *Baal*
J.-C. Dunyach. *The Night Orchid; The Thieves of Silence*
Henri Duvernois. *The Man Who Found Himself*
Achille Eyraud. *Voyage to Venus*
Henri Falk. *The Age of Lead*
Paul Féval. *Anne of the Isles; Knightshade; Revenants; Vampire City; The Vampire Countess; The Wandering Jew's Daughter*
Paul Féval, *fils. Felifax, the Tiger-Man*
Charles de Fieux. *Lamékis*
Arnould Galopin. *Doctor Omega; Doctor Omega & The Shadowmen*
G.L. Gick. *Harry Dickson and the Werewolf of Rutherford Grange*

Nathalie Henneberg. *The Green Gods*
V. Hugo, P. Foucher & P. Meurice. *The Hunchback of Notre-Dame*
Michel Jeury. *Chronolysis*
Octave Joncquel & Théo Varlet. *The Martian Epic*
Gérard Klein. *The Mote in Time's Eye*
Jean de La Hire. *Enter the Nyctalope; The Nyctalope on Mars; The Nyctalope vs. Lucifer; The Nyctalope Steps In*
Etienne-Léon de Lamothe-Langon. *The Virgin Vampire*
André Laurie. *Spiridon*
Gabriel de Lautrec. *The Vengeance of the Oval Portrait*
Georges Le Faure & Henri de Graffigny. *The Extraordinary Adventures of a Russian Scientist Across the Solar System* (2 vols.)
Gustave Le Rouge. *The Vampires of Mars*
Jules Lermina. *Mysteryville; Panic in Paris; To-Ho and the Gold Destroyers; The Secret of Zippelius*
Jean-Marc & Randy Lofficier. *Edgar Allan Poe on Mars; The Katrina Protocol; Pacifica; Robonocchio; Tales of the Shadowmen 1-7*
Xavier Mauméjean. *The League of Heroes*
José Moselli. *Illa's End*
John-Antoine Nau. *Enemy Force*
Marie Nizet. *Captain Vampire*
C. Nodier, A. Beraud & Toussaint-Merle. *Frankenstein*
Henri de Parville. *An Inhabitant of the Planet Mars*
Georges Pellerin. *The World in 2000 Years*
J. Polidori, C. Nodier, E. Scribe. *Lord Ruthven the Vampire*
P.-A. Ponson du Terrail. *The Vampire and the Devil's Son*
Maurice Renard. *The Blue Peril; Doctor Lerne; The Doctored Man; A Man Among the Microbes; The Master of Light*
Jean Richepin. *The Wing*
Albert Robida. *The Adventures of Saturnin Farandoul; The Clock of the Centuries; Chalet in the Sky*
J.-H. Rosny Aîné. *Helgvor of the Blue River; The Givreuse Enigma; The Mysterious Force; The Navigators of Space; Vamireh; The World of the Variants; The Young Vampire*

Marcel Rouff. *Journey to the Inverted World*
Han Ryner. *The Superhumans*
Brian Stableford. *The New Faust at the Tragicomique;The Empire of the Necromancers (The Shadow of Frankenstein; Frankenstein and the Vampire Countess; Frankenstein in London); Sherlock Holmes & The Vampires of Eternity; The Stones of Camelot; The Wayward Muse.* (anthologist) *The Germans on Venus; News from the Moon; The Supreme Progress; The World Above the World*
Jacques Spitz. *The Eye of Purgatory*
Kurt Steiner. *Ortog*
Eugène Thébault. *Radio-Terror*
C.-F. Tiphaigne de La Roche. *Amilec*
Théo Varlet. *The Xenobiotic Invasion*
Paul Vibert. *The Mysterious Fluid*
Villiers de l'Isle-Adam. *The Scaffold; The Vampire Soul*
Philippe Ward. *Artahe*
Philippe Ward & Sylvie Miller. *The Song of Montségur*

MYSTERIES & THRILLERS

M. Allain & P. Souvestre. *The Daughter of Fantômas*
A. Anicet-Bourgeois, Lucien Dabril. *Rocambole*
A. Bisson & G. Livet. *Nick Carter vs. Fantômas*
V. Darlay & H. de Gorsse. *Lupin vs. Holmes: The Stage Play*
Paul Féval. *Gentlemen of the Night; John Devil; The Black Coats ('Salem Street; The Invisible Weapon; The Parisian Jungle; The Companions of the Treasure; Heart of Steel; The Cadet Gang; The Sword-Swallower)*
Emile Gaboriau. *Monsieur Lecoq*
Steve Leadley. *Sherlock Holmes: The Circle of Blood*
Maurice Leblanc. *Arsène Lupin vs. Countess Cagliostro; Lupin vs. Holmes (The Blonde Phantom; The Hollow Needle)*
Gaston Leroux. *Chéri-Bibi; The Phantom of the Opera; Rouletabille & the Mystery of the Yellow Room*
William Patrick Maynard. *The Terror of Fu Manchu*

Frank J. Morlock. *Sherlock Holmes: The Grand Horizontals; Sherlock Holmes vs Jack the Ripper*
P. de Wattyne & Y. Walter. *Sherlock Holmes vs. Fantômas*
David White. *Fantômas in America*

SCREENPLAYS

Mike Baron. *The Iron Triangle*
Emma Bull & Will Shetterly. *Nightspeeder; War for the Oaks*
Gerry Conway & Roy Thomas. *Doc Dynamo*
Steve Englehart. *Majorca*
James Hudnall. *The Devastator*
Jean-Marc & Randy Lofficier. *Royal Flush*
J.-M. & R. Lofficier & Marc Agapit. *Despair*
Andrew Paquette. *Peripheral Vision*
R. Thomas, J. Hendler & L. Sprague de Camp. *Rivers of Time*

NON-FICTION

Stephen R. Bissette. *Blur 1-5; Green Mountain Cinema 1; Teen Angels & New Mutants*
Win Scott Eckert. *Crossovers* (2 vols.)
Jean-Marc & Randy Lofficier. *Shadowmen* (2 vols.)
Randy Lofficier. *Over Here*

HEXAGON COMICS

Franco Frescura & Luciano Bernasconi. *Wampus*
Franco Frescura & Giorgio Trevisan. *CLASH*
L. Bernasconi, J.-M. Lofficier & Juan Roncagliolo Berger. *Phenix*
Claude Legrand, J.-M. Lofficier & L. Bernasconi. *Kabur*
Franco Oneta. *Zembla*
L. Buffolente, Lofficier & J.-J. Dzialowski. *Strangers: Homicron*
Danilo Grossi. *Strangers: Jaydee*
Claude Legrand & Luciano Bernasconi. *Strangers: Starlock*

ART BOOKS

Jean-Pierre Normand. *Science Fiction Illustrations*
Raven Okeefe. *Raven's L'il Critters*
Randy Lofficier & Raven OKeefe. *If Your Possum Go Daylight...*
Daniele Serra. *Illusions*

www.ingramcontent.com/pod-product-compliance
Lightning Source LLC
Chambersburg PA
CBHW060350030726
47497CB00003B/664